drowning man as both a: ☑ W9-DJP-432
through one of the tunnels; he
catches another in mid-air who has
fallen from the canyon's face. Lynn's
feats of heroism, his energy and
skill, attract admiration, earn him
promotions — and lead to trouble.

From a badly shaken cowboy in
the hospital with a broken leg and
memories of brutal gang terrorism,
he learns that there is a powerful
gangster network operating at the
dam with the object of blowing it
up. Is this a frightened man's fan-
tasy or the naked truth? While drilling on the face of the canyon wall
hundreds of feet up, Lynn keeps an
eye out for strange activities, and
finds them. Soon he is involved in a
plot with far more personal conse-
quences. Anne is kidnaped again,
and in a rousing climax Lynn is
faced with the frantic effort to get
her back unharmed.

As in all of Zane Grey, there are
wonderful descriptions of the West
and of man's heroic efforts to tame
nature. In this new book, the building of Boulder Dam becomes an
inspiring drama in its own right.

BOULDER DAM

Books by Zane Grey

Novels

Boulder Dam
Blue Feather and Other Stories
The Ranger and Other Stories
Horse Heaven Hill
The Arizona Clan
The Fugitive Trail
Stranger from the Tonto
Lost Pueblo
Black Mesa
Wyoming
Captives of the Desert
The Dude Ranger
The Maverick Queen
The Deer Stalker
Rogue River Feud
Valley of Wild Horses
Shadow on the Trail
Wilderness Trek
Stairs of Sand
Majesty's Rancho
Twin Sombreros
30,000 on the Hoof
Western Union
Knights of the Range
Raiders of Spanish Peaks
West of the Pecos
The Lost Wagon Train
The Trail Driver
Thunder Mountain
Code of the West
The Hash Knife Outfit
The Drift Fence
Robber's Roost
Arizona Ames
Sunset Pass
Wild Horse Mesa
The Shepherd of Guadaloupe
Fighting Caravans
Don
Nevada
Forlorn River

The Border Legion
The Call of the Canyon
The Day of the Beast
Desert Gold
The Desert of Wheat
Heritage of the Desert
The Light of Western Stars
The Lone Star Ranger
The Man of the Forest
The Mysterious Rider
The Rainbow Trail
Riders of the Purple Sage
Tappan's Burro
The Thundering Herd
To the Last Man
The U.P. Trail
Under the Tonto Rim
The Vanishing American
Wanderer of the Wasteland
Wildfire
The Wolf Tracker

Out-of-Door Books

Zane Grey's Adventures in Fishing
An American Angler in Australia
Tales of Fresh-Water Fishing
Zane Grey's Book of Camps and Trails
Tales of Tahitian Waters
Tales of Fishes
Tales of Fishing Virgin Seas
Tales of Lonely Trails
Tales of Southern Rivers
Tales of Angler's Eldorado
Tales of Swordfish and Tuna

Books for Boys

Ken Ward in the Jungle
Roping Lions in the Grand Canyon
Young Forester
Young Lion Hunter
Young Pitcher

BOULDER DAM

by Zane Grey

HARPER & ROW, PUBLISHERS

New York, Evanston, and London

BOULDER DAM

Prologue

That first upthrust of the slope of the western hemisphere formed a vast inland sea which gave birth to a rapacious and terrible river. Throughout the ages in its work of draining that immense area of water it cut wide and deep into the bowels of the earth.

Then after millions of years came the second upthrust. It added velocity and grinding power to this sinister and irresistible stream, and the inland sea shrank to a salty lake in the midst of a desolate wasteland. But the river flowed on in lessened volume, grim in its task, still mighty and insatiate, fed by the rains and snows from the mountain heights. It was a river of silt. It had teeth of sand. In the thousands of centuries that nature bent to this slow and inscrutable travail it gouged a dark canyon down to the black archaic rock, and there on the very floor of the earth crust, harder than iron and as enduring as the firmament, the great river thundered and ground in vain. It must wait for another cataclysm of the elements.

In time strange living creatures appeared out of the north and

1

wandered into the branch canyons of the great chasm. They were little men, dark-visaged and slant-eyed, and they perished almost without leaving trace of their struggle. The cliff dwellers followed, building tiny houses of stone and cement that withstood the weathering processes of time long after a stronger race out of the south drove them over the precipices. And this race gave way to the Indians.

The Spaniards found savage redskinned tribes all over this arid region. And they guided Coronado and his armored followers to the brink of the abyss from the depths of which floated up the sullen roar of a mighty river.

Coronado was the first white man to gaze down into that awful red rent in the earth. The solid ground appeared divided, and there was no way across to the other side of the world. The scene was of such sublimity that the Spanish explorers stood spellbound. Nothing had ever been known of such a terrible place. Coronado could not at first accept the evidence of his own eyes.

A ragged rim of yellow limestone ran north and south. Grotesque cedar trees, with gnarled and bleached tops, reached out with clutching hands of dead men. Down sheered the precipitous cliffs, to merge into a zone of red, where strange plateaus and slopes, and mountains of naked rock, led the fearful gaze down into the purple and obscure depths of chaos. It was a ghastly exposure of the naked ribs and bowels of the rock-bound earth. But it had an appalling beauty. A million facets of red and orange and brown caught the sunlight in brilliance too strong for the gaze of man. The unknown depths were mantled in dim mystic purple. The far slopes sheered up with vast and tremendous sweep to a golden band crowded by a wandering fringe of black. Coronado named the abyss *Grande Cañón del Rio Colorado*.

White men as daring as the armor-clad Spaniards in due time explored the bottom of that canyon. Powell, with his intrepid band, ran the mysterious river in boats, a voyage that entailed terrible risk and hardship and loss of life. The red river of silt was a succession of dangerous rapids for two hundred and seventeen miles. Powell named them, and the intersecting gorges, and the superb peaks and domes as well as the differing reaches of the canyon.

In our modern day men even more daring than Coronado and Powell stood upon the black rim of the lower canyon and conceived an idea as strange and wild as any vague dawning thought of the cliff dwellers, or of the dreaming redskinned savage, an idea born of the progress of the world, as heroic and colossal as the inventive genius of engineers could conjure, as staggering and vain as the hopes of the builders of the pyramids, an idea that mounted irresistibly despite the mockery of an unconquerable nature—and it was to dam this ravaging river, to block and conserve its floods, to harness its incalculable power, to make it a tool of man.

Chapter 1

It was early in the evening of a spring night in Las Vegas, Nevada, 1932. The town roared with thousands of workers in from Boulder Dam to buck the tiger and have themselves a good time.

No Western town during the gold rush or the later frontier days could have held a candle to this modern wide-open city, which owed its mushroom growth and boom business to the great government project of damming the Colorado River.

Throngs of men paraded up and down the pavements under the glare of brilliant neon lights that turned night into day along the wide main street. The scene resembled Broadway on New Year's Eve, except for the horns and hilarity. This Boulder Dam crowd was noisy enough, but grim and hoarse, with the stride of men not easily brushed aside from the intent visible in gleaming eyes and on bronzed faces. A steady stream passed to and fro, congested and blocked every little way before the swinging doors of the gambling palaces.

Lynn Weston, young Californian, stood outside the Monte

Palace, indulging in his peculiar penchant for watching the passers-by. This habit had grown in Lynn during his frequent visits in from Boulder Dam. He belonged to this heterogeneous throng, and for the endless year of his toil at the dam he had been actuated by their common weakness for excitement and oblivion, yet in his way he was a lone wolf. The ignominy of the catastrophe that had forced him into the ranks of these raw workers weighed upon him less and less as time went on, and unaccustomed hard labor had begun its mysterious alchemy of change in him. Disappointment at unrealized opportunity for his ambition and bitterness at the misfortune of not completing his engineering course at college both had somewhat lost their sting. College man, famous football player, scion of an old California family whom the depression had reduced to unfamiliar and insupportable straits, and lastly a jilted lover who had welcomed his dismissal but who chafed under the shame of it, Lynn Weston looked on the passing throngs with slowly clarifying eyes, an awakening mind, and a strange sense that the something evermore about to happen to him was due. This mood never troubled him through the strenuous hours of rough labor, nor when he looked upon red liquor and the bright face of the gamblers' lure.

With a shrug of his broad shoulders Lynn went into the Palace. The glaring hall was full of a blue haze of smoke, the sound of men's voices, the clink of silver coins and the rattle of roulette wheels. Men stood ten deep around the gambling games. As Lynn elbowed his way back toward the rear his keen sight met the same weathered visages of his fellow workers and the same pale-faced, hard-eyed, thin-lipped parasites he was used to seeing there. In the rear of this long hall he knew where and how to get the bottle that had become a habit and which he despised for the very thing he found in it. Here in the rear lounged men for whom Lynn had no name but whom he always wanted to beat down and throw into the dirt. They were the dregs of humanity, outcasts, criminals, hopheads, men of a type he had taken care not to meet in the dark.

5

At length Lynn found a vacant chair at one of the poker tables, but the players there were too slick for him, and after dropping ten dollars he quit. He lost at monte too, and the big roulette wheel reduced his month's wages to a five-dollar bill. Lynn was gambler enough to grow cooler as luck held aloof. But he had another stiff drink.

At the faro table the fickle goddess of fortune smiled upon him. Lynn knew this dealer and that the game was crooked, but with the perversity of a gambler who was winning he kept backing his luck. And it stayed with him until he was far ahead. This was the time to quit. But Lynn was reluctant to turn his back upon a game that owed him much and which he wanted to beat, as much perhaps to get even with the crooked house as to square accounts. So he took another whirl at the game. This time Lynn's sharp trained eye caught the dealer in a flagrant bit of cheating. Quick as a flash he snatched at the dexterous white hand and with a wrench turned up the cupped palm. The dealer let out a half-stifled cry of pain and anger.

"Caught with the goods, Hevron!" Lynn rasped out piercingly, and he held the trapped hand for players and spectators to see. "There, plain as your hawk nose! This is the second time. If I hadn't beat your rotten game I'd take a sock at your ugly mug. . . . Here, cash these."

With lowered face clouded and ashen, Hevron made the exchange with white hands less dexterous than nervous.

"Young fellow, you're drunk. Better hold your tongue," he declared threateningly.

"No, I'm not drunk," returned Lynn. "You pulled a crooked trick. Some of these men saw it. You're crooked. This joint is the crookedest in Las Vegas. Everybody knows it. I was a sucker to come in here. But I'm even now, and I never will come back."

"You'll never get in my game. Beat it now or I'll have you thrown out."

"Is that so?" Lynn queried coolly, and he flashed out a brown hand that fastened in the dealer's shirt. With one powerful pull

6

Lynn dragged Hevron over the table into the scattering crowd. Then he swung at him. Hevron collided with a bystander, spun around and fell, striking his head hard upon the brass footrail of the bar. He collapsed there, with blood running from a gash over his ear.

"Say, Big Boy, look out how you slam people around," cut out a crisp voice to silence the noise.

Lynn looked up from Hevron into the cold face of Ben Sneed, lately come into notorious prominence as the boss bootlegger of the Boulder Dam project.

"How do, Sneed," replied Lynn. "Sorry he jostled you. But I wasn't looking at the backfield."

"What'd you sock him for?"

"Cheating. Then he threatened to throw me out. The other players will confirm my stand. . . . What's it to you?" Lynn replied curtly.

"Excuse me, Weston. It's none of my mix. I was beefing because he nearly upset me."

Lynn broke through the circle of spectators and hurried down the hall to go out the back door. He crossed the open plot of ground to the police station and entered. Logan, the night sheriff, a burly Texan with strong brown face and shrewd eyes, sat talking to several men. Lynn was relieved to find Logan, with whom he had some acquaintance.

"Howdy, Weston. What's it all aboot?" drawled the sheriff.

"I just socked Bat Hevron," Lynn returned hurriedly. "Caught him cheating, Sheriff—the second time. I was ahead of the game—and if he hadn't got sore nothing would have happened. But he was ugly—said I was drunk and threatened to throw me out."

"Wal, thet's too bad," Logan replied slowly, stroking his square chin. "I reckon you had it on him."

"Yes. I'm sure I can prove it. . . . The punch I gave him wouldn't have hurt much, but he fell and cut his head. For all I know he might have fractured his skull. He was out, all right."

"What you want me to do, son? Lock you up?"

7

"I should say not. I just wanted you to have my story first."

"Weston, you go back to Boulder and stay there till this blows over," advised Logan. "Shore, I wouldn't pinch you—not on Hevron's say-so, or the house either. But thet's a bad outfit, son. As a matter of fact the Monte is the crookedest joint in Las Vegas. Most of the gambling halls here give you an honest run for your money. But there are big shots behind the Monte. We couldn't shut them up if we wanted to. There's been some tough fights. I've been beat up bad a dozen times."

"How come, Sam?" asked one of his companions. "That's funny, from you."

"I don't reckon it's funny. You see, my town bosses won't let me use a gun. I had hell not long ago for shootin' a hombre's laig off. I had to. He pulled a knife on me. But the fact is every time we have to make an arrest an' get into a jam we have to use our fists. How's thet for as wild a burg as Tombstone or Ely or Tonopah ever was?"

"If I don't miss my guess you'll not live long here," the other rejoined tersely.

"Sheriff," spoke up Lynn, "when I let Hevron have it he upset Ben Sneed. And Sneed called me pretty sharp. Could he have any interest in the Monte joint?"

"He could, shore, but I reckon not. Sneed is the squarest bootlegger that we've had heah. Fact is he's a good chap. I like him. Says he buys an' sells booze. Thet's all. Runs a swell night club oot at his ranch. But no gamblin'. . . . I'll tell you, Weston, you've made an enemy in Hevron. He came heah from Chicago. He's a bad egg. An' his dealin' faro is just a blind. He could hire one of thet lousy ootfit at his hangoot to slit yore throat for a dime an' get back some change. You beat it back to Boulder City an' stay there."

"Thanks, Sheriff. I'll do that little thing," Lynn replied soberly, and went out. Cutting across the block he reached a side street and went on to the corner. There he halted a moment. It was nothing for Weston to slug a man. He had done it often, but he

8

feared that he might have done it once too often. Sheriff Logan had been outspoken, and concerned, which was enough to give Lynn a case of the jitters. Just what had Logan meant by Hevron dealing faro as a blind, and who were the men that would slit a throat for a dime and give back some change? All kinds of rackets had grown up like weeds since the great influx of workers to the Dam. Bootlegging was carried on open and aboveboard. But Lynn had heard rumors of rackets that cast bootlegging in the shade. There was a tough gang from Oklahoma that hung out in the hills above the Pass some twenty miles from Las Vegas and just out of the Boulder Dam Reservation. This gang was suspected of holding up laborers on their way to town. A number of men had been found dead along the roadside, apparently having been struck by a speeding car when they were going back to camp drunk. There was a Montana outfit of wild cowboys somewhere in the district. Least known of all was a bunch of Chicago gangsters who worked at the dam and operated in Las Vegas. Rumor had it their women were with them.

Lynn thought about those elements, now that he had allowed his temper to get the better of him. And he made up his mind to keep a keen eye about him and pass up the bright lights for a while.

On his way down the main street, when he got beyond the crowd and near the side street where he had parked his car he felt he was being followed by two men. Crossing the street he went back uptown. No doubt some of the thugs at the Monte had seen him win the several hundred dollars and were bent on relieving him of it. Lynn did not relish the idea of being bumped off for some ill-earned money. Before he got to the center of town he made sure he was being followed. This caused a slow fire to burn out the cold constriction in his veins. He ought to have a gun, but he did not dare risk going into a store. Instead he ducked into the crowded Blue Eagle and got out the back way before his shadowers had time to enter at the front. Then he ran up the alley to the next side street. By the time Lynn had gotten back to the main thoroughfare he was sore. This running from a couple of footpads did not strike him pleasantly at all. He had had just enough whisky to be easily roused.

Whereupon he strolled along under the flaring lights, keeping to the outside of the stream of noisy men. His cap afforded poor concealment for his eyes, so he went into a store and bought a sombrero. Resuming his walk he went on down to the Monte. Here Lynn stood back in the shadow of a projecting corner of wall.

He had been there scarcely a moment when three hard-looking customers hurriedly came out of the Monte, followed by Ben Sneed, his keen face dark as a thundercloud.

"If Ben Bellew gets that girl I'll scramble you saps all over the place," Sneed hissed into their ears.

"Aw, Ben, you shouldn't have left thet dame," returned one, with the fear of death in his hoarse voice.

"Hell! She was naked, wasn't she? I had to buy her some clothes. And I locked her in, didn't I?"

"Bellew must have trailed her."

"Scram! Get the car, you . . ."

The quartet passed on out of hearing. Lynn, his ears ringing, leaned there shot through with curiosity and speculation. He was always seeing or hearing something to stir his feelings. In this instance he had to fight a strong impulse to follow Sneed. There was deviltry afoot every dark hour of this raw Las Vegas night. But he had his own risk to think of. Lynn watched vigilantly for the men he had caught dogging his footsteps, and he was not at all sure that he could recognize them.

After a goodly wait, during which his anger and alarm eased, he hurried down the street. At every cross street he turned to look back. When he was four blocks down he decided he had given them the slip, and he reached the outskirts of town without renewed alarm.

Lynn turned off at the last side street to find his car. There were no lights near, which was the reason he had chosen this dark

10

place to park. Cars had a habit of disappearing around Las Vegas. He walked clear out into the desert without locating the anti-quated automobile that he called his own. Turning back he concluded he had missed the street. Perhaps in the darkness he had gotten turned around. He went clear to the electric light which marked the corner where he had turned off. As his brain was a little befogged he could not be sure of direction.

As he nearly reached the corner a big car whirled up and stopped with a roar. Three men leaped out. One ran across under the light to disappear up the side street. The other two halted to peer in Lynn's direction.

"She went this way."

"I saw her run under the light. She had a blanket round her."

"Not down that street," came a sharp voice from the car. "She went across here. Hurry!"

Lynn had halted under a tree. He knew he could be seen if they looked in his direction, and he did not want to be caught in a suspicious position, so he walked boldly out.

"Wait! Someone comin'," whispered the nearest of the two men.

"Halt! Who're you?"

Lynn found himself confronted by two men whose faces he could not see distinctly under their wide-brimmed hats. His quick eye detected the menacing right hand of one thrust into his coat pocket, which protruded ominously. There was a gun there in the grip of a man with murder in his heart.

"What's this—a holdup?" asked Lynn.

"Oke, you guessed right," came the rough reply, and the man poked the concealed gun against Lynn's abdomen. "Look him over, Gip."

The second ruffian leaned close to scrutinize Lynn's features. "Never seen him before," he said.

"Talk!" ordered the other, punching Lynn with the gun.

"Well, I'm a little—nervous to talk—if I knew anything to say," replied Lynn. And the fact was that he could scarcely restrain from hitting out with all his might. On the instant, then, the man

11

in the car leaned out, bareheaded, his face in the light. Lynn recognized Ben Sneed.

"Did you see a girl runnin' along here?"

"No," replied Lynn.

"We're losing time," called Sneed from the car. "Jump in. We'll follow Ring."

In another moment Lynn found himself watching the red tail-lights of the car vanishing in the direction the man called Ring had taken.

"Well, what do you know about this?" he muttered. "If I ever meet that bozo again I'll know him, and will I sock him? I'm telling you. . . . Whew! A gun shoved in your belly doesn't feel so hot."

Lynn watched for the car to come back. He heard it for a moment longer. Then the hum ceased. He wondered if Sneed had caught the girl in the blanket.

"A naked girl running away in a blanket!" he muttered, perplexed and wondering. "By gum! That's the white-slave stuff! But Sneed didn't strike me as low-down as that."

He waited there for a little while, watching and conjecturing. Several cars passed, traveling in both directions. At length Lynn decided he had better find his own car if he didn't want to walk half the night to get home to his cabin. A search down the side street in the direction Sneed had taken failed to locate the car. He began to fear it had been stolen. The loss of the ramshackle vehicle would not concern him, but he wanted to get home. Then he retraced his steps down the street he had first searched, but on the opposite side, and found his car against a background of brush that had made it difficult to distinguish in the dark. Hopping in, he was soon on the move and turned on the road toward Boulder Dam.

Lynn had not noticed the cold until he got going, but with the desert wind whipping in at both sides of his car he became chilled through. He had a comfortable warm sensation, however, where the bulging pocket full of silver dollars sagged heavily against him.

12

Excitement lingered with him, despite his relief. It had been rather a momentous evening, and no doubt that augmented his thrilling sense of the desert. The bare windiness stretched vague under the stars to the black mountains on the horizon. The dry sweet tang of sage and greasewood stung his cold nose. Far ahead two bright eyes of a car pierced the darkness, and still farther on twinkled a couple of pinpoints. Five miles or more out the red-gold lights of Ben Sneed's ranch burned against the white-walled hacienda with its dark arches. Lynn had dropped in at the resort several times, but not to stay long. Sneed did not run games of chance.

"I'm curious about that guy," he mused, as he passed the notorious night club. "Wonder if he got the girl with the blanket? Some life round this Boulder Dam diggings!"

The tremendousness of that engineering project and the magnificence of its setting in the Black Canyon of the Colorado had struck Lynn with staggering force at his very first sight and conception of them. They had changed the direction of his life; they had set him at a man's job; they had been responsible for the gradual development of his character; they had at length replaced the bitterness of failure and drifting to some vague dream of finding himself on the ladder to success.

It was the desert then that had taken intangible and subtle hold of Lynn Weston. Looking backward he could realize how by imperceptible degrees he had learned to love the lonely and desolate wasteland of rock that the torture of hard labor had blinded him to at first. There seemed to be something permanent for him out here in this Nevada. He conceived the idea right there—why not let this large sum of money he had won be a nucleus to a stake which he could add to during the years Boulder Dam would be in building? Then he could buy a ranch, or start a gold mine, or develop some business on the big inland lake which the dam would flood back into the canyon and basin and which in time would become a sportsman's paradise. And suddenly he recalled what he had long forgotten—the scorn with which Helen Pritchard had ended their engagement and the more

13

grievous fact of his family evidently having shared her conviction of his hopelessness. But she was wrong, thought Lynn, strangely finding himself free of the old pain; and his family might yet be embarrassingly forced to change their minds, if they did not actually receive help from him.

How this old desert brought home to a man the things that counted—endurance and strength and guts to make life possible and worth living!

Lynn slowed down at the government inspection post, where record was kept of all workers going and coming. He had a cheery word for the guard who passed him.

"Back early, Weston," was the grinning reply. "Sober an' broke, I'll bet."

"Wrong both ways, Dan. . . . How many cars ahead of me the last hour?"

"Two, I reckon. A truck, an' a Ford full of micks."

"So long. I won't be seeing you for a spell."

A few miles farther on Lynn clattered up a grade to the pass. That was a gateway to the rough brakes of the canyon country. Back from the road from benches and in coves between the hills gleamed the lights of the camps of the riffraff drawn from all over the United States. It was not a safe place to pass late at night. But Lynn drove slowly because he did not want to hit some murdered workman or outcast whose body might be tumbled from behind rock or brush out upon the road. Where the pass opened wide beyond the black hills he sped by Rankin's Palace, a huge rambling structure gaudy with its many different-colored lights. Music came on the cold wind. If law had any jurisdiction over Rankin's resort it had never been called upon. Money could buy anything there. But the laborers had learned to give it a wide berth. Visitors, tourists, adventurers, gamblers, rich men's sons and society women out for a kick furnished Rankin with his pickings.

Beyond this no man's land Lynn entered the government reserve and approached the broad plateau where a model town, Boulder

14

City, was in the course of construction.

Lynn turned off the smooth asphalt thoroughfare into a gravel road that headed down into the huge desert basin back of Boulder Dam. Here he entered the canyon country. The road was lighted, but the lamps appeared only to accentuate the lonely desert. For miles downgrade there were no buildings, no works of any kind, until he crossed the railroad track which had been built twelve miles down into the basin. This railroad forked below the crossing, the right-hand branch running down to the river and along the shore into the canyon to be dammed; and the left branch turned off into the basin toward the gravel pits from which millions of tons of sand and gravel were to be transported to the site of the dam.

Sand and gravel were Lynn's job, but he did not think of them then. As always, and especially at night, he felt the call of that wonderful country. The hills along which he drove would soon be submerged under the largest body of water ever artificially made by labor of man, but Lynn did not think of that, either. He caught glimpses of the Colorado, gleaming palely under the bright stars and mirroring the great walls. Lynn did not trust that swirling, sullen, muddy river. He had worked along it for a year now. He had seen it once in flood. He questioned the effrontery of man's egotism. The Rio Colorado had a voice, a low sullen murmur of unrestraint. In Lynn's secret opinion only the elemental forces that had given birth to this strange river could ever change its course or dam it permanently.

On the Arizona side the black walls stood up ragged and bold, and beyond them, touching the stars, lifted the stark and ghastly mountains. The basin on Lynn's left opened out into dim and obscure space, bounded by the distant Nevada hills. Across it the cold wind whipped, carrying alkali dust and grains of sand to sting Lynn's face. He used to gaze out upon that lonely vague gloom as if it were his future. But that thought had gone, he didn't remember when, and when he looked now it was to feel something vital and compelling to which he could give no name.

15

The night gravel train went puffing and rattling by, carrying its thousands of tons down to the mixing mill above the site of the dam. A bend in the road brought Lynn into a zone of electric lights that shone upon the gravel mounds, like gray foothills under the huge iron structures. At the moment a swinging car from high on the bridge tumbled its load with a thunderous roar. Out of the darkness and peace of the desert Lynn had come upon the inferno of man's creation—yellow light and glare, roar of machinery, ceaseless action of men at work. No moment of cessation of continuous labor on the building of Boulder Dam! The big dormitory appeared to shine with a hundred window eyes, and the camp beyond further attested to the fact that there was no darkness or rest here.

Lynn drove by the camp to his rude cabin. He had preferred this shack of boards to a tent, in which he had sweltered and frozen by turns.

"Once again, old Tincan!" he said, as he brought his car to a jolting halt. Then as he got out he heard a moan. "Hello! Have I got them?" Listening a moment he was amazed and transfixed by a low sound, like a sobbing intake of breath. It came from the back of his car, and it galvanized him into action.

He peered over the door. There was something on the floor—an indistinct shape, mostly dark, but lighter toward him.

"For the love of Mike!" Lynn whispered incredulously. And he thrust a swift hand over the door. It came into contact with curly soft hair on a small round head. An unaccountable thrill checked him for an instant. He bent over, trying to see, feeling farther. His forceful hand encountered a fold of woolen blanket that fell back to let him touch the outline of a woman's body.

16

Chapter 2

With a start Lynn hastily withdrew his hand. His first whirling thought was that thugs had used his car as a means to get rid of a murdered victim. Then his straining eyes distinguished the dark little head and the white shoulder. He sustained a strong shock. And on the instant when he sought to find his wits another gasping intake of breath routed his fearful consternation.

"Alive, by God!" he cried under his breath, and he ripped open the door.

Lynn put his arms under the girl, and lifting her out he carried her toward his cabin, bending a searching glance all around. The flare of electric lights did not extend that far. He could not be seen in the gloom. The girl felt like a lightweight in his arms. Holding her in one arm, he opened the door, went in and laid her on his bed. His next swift move was to bar the door, after which he let down the canvas curtains to his two windows. After that he reached up to turn on the electric light.

The girl was recovering consciousness, if she had lost it. Then

17

her eyes opened, wide gray gulfs of terror.

"Don't let them—get me," she begged almost inaudibly.

"I'll say they won't, young lady," Lynn burst out in relief as well as haste to reassure her. "I found you in my car—just now. Drove out all the way from town."

"Where am—I?" she asked.

"You're in my shack at the gravel pits above the dam—thirty miles from town. I work here. My name's Lynn Weston. I'm from California. . . . You're safe, girl."

"Oh, thank heaven!" she cried weakly and appeared about to faint.

"Don't—don't pass out. Tell me quick—are you injured?" And he leaned over to shake her gently.

"No, I'm not hurt."

"Did they—Bellew or Sneed—any of that rotten gang—harm you?"

"Oh, you know—!"

"I overheard enough to—to give me a hunch. Quite by accident I happened to hear Sneed and his men as they came out of the Monte. They spoke of Bellew. Then down the street where I was looking for my Ford. Ran into Sneed again—his car—three men jumped out. They had seen you run by under the light. They held me up—with a gun—the thugs! Asked if I'd seen a girl. You must have hidden in my car then."

"Oh! I've gotten away," she exclaimed, staring up at him. Her white hands shook as she held the blanket close.

"You sure have. But tell me—did they? . . . How'd you happen to be—this way? Surely you don't belong to Bellew or Sneed?"

"Bellew's a white slaver."

"Oh! So that's it? Now we're . . . Say, girl, did he—they harm you?"

"No. I'm all right—only scared—and frozen stiff."

"What a sap I am!" Lynn said, and sprang into action. He kindled a wood fire in his little stove and put water on to heat. Then he got out a pair of pajamas and spread them upon his rude

18

rocker to get warm. He found his slippers, also, and a fleece-lined coat. "There! Soon as the fire's hot you get into these—and put the blanket over your knees. I'll go outside. Then I'll come back say in ten minutes and make you a cup of coffee."

With that Lynn stalked outdoors to pace up and down before his cabin. It was not likely that anyone would come along at this hour, but he kept strict lookout, while he marveled and pondered over the adventure that had befallen him. Who was this girl, and how had she gotten into such a predicament? She appeared to be about nineteen years old and she was strikingly beautiful. He could not forget her large gray eyes stained dark in fright.

He walked up and down beside the car. What would he do now that he had accidentally saved the girl? He did not know. But it dawned vaguely upon him that the something he had felt coming must have had its inception in this adventure. The whole year he had toiled there, from almost the very day he had turned away in bitter contempt from Helen Pritchard there on the rim of Black Canyon where he had sustained the crucial shock of his life, had been one of inscrutable pangs and dawnings, of a grim stubborn resolve, of fleeting dreamful glimpses of the reward of a newer different life. Could this girl have been dropped out of the clouds to react in some way upon him? Every hour of toil, every bit of suffering, everything that had happened during this eventful year, looked back upon, seemed to have been intended to test him in some inexplicable way. Lynn had to ridicule the fact that inside his cabin was a young girl whom fate had thrown in his way and had given him the good fortune to serve, perhaps to save, her.

"I'm a queer sap," he thought, gazing across the dark void toward the bold mountains. "Finding out I never knew myself. Sentimental—and full of mush in this modern day! Maybe I'd be well to trail along with this unknown self. It's a cinch the other side was a flop."

Presently he went back into the cabin, barring the door behind him. His guest sat in the old rocker before the roaring stove,

19

dressed as he had expected to find her. But Lynn was wholly unprepared for the prettiest girl he had ever seen.

"Well, how you making out?" he asked gayly.

"I'm warm and comfortable—thank you," she replied gratefully. "And that awful something—here—is leaving me."

"A hot cup of coffee will help it go," Lynn said cheerfully and proceeded to lift the steaming pot off the stove. "I don't batch it here. But I've a few camp utensils I found in this shack, and I amuse myself making coffee occasionally. . . . But perhaps you'd prefer a drink?"

"No, thanks."

"That's lucky. Now that I think of it, I haven't anything to offer you. . . . Here's your coffee. It's hot, so be careful. And here's sugar. . . . I guess I'll drink a cup myself. It sure was cold driving out tonight."

Presently Lynn drew a box up to the stove and seating himself upon it sipped his coffee and watched the red fire through the little barred door. What he wished most at the moment was to look at this girl so strangely thrust upon him and next to that to question her. Nevertheless he refrained from either.

"I'll go outside presently and let you have my bed," he said. "I can find a place to sleep. I'll be right close, in the woodshed in case you want me. Then in the morning we'll talk over what's best to do."

"You're very good," she murmured. "What can I do? No clothes—no money!"

"We'll get the clothes," Lynn said quickly. "Just you write out what you need—what things, size, you know, and I'll get someone to go to the store."

"I'll pay you back if I can only find a job," she replied gratefully. "Only I'll always be afraid to hunt for a job again. Because that is how I fell into this terrible fix."

"Miss, you needn't tell me if you'd rather not. Only I—"

"Oh, I must tell you," she interposed earnestly. "You're kind—and nice . . . I can trust you. I'm alone—no friends—no relations

20

—no home. You might be the friend I need so dreadfully."

"I will be," rejoined Lynn. "As I told you, Lynn Weston is my name. Did you ever hear of it?"

"No. But your face is familiar. I've seen it somewhere. Are you in the movies?"

"Good Lord, no. I was just a football player—soon forgotten."

Apparently the girl had gotten over the worst of her fright by this time for she began, eagerly. "My name is Anne Vandergrift. I'm nearly twenty. I was born in Salem, Illinois. My mother died when I was little. A few years ago my father followed her. But before he died he arranged for a friend of his, Henry Smith, who had gone to Los Angeles, to give me work. I came West. Mr. Smith sent me to business school for six months and then employed me. I lived with his family and was happy. Then came the Depression. It ruined Mr. Smith. He committed suicide. His family had to get out and fare for themselves. So did I. Jobs were easy to get. But I couldn't keep them—I—I couldn't—"

"Why not?" Lynn interposed deliberately and turned to look at her. That done he had neither inclination nor power to avert his fascinated gaze.

"Because the men who offered me jobs or tried me out wanted me to—to go out with them. I just couldn't see it their way. So I kept tramping the streets. I lived on my savings, and they dwindled until I was broke. My landlady kept my few belongings and turned me out. . . . That day on Main Street I found an employment agency with a sign in the window, GIRLS WANTED. I went in. A woman told me she had jobs for waitresses in Las Vegas. That the town was booming with the building of Boulder Dam. I said I'd be glad to take any wages and go at once. Then she questioned me sharply, asked about relatives or friends in Los Angeles. When I explained I had none she said she would send me to Las Vegas that day by bus. She'd pay my fare and have someone meet me in Las Vegas. I had only an hour to get ready. I *was* ready, right then, and so I told her."

"Well, Anne," Lynn spoke up dryly as she paused for breath.

21

"Strikes me you were pretty much of a tenderfoot to fall for that line so easily."

"I was. . . . That woman went with me, put me on a bus. There were several other girls, two that I didn't care to talk to. And one who couldn't speak English. Other passengers got on at San Bernardino and Barstow. But I didn't get acquainted with them. It was after dark when the bus got to Las Vegas. A man with a thin dark face and sharp dark eyes met me as if he knew me and took me to a house and gave me a room upstairs. He said he'd send my supper up to me—that Las Vegas was a wild town and I mustn't go out. I was too tired and excited even to eat much."

"Anne, you don't look like a dumbbell," Lynn burst out almost heatedly at the girl's evident innocence. "Why, any kid would have been suspicious of that situation."

"I thought it was strange, but I had no choice," she went on mournfully. "I slept like a log. And I was awakened by a hard-faced woman who brought my breakfast. She told me to hurry and eat and said she'd be up again right away to talk about work. I ate my breakfast in bed and was just about to get up and dress when the woman came in again. She locked the door and gathered up my clothes. Then she went out and locked the door. I was horrified. But still I didn't quite understand. When I began to look around I discovered the only window was a skylight in the ceiling. The walls were thick—the door heavy. Then I realized I was a captive. I wrapped a blanket round me. It seemed a long time before I heard any noise. Then I heard voices outside the door. It was a young man that entered—a well-dressed, smooth-faced chap, good-looking except for his eyes. They were hot, like molten metal. He carried a thin shiny whip in his hand. He talked sweet—I forget his words—tried to get fresh, and when I flung him off he cut me across the leg with the whip. . . . Look here."

Whereupon the girl, now pale and earnest in her story, dropped the slipper off her right foot and let the blanket fall from her knees. She pulled up the pajamas Lynn had lent her and showed a shapely leg with a cruel red welt marring its white beauty.

Lynn bit his tongue to keep back a wrathful curse and could only stare in amazement and anger.

"That cut hurt so terribly I fell right down on the floor," resumed the girl, once more lifting the blanket over her knees. "He would have struck me again, surely, when another man entered. He was older and had a face like a hawk. His right hand was in his pocket, and he stuck it out at the younger fellow. 'Beat it!' he said. As the first man ran out a third man came in. He was not young and somehow he was different. He looked only at my face. 'It's the girl I want, Bellew,' he said. 'She's the one I saw brought off the bus. . . .' Bellew said, 'Cost you ten grand, Ben Sneed.' 'Listen, hophead,' replied Sneed, and his voice cut like a blade, 'I'll pay the ten grand, but right now—and take her away as soon as I can.'

"I remember every word they spoke. And I saw how Bellew stood with that pocket of his pointed toward Sneed. He had a gun in it, because I'd seen that in the movies. . . . 'Bellew, I'll talk turkey with you,' Sneed said, cold as ice. 'You lock this girl in here. You can go with me while I dig up that ten grand.' 'Ben you're not the big shot in this burg,' snarled Bellew. 'You're only a booze peddler. This is my racket.' 'Yes,' said Sneed, 'this racket is yours, all right, along with other dirty rackets, one of which is hijacking my trucks. I'm wise to you. And one more blow like that will be curtains for you and all of your gang. It's not my way to talk turkey with men like you. That's on account of this girl. . . . Come on, now, scram.'

"They left the room," whispered Anne Vandergrift, moistening her lips. "I was alone. I don't know whether the time dragged or flew. But the room began to get dark. I knew the sun had set. It grew night. I could only wait and pray. After a while I heard loud voices—footsteps. I listened. The woman was being dragged up the stairs. More men came running up the stairs. A fight followed. Blows, curses! I found myself free and stumbled down a stairway that opened into an alley. From there I got on the main street. I ran as fast as I could, holding the blanket round me. At

23

first someone followed me, I was sure. But I got away—up that side street—where I found your car. I tried to start it, but couldn't. I only had enough strength to crawl in the back and hide. . . . That's all, Mr. Weston—and here I am."

She sat back in the rocker, pale and breathless from her recital, her gaze intent upon Lynn. He saw that her eyes were unusually large and gray-green in color. She had nut-brown hair, curly and disheveled, with glints of a lighter shade in it. Her face was cast in a mold that would have been beautiful even without expression or glow. Her eyes were wide apart under level brows. Cheek and chin and neck all merged in a perfect contour without line or blemish, and a faint blue tracery of veins showed through the pearly skin.

"Some story!" Lynn exclaimed huskily. "You had a lucky break! . . . Let me find you pencil and paper so you can write out that list before you go to bed."

"Won't it look strange—you buying all these woman's things?"

"I'll get a woman to do it."

"What will she think?"

"By George! I'll have to fix that somehow. Because I want to find a job for you over at the supply camp. I'll puzzle it out. . . . Slip out of that coat, please. I'll need it. And I'll take this blanket you brought with you. Go to bed now and sleep. You'll be warm —and safe."

She stood up to comply with his request, and despite his ill-fitting pajamas she presented a picture he would not soon forget.

"And you—you'll be where you can hear me?"

"Just outside."

"Won't you freeze?"

"I'll be okay. Let's see now. I'm on the job from nine until five. I'll have to come in early, start you a fire and get the list and beat it to camp. Maybe I can get an hour or two off. Then after work I'll see you. . . . Good night, Anne Vandergrift."

She murmured an inaudible reply, and he felt her eyes on him as he saw to the stove, and then as he backed toward the door

24

he looked up to see her earnest, unutterably grateful face.

Lynn went out to get in the car, and wrapping the blanket round his legs he slid down to rest and think, if not to sleep. After a few minutes the light went out in the cabin. A dull rattle and roll of wheels, with an occasional roar, filled Lynn's ears. The immediate problem concerning this girl did not seem to present any particular obstacle. He could place her in one of the boarding houses over at camp and take care of her till he had found work for her. Boulder Dam was known to try all the workers who applied. But what concerned Lynn was these damned racketeers. Since his advent at Las Vegas he had heard gossip about them. They were princes of crime. They had a system of extortion the laymen could not understand. If the little booze-peddling agents had money to burn what vast sums Ben Sneed must command! If he offered ten thousand dollars to Bellew for this singularly attractive and innocent girl he would pay ten times that amount. These men carried on their nefarious trades with no regard for the law whatsoever. For them there was no law. Their rivalries, jealousies, greeds, had them continually at each others' throats.

Pondering over this serious phase of the situation Lynn fell asleep. Late in the night he awoke, cramped and cold, and shivered and dozed and waited until daylight. Then he went to the gravel camp cook house and had his breakfast, filled his pockets with fruit and made some sandwiches. After that he hunted up his boss and asked for a little time off. The camp rules were strict, but he succeeded in his mission and then hurried back to his cabin.

When he entered, Anne was sound asleep. Lynn carried a basin of water and his shaving things outside, where he proceeded to break his usual routine. He had never shaved very often and never until after work. He was aware of this departure, but did not question it. When he got through, the sun burst rosy and bright over the Arizona mountains. Lynn went indoors again, not tiptoeing this time. But the girl did not stir. He rolled up the

25

eastern canvas blind which let in the sun upon Anne's face. Lynn was compelled to halt and gaze at her. Something more than a natural admiration stirred in him. How young, fresh, helpless, sad and lovely she looked in that rosy morning light! Lynn had to give her a little shake to awaken her.

The big eyes fluttered open. Shadows of slumber succeeded to shadows of doubt and fear. Her gaze flashed from Lynn round the cabin and back again. "Oh! Where am I? Who . . ."

"Wake up, Anne, and remember," he said cheerily. "I'm the lucky guy who found you in his car last night. . . . Listen, I'll lay a fire for you to start when you want to make a cup of coffee. Here's some fruit and sandwiches, all I could swipe. Bar the door after I go out. My luxurious bathroom is in that compartment through the window there. . . . Where's your list? Ah, there it is! It doesn't appear long for a young lady at the moment absolutely dependent upon a Boulder Dam laborer's pajamas."

"I don't need—very much," she faltered, and the color in her face was not all a sunrise flush.

"Okay. I'm off. You were hard to wake up. Sleep all day."

"Will you be gone so long?"

"I have to work, you know, mysterious stranger. And drive in for your things after hours. So long. And don't worry. It's all right."

Lynn hurried out, somewhat amused and puzzled at his feelings. He had been in haste to leave the cabin, yet he wanted to stay. Tincan appeared cantankerous that morning and did not want to get going. She was always presenting Lynn with new and intricate mechanical problems to solve. At last the engine thawed out, sputtered and roared. Once beyond the great dunes of gravel Lynn stepped on the gas and put the old tin horse to its best paces.

The spring morning must have been unusually beautiful. Lynn found the sunrise glamour on basin and range like rose-colored glasses to delight the eye. The hard picture of the desert appeared softened. Sage and greasewood, and bare swales of sand, and rolling ridges were crested with tints of fire. The Colorado flowed

26

out of a red gap in the frowning walls and slid with ruddy gleam on toward the black canyon which still slept in somber shadow.

Lynn made the run up the grade to the main road in record time. Then he slowed for the turn down on the bench where Boulder City was in course of construction. It took vision to make of all the heaps of earth and piles of lumber, the bare skeletons of buildings rising like a denuded forest, the trucks roaring to and fro, the big steam shovels clanging, the action of workmen thick as a swarm of crawling bees, the acres of shacks and tents stretching far along the level—it took eyes to picture the shining and model city that was to become famous there.

A long street of stores terminated in the finished dormitories and the great dining house that took care of thousands of men. Lynn halted his hot car at the largest store.

After buying some food supplies and the list of clothes for Anne, he found upon applying for information that there were several hundred married men among the builders there, and they kept house in the little cabins that were being rapidly built for their accommodation. He was furnished with a list of names of those who would take a boarder. One of these was a pipe fitter named Brown, who lived with his wife in the camp at the gravel mills. Lynn drove back to the basin.

At ten o'clock he climbed the steel crane to relieve the engineer who had been put on his job. Lynn had graduated to this job by the hard apprenticeship he had served as a common laborer. And his job was to run one of the lofty carriages that swung the big tanks of graded sand and gravel from the huge piles to the freight cars which were loaded under the steel bridge. It was a job of concentration and precision. Lynn had to be alert all the time. The sand and gravel came in carloads from the pits of the river, were dumped from the high trestle into the mills, to come out cleaned, assorted, into the rounded glistening mounds, from which they were loaded again into freight cars and hauled down to the canyon, to the electric cement mill, most marvelous of Boulder Dam's many magic machines.

Lynn took a nameless pride in the fact that he was a little cog

27

in the vast system of wheels which must whirl ceaselessly for years, without ever a stop, until Boulder Dam was completed. How he had arrived at that stage he scarcely understood, unless the contrast from former toil and its accompanying pangs had developed it in him. That day, as the humming and roaring hours passed, he conceived the idea of having a hand at other and perilous jobs down in the canyon. The great diversion tunnels that were to carry the waters of the Colorado under the walls and around the dam, these haunted him, and the work had only begun. He wanted to ride one of the carriages that dropped a thousand feet down into the canyon, to perch like an eagle above it all and watch. He intended to be a driller, a dynamiter, a scaler, most perilous of all work on the dam, and lastly to rise to some competent and permanent job.

These plans coalesced and fixed in his mind that day, and he admitted that it was because Anne would be working at Boulder City and he wanted to be near her. It was just a kindness on his part, he thought, a desire to serve her and outwit those villains who trafficked in the souls and bodies of American girls.

That day turned out to be the most endless Lynn had ever spent there. But it wore to a close, and then he made for his car. Sunset burned in his eyes all the way to the construction camp.

At last he hauled up short before his dark cabin. He had not thought of it, but he should have expected it to be dark. The girl would hardly have risked turning on the lights in his absence. Lynn lifted out the big parcels of supplies and rapped on the door.

No response! He rapped again anxiously. Still there was no answer. She must be asleep. He tried the door and to his amazement it was unbarred. He went in, and called in a low voice. Then alarm seized Lynn. He flashed on the lights and in consternation saw the cabin was empty. No fire in the stove! His pajamas lay on the bed unfolded, as if hastily thrown there. Anne Vandergrift was gone.

"My God!" he thought. "Is it possible those thugs could work so quickly!"

Chapter 3

Bewildered, and suddenly sick with the conviction of catastrophe, Lynn absurdly searched the empty cabin with hopeful eyes. Then he flung aside the curtain that hung before the opening through the partition at the back. The little storeroom and woodshed were likewise empty.

"She's gone!" he admitted, and spying the garments he had lent her and both his blankets and the one she had arrived in, he was further staggered. "Gone! Without a stitch on her! Good heaven, what's to be made of this? . . . I'll kill those crooks."

Lynn sank in the old rocker and gazed blankly at the packages he had dropped to the floor. A cold sweat broke out all over him. He endeavored to still his agitation so that he could think what he must do. But it was futile. His grief and fury, and another emotion unfamiliar to him, would not be assuaged at the moment. He could not sit still. He got up to pace the floor. What had happened to Anne Vandergrift? Helpless before that one poignant query he could only reiterate it.

A rustle outside the open door brought Lynn upright. A white face appeared against the black background. It flashed across the threshold. Anne Vandergrift ran in with softly thudding feet. She closed the door and dropped the bar in place, then turned to come to him, her gray eyes unnaturally wide and bright.

"*Anne*! . . . You're not gone? They didn't get you?" Lynn burst out.

"No. But have I had a scare! Oh, I thought you'd never—never come," she replied.

If the moment had not been so vital and compelling Lynn would have laughed at the girl's ludicrous appearance. She looked lost in his fleece-lined coat, and she had donned a pair of his overalls and had tucked the bottoms in heavy woolen socks. She kicked off his loose slippers and then slipped out of the coat. Under it she had on his red blouse, which completely hid her femininity. But after a second glance at her flashing face and tumbling hair Lynn did not see anything else.

"I borrowed your clothes," she said, her gravity breaking.

"So I see. You look—swell," he rejoined haltingly and then flounced onto the chair as if weak in his relief.

"By George, but I'm glad you're here safe."

"You couldn't be half as glad as I am."

"I thought . . . Well, never mind. . . . How come, Anne—that I found you gone?"

"I slept almost all day," she replied hurriedly. "When I got up I thought I'd better put on these. It was a good thing I did. I'd hardly got dressed when I saw a big car down by that long house across the road from the tents."

"That's the mess hall where we eat."

"I saw men get out. There were five of them. Gangsters! Oh, I could recognize a gangster now in a burlap sack. They looked like wolves on the scent. Four of them went in. And the one who stayed by the car was Bellew."

"Bellew!" ejaculated Lynn, leaping up.

"Yes. I knew him, even at that distance. I nearly dropped. All I could think of was to run and hide. I went out the back way

—out into the brush—where I hid behind a rock. I was not able to see the car, but I could have seen it come down the road toward the cabin. It didn't come. And after a while I lost some of my fright, but I stayed out there till I saw the light show from your window. I'd heard a car—a sputtering, rattling car which I thought was yours. But, believe me, I made sure it was you in here."

"Anne, what was Bellew doing out here?" demanded Lynn.

"He was after me. He *might* have been on some other errand. That's possible. But I felt he was after me."

"What made you feel that way?"

"I—I don't know. Only I saw him—I heard him. He wasn't like a human being. He's steel and—and flint. A terrible man! It made me weak just to know he was out there. . . . Mr. Weston, please —please don't let him get me."

"Cut the mister," responded Lynn, gruff in his confoundment and apprehension. "My name's Lynn. I fetched your things and some supper for both of us. But we'll have to cook it."

"I can cook," she said seriously.

"I'll build the fire and get some water in. Then I'll go out and snoop around. I didn't see any cars, only trucks as I drove in. . . . I wonder—had I better take you away tonight?"

"Oh, let me stay," she pleaded wildly. She appeared terribly unstrung.

"That'd really be best. I didn't have time to find you a boarding-house."

"Lynn, why not let me stay here a—a little while. . . . Let me hide here till Bellew gives up searching?"

"*Here*! . . . In my cabin—with me?" exclaimed Lynn, aghast.

"Yes," she importuned, her eyes gravely upon him. "You're the only decent man I've met since I worked for Mr. Smith."

"Thanks. . . . Say, L.A. must have been as bad to you as Shanghai," returned Lynn, and he considered her suggestion a moment. It struck him singularly that he did not instantly repudiate the idea. But he nipped an insidious and pleasing temptation in the

31

bud. "No, Anne, that wouldn't do at all."

"Why wouldn't it—unless I'd impose upon you. But I could sleep in your woodshed—take care of your cabin."

"I daresay you could, Gray Eyes," he replied, regarding her with a growing realization that her personality equaled her charm. He could not help contrasting her with Helen Pritchard, whose memory only an extraordinary allusion could invoke. "Suppose you were caught here."

"I wouldn't care—for myself."

"Well, I would. It'd ruin your good name."

"With whom? Some of these workingmen? Possibly your boss or some officials? But I'm unknown here and alone in the whole world."

"Anne! It's not the thought of myself that makes me disapprove. Or lack of—of feeling for you. It's principle. Lord knows, I'm not much. I'm a failure myself—and also alone in the world. But I won't risk disgracing you."

"You're risking more by taking me to Boulder City. More than my life! . . . That Bellew will find me. He *will*. . . . Oh, I'd kill myself the minute I had a chance. But those beasts do not give a girl a chance even for that."

"I could drive you to a railroad and put you on a train," he replied, unable to meet the eloquent beseeching eyes.

"That would be as bad. Where can I go? What can I do? There's no work these days. I'd be worse off than when I tramped the streets of Los Angeles."

Lynn bent over to light the fire. He was in a tight spot, and he felt himself yielding. He ought to have been glad to shelter and protect this girl, and he wondered what besides his thought of her good name was at the root of his reluctance. Having lighted the fire he slowly got up to find her close beside him, waiting in a suspense that made him blurt out, "Anne, you're distractingly pretty!"

"What of it?" she cried, almost in desperation. "I can't help that. . . . Oh, I hate my face—all of me! If it weren't for *that* I'd

32

have missed this horrible experience."

"Yeah? Well, any other girl having your beauty wouldn't hate it, believe me. . . . I'll go out now, Anne, and have a look around. Fasten the door. I'll be back in half an hour. Meanwhile you get supper."

Lynn put on the fleece-lined coat and strode out. The night was dark and cloudy, with a damp breeze off the river. Before he had gone halfway to the mess hall he realized he would have to give in to Anne's proposition, at least for the moment. The poor kid was so frightened that she wanted to stay near the one man who had been kind and brotherly to her. Lynn persuaded himself anew that he had not refused on his own account. It really was the best and safest way out of the difficulty for the time being. And once having submitted to the idea he got something out of it, a warm, fine sense of another opportunity to prove to be what he had once hoped he might be, a relief not to take her away to a sleepless fear. What if some of the laborers discovered her in his cabin, or the boss, or even Mr. Carewe himself? The security for Anne would be sufficient until the evil hour came.

The doorman, Duncan, a cheery Scotchman, hailed Lynn: "Where have you been, me boy, these days?"

"Been to Vegas, and I'm batching it at my shack. Anybody asking for me, Dunc?"

"Lots of vistitors today, but none for you, Weston."

"Do you remember a big car driving up around four this afternoon? Bunch of young men?"

"Shure. They had dinner. Gave me a dollar for showing them around."

"What'd they ask you?"

"Nothin' particular."

"Did you see them leave in their car?"

"I did that. And watched it. Their driver shure balled the jack."

"Dunc, I want a mattress and a couple of blankets. Mine are not so hot. Guess I drew some old stuff when we moved down from the dormitory. Where'll I get them?"

33

"There's plenty of unoccupied tents since Boles took off that bunch of hands. Out at the end of camp. Help yourself and don't say nothin'!"

Lynn walked around before he went in search of the needed articles. Over by the mill the clouds of pale dust hung over the noisy scene, obscuring the electric lights. The roar went on unceasingly, and to make out the swinging of carriages, the lifting giant arms of the cars and the looming through the gray shroud of huge trucks, all without a visible man in sight, gave the place an uncanny magic. Presently he hurried back to the camp, and after some search he located an unused tent from which he appropriated a mattress and blankets. These he carried to his cabin.

Lynn took care to go around to the side window and call low to Anne. She let him in, her eyes shining upon him as she grasped the meaning of the burden he carried.

"Oh, Lynn, you'll let me stay!"

"Yes, I crawl. . . . Lord, I hope I'll never be sorry. But I guess it's the best thing for a few days—till I can get some woman to take you in."

Her mute gratitude added to the thought-provoking mood she had fastened upon Lynn. He carried the mattress and blankets back into the shed, where he found room to make his bed. The fact that only a hanging piece of canvas would separate him from the cabin did not now disturb his equilibrium. He was astounded to find that she had put on the dress he had fetched from Boulder City. In fact upon his return from his half hour at the mill he had come in without noticing that she had changed. He had seen only her face, her eyes, her look of gladness.

"Say, but you're a peach!" he broke out, in sincere admiration. "No wonder Bellew and Sneed fell for you!"

"Oh, Lynn—don't," she faltered, with a blush that was not all shame. "Don't spoil any—any nice speech with the names of those men. . . . Does it fit me? The shoes do—and the stockings are all right, if they'll stay up."

34

She turned round anxiously for his benefit. Lynn, gazing at the trim form, and remembering that he had seen her only in a blanket, and his pajamas and then outrageously clad in his work clothes, wondered if that was why she burst upon his sight such a perfect beauty of a girl.

"Anne, I went to a great college for three years," he said, "one noted for being the stamping ground of the swellest girls in California. Even in Hollywood they don't show any more stunning girls, though they have plenty of them. But you've got any girl I ever saw there skinned to a frazzle, if you know what I mean."

"Supper is ready," she replied, with heightened color, "if you'll help me find things to serve it on."

Lynn's resourcefulness was put to a full test. Tin cans and chips of clean wood were requisitioned. They sat down on the two box seats with one plate, one cup, one knife and fork and spoon between them. The tragic shadow that had hovered over Anne seemed to lift for the hour. She was young, and she responded to the situation almost with gaiety. Lynn felt her unconscious leaning toward a something stronger than a deep gratefulness for his help and protection. He was the one who sustained embarrassment. Many had been the bright eyes to look at him across luxurious tables at the Roosevelt, the Biltmore, the Coconut Grove and places too numerous to recall, but he had never met eyes that could compare with these gray-green ones of Anne Vandergrift's, that shone like stars upon him here in this dingy bare shack. The situation seemed incredible, yet while Anne forgot her peril and revealed herself as a simple and unsophisticated girl, glad to be dependent upon him for shelter and protection, Lynn found it stingingly real and sweet.

After the meal they turned out the light and stole through the woodshed to the back, where they walked into the cool, windy hall of the desert. Lynn said it would be safe for her to walk there after dark, but she must not go outdoors during daylight nor risk being seen at a window. Anne seemed to grow quiet out under the stars. He saw her tear off a bit of sage and press it to her lips and nostrils. The basin floor was hard-packed gravel covered with tufts of sage and clumps of greasewood far apart. Lynn led around back of the mills, across the railroad tracks to the bank of the river.

"This is the Colorado, Anne. Some river, believe me!" said Lynn. "Listen now."

Up from the gloomy gleam of water came a gurgle and murmur that was musical as all running water is, but from the bend beyond, the current roared low, and from the black gap below even the silence seemed sullen, waiting, forbidding. It was so broad there, too, that Lynn could not see the opposite bank. In the starlight it flowed on ponderously, majestically, supreme in its power.

"It makes me afraid," whispered Anne.

"Me too, now. At first I didn't get that. Funny how this river grows on one. I've seen the Columbia up in Oregon, which is much larger. But it did not affect me. This Colorado is red in color, one third sand, and it runs with strange currents, whirlpools, holes and bulges that cannot be gauged or explained. It's not like any other river. I studied engineering at college, and this job fascinates me. I can't grasp it. I think Carewe, the chief engineer, must have a colossal egotism, a monumental gall besides his genius, to imagine he can stop the Rio Colorado."

"I'm cold," said Anne, shivering. "I don't know whether or not it's the breeze, or the river, or something. Let's walk."

They turned to face the flare of lights against which the dark spiderlike skeleton structures stood out and the clouds of dust rolled up like smoke. Presently they were near enough to hear the din of a vast mechanical system handling tons of sand and gravel every minute. They half circled the mill and camp back to Lynn's cabin.

"Just as well not to turn on the lights," he said. But he replenished the fire in the stove and drew up the one chair for Anne, who stretched cold hands to the heat. After a little while he could see her dimly. And it seemed to him that he was dreaming.

36

"Anne, I'm not very practical," he said in low voice. "It only just occured to me that you'll need things a girl needs. And I must buy cooking utensils and tableware."

"I thought of it—and how I am ever to pay you back."

"Never mind that. . . . I've an idea. Tomorrow night I'll drive you in to Boulder. You can buy what you need at one store while I'll go to another. Sue, the clerk I know, goes off at six o'clock. So we run very little risk."

"Lynn, I—I can't tell you how I feel—what—" she faltered. "But if you only could know my worry and disgust for weeks in L.A.—and then—the tortures I suffered when that woman took my clothes—and last my fright . . . This cabin seems like heaven. Every little bit I wake up and wonder if it's true."

"Well, I've a faint idea what you've been through," Lynn rejoined sympathetically. "We can put this stunt over for a little, if we're careful. Then, would you let me send you back to L.A. or Frisco, or some Arizona town where Bellew and Sneed couldn't find you?"

"If you wish, of course, I'll have to go. But . . ."

"But what?" queried Lynn, as she hesitated.

"I'll never meet anyone again so—so kind as you," she said.

"Oh, nonsense," blurted out Lynn. "Sure you will. At that, I never heard before I was so kind. I was a flop with the girls on the campus. . . . Anne, it's not that you—I want to get rid of you. Honestly, this situation is intriguing, to say the least. You're a peach. Circumstances have thrown you with me. Well, what kind of a fellow would I be to take advantage of it?"

"I understand you—but I'm afraid I'm pretty ignorant. . . . My mother died when I was little. My father never told me anything. He kept me in—never let me meet anyone. And when I came out to work for Mr. Smith the men and boys I met at business school and his office annoyed me. I might have liked them if I'd have known how to take them. But I didn't. I always wanted to be a boy. But I'm a *girl*—homeless, friendless, helpless. That's why

I hate the thought of your sending me away. Still I couldn't ask you to take care of me indefinitely."

"I might be as rotten to her as any other man," he replied somberly, as if speaking to himself.

In the dim fire-lit obscurity of the cabin Lynn saw her big eyes, like haunting holes in a blanket, fix upon him intently.

"I don't believe—that," she whispered.

"You don't?" he rejoined thickly.

"No. I shall not."

"But you have no idea of what kind of a fellow I am."

"Oh, yes I have. You're just—just splendid."

"Anne, my doubt of myself is only bitterness. Someday I'll tell you my little tale of failure. I used to grovel in morbid brooding. Hard work has almost cured that. Honest to God, I'd like to be good and splendid. I'd like to be worthy of a helpless girl like you trusting herself alone with me in this camp shack out on the desert. But I don't trust myself. . . . Suppose I should come home drunk some Saturday night?"

"I'd be sorry—but not afraid."

"Oh hell! What am I talking about? I won't come home drunk."

Anne leaned in the dusk to press his hands. Then as if divinely startled she flashed up to go to the window. Lynn hunched over the stove, hugging to his breast the fine emotion she roused in him. He must cling to that. Anne Vandergrift might be another of the influences come to help him rise.

"I'll hit the hay now," he said. "I'll be gone tomorrow before you are awake. Out the back door, which I'll lock. Don't forget to be careful. I'll be here by five. We'll get supper and beat it for Boulder City. Good night, Anne."

She murmured in reply, came softly back to him, as if to repeat her former impulsive action. But she checked it. The last ruddy glow of the fire shone upon her face and the speaking shadows where her eyes hid.

Lynn left her standing there and sought his bed behind the partition and the woodpile. The place was not half bad. He would

38

be as snug as a bug in a rug. It was almost like camping out, a kind of sport he had known so little and would have loved. Mice ran over his bed, friendly inmates of his cabin he had been fond of feeding. The distant hum of the mill filled his ears. Before he fell asleep he realized that the events of the last few days had incalculably heightened the spirit which had had its inception in his contact with Boulder Dam.

Work next day was something for Lynn to eat up. He was on the job every instant, keen as a whip, careful as always but of swifter and better judgment in swinging and emptying his loads. He felt glad that he did not have to part with this engine for a while. Before he had any idea of the nearness of the shift the whistle blew, and he was free.

The instant Anne opened the door and he met her eyes in the sunset light he knew she had been waiting for him. And there came a quick return of the pleasurable excitation that he had now to associate with her presence.

"Let's step on it, Anne," he said gaily. "It'll be dark in half an hour. And you know we have a heavy date."

"The day has been so long," she replied, with a smile warming the wanness from her face.

"Anything doing to worry you?" he asked quickly.

"No. . . . It's gone."

The two of them speedily dispatched what was left of the food Lynn had brought back from Boulder. Dusk found them ready for the drive in, Anne quiet and intense with emotions that must have been happy, Lynn gay and voluble with a levity quite foreign to him. Nevertheless he was exceedingly vigilant about getting Anne out unseen by any laborers. As he drove by the mills he made her slide down in the seat until they had passed the zone.

"Sit up now, Gray Eyes," he said.

And silently he thought he should kick himself into an appreciation of this rare treasure the winds of chance had blown into his life. Lynn's gaiety suffered an eclipse with that thought. He drove on, giving the car all it could stand, keenly aware of the clean-cut pale profile close to his shoulder. In less than half an hour he turned across the main road into the one street of Boulder City that was finished. It was Sunday night, but just the same as Saturday or any other night. Boulder Dam activity never ceased. Night was the same as day. He parked the car before a dark building far down the street.

"Here we are, Anne. Swell ride, wasn't it? And I once owned a Lincoln and had a girl who fitted the upholstery. . . . Hop out, child. This will be duck soup for us. . . . Take this money. There's your store—five doors up. The big well-lighted store. Mine is here on this side—the one with the red sign. I'll be in there if you don't find me here in the car. As you belong to the feminine class you'll be longest. Ha! Ha! So you can expect me to be waiting. . . . A last word. If any young men accost you—which is a cinch will happen—you be deaf and dumb! Get that!"

"I may not be deaf but I'll be dumb," she returned with an adorable smile. As she started she wheeled to whisper anxiously: "Don't wait very long for me. Come after me!"

Lynn watched the graceful shape move swiftly across the street. Would she ever again be free of fear? What blackness of consciousness must have been forced upon Anne! Lynn cursed under his breath. If he ever got his hands on this Bellew it would be too late for one thug to pull that pocket gun stunt.

It did not take Lynn long to purchase an assortment of utensils, tablecloth, paper napkins and a generous supply of canned goods and vegetables, fruit, butter and bread for at least a week. These he carried out to the car and stowed away in the back seat. Then he paced up and down, close to the building, so that the numerous passers-by would not get a good look at him. Lynn regretted that his build, if not his looks, rendered him conspicuous.

Anne did not come. Lynn waited fifteen minutes, and that, counting the time he had taken for his purchases, seemed to be quite enough for Anne to accomplish her errand. But Lynn held himself in hand for another quarter of an hour. Then he made for the big store.

40

As he looked in the wide door of the well-lighted store he saw Anne laden with packages attempting to get by two young men. At that moment one of them, a tanned grinning boy like hundreds Lynn had seen, drew back with a parting shot to his comrade.

"Snowballs, Bo. Nothin' doin'."

But the other, a handsome bold-eyed fellow, persisted without the ingratiating gaiety that had set well upon the younger man.

"Where'd you spring from, Lovely?" he asked. "I never saw you before. Let me help you carry those bundles?"

Anne appeared not to hear him, but her gray eyes belied that with a darkening flush. As she swerved to get aside, the young man, apparently by accident, knocked some of her parcels from her arms. With profuse apologies he made as if to help Anne gather them up when Lynn intervened.

"Fade, you masher!" he said, and he shoved the fellow back with a hand that must have impressed its latent power. "I might take a crack at you."

"No offense, sir," returned the other, red in the face. "I was only offering to help the lady."

Lynn turned to Anne, who appeared in the act of rising with her array of parcels. But now her poise was destroyed by a vivid blush.

"Tough luck, Sis, that you can't enter a store without running into these ———" Lynn said and bent to relieve Anne of her burden. As they went out Lynn's sharp ears registered some disturbing remarks.

"Bo, that was Biff Weston, the old All-American fullback," rang out an excited voice. "I've seen him here before. . . . Did you get off lucky? I'm telling you."

Anne heard Lynn's caustic imprecation, and as they drew beyond the store she looked up. "I heard what he said. Biff Weston. What'd they call you that for?"

"I'm afraid I had a bad rep for biffing fellows. It sure was hard to keep from handing that guy one. But, Anne, please overlook it. I didn't want to draw attention to you."

41

"Oh! I wonder. Would I have been distressed if—if you—biffed him—as you call it? . . . Oh, dear, it makes me miserable. It enrages me!"

"What does, Anne?"

"I can't go anywhere. I can't poke my darned face outdoors that I'm not followed or annoyed or insulted—or—or kidnaped."

"Child, if you were older and vainer you'd get a tremendous kick out of that. You've got what every woman would give her soul for. You've got what Helen of Troy had."

"And that was—Lynn?" asked Anne, stumbling along, as she tilted up her head.

"A lovely face and beautiful body. It's a tough break, Anne. But I confess I wouldn't change them if I could."

"Well, *I* would," Anne averred stoutly.

Anne's bundles on top of those that Lynn had deposited in the back of the car filled it completely.

"Anne, what'd you have done that night if my car had been as full as it is now?"

"Oh, I don't know," Anne wailed at the very thought.

"Would we dare go . . . No, we wouldn't. Anne, you're playing he—havoc with my will power. . . . Get in, girl. Aren't you going back with me? *Home?* . . . Don't sit so faraway. It'll be cold, and you have my fleece-lined coat."

"I'm afraid to be happy," she whispered to herself. And all the rest of the way down into the basin and across to and beyond the camp she was silent.

That evening passed somewhat like the preceding one except that Lynn did not take Anne for a walk. The many packages lay unopened on the floor and table.

Next afternoon Lynn rushed back to the cabin, eager to see Anne again and to do some wood chopping and other chores. He had gotten by the first happy circumstance, but no more, when Anne called his attention to a big shiny touring car coming down the road.

"Visitors. They're always butting in," muttered Lynn. The car came on to the mess hall, where it halted, evidently to allow the chauffeur to ask directions. Then it came on by the tents, straight for the lonesome cabin beyond.

"It's coming here," Anne whispered with agitation.

"No! Who'd want to see me? . . . But by thunder, it's come past the tents! . . . Anne, hide in the woodshed."

Presently Lynn could no longer see the car from his window. But he heard it come on and stop. The snap of a car door and the sound of a girl's quick high-pitched voice sent Lynn's heart thumping into his throat.

Then followed a nervous rapping on his door. Lynn pulled it open with a sweep. A fashionably attired young woman, with blond hair waving superbly under her little hat and blue eyes darkly expectant, stood before his threshold.

"Biff! How perfectly fine you look—you big bronzed giant," she said with a dazzling smile.

"*Helen!*"

Chapter 4

The long year of toil and travail rolled back as if it had never been. Lynn found the power of mind to remember a fearful and a marvelous thing. And he discovered then that it was not Helen Pritchard's shallow infidelity that had been the shock which had shook the very foundation of his being, but his first gaze down into the purple depths of Boulder Dam Canyon, with its puffs of smoke and roar as from great guns, its thousands of crawling ants that were men, toilers under the walls, its beginning of the incredible transition of the engineer's dream to actuality.

One day long ago Helen had followed Lynn out of the car, where she had left her mother and the languid college swell she had recently attached, and had come to his side to look down from the height of the canyon rim to the scene below.

Lynn had then scarcely been aware of her elegant presence.

"Grand! Grand idea, but . . ." he muttered to himself.

"Isn't nature grand, Biff?" Helen queried with a low laugh, somehow mocking. And then he saw her, with slow gesture, flip

44

her cigarette over the low wall down into the canyon. That was like Helen. This stupendous hole was no more to her than an ashtray. The significant little action angered Lynn more now than all her nagging on the ride from Riverside to Boulder Dam.

Propelled by the deepest emotion Lynn had ever felt he went back to the car and took out his small bag. Then he bared his head to Helen's mother: "Thank you for the ride, Mrs. Pritchard. I'm stopping out here. Goodbye. . . . So long, Larry," he added curtly to the pale young man beside her. "Wish you luck."

"Why, Lynn! What are you doing?" expostulated Mrs. Pritchard, mildly perturbed. "If you must leave us surely it need not be here in this dusty wilderness of rock. At least wait until we return to Las Vegas."

"Helen has broken our engagement," returned Lynn. "And it just struck me that *this* is the place for me to go."

He bowed again, courteously, but with a cold firmness that seemed to come strangely to him there, and as he stepped toward the parapet he found Helen's eyes on him.

"Biff, what did you say to Mother?"

"I told her you had given me the gate."

Helen flushed. "Very dramatic of you here on this dump. Couldn't you wait until we got back home? Larry will tell it—that you left me in a jealous huff—here on this ghastly desert."

"Let him. But jealous? Not a chance, Helen. I wish him joy and a better break than you ever gave me."

"Lynn, you might be decent enough to take into consideration my disappointment in you."

"Just how, Helen?" he blazed at her with accusing eyes.

"You know. Haven't I told you a hundred times. You hated my crowd. You were bored to extinction by the things I like so well. You had no head to make contacts that would have helped you socially and in business someday. Why, Biff Weston, the only pleasure you *ever* gave me was to let me see you run with a football. That was great, I admit. But even in football you could not take advantage of opportunity. If you hadn't joined that lousy

45

fraternity you'd have been captain of the team. Worse, you were a rotten student. You flunked in your major course. . . . All the publicity! Oh, it made me sick."

"That's all true, Helen," he replied sadly. "To my eternal shame and regret I admit it. I failed in everything, except when I got my hands on a football. . . . Can you be as truthful about your disappointment? Hasn't the financial ruin of my father a little to do with it?"

"Biff, I didn't care a damn about the money. But my family . . ."

"Don't say any more, Helen. Really you let me off easily!"

"But what are you going to do?" she flashed with the passion of a woman who could not wholly give up to a calculating mind.

"You said it, darling," he rejoined. "I'm going to work down in this ghastly hole."

"Work! . . . As a common laborer?" she gasped.

"Yes, by God! At anything I can lay my hands to. . . . I'll owe it to you, Helen. One good turn you did me! . . . Go back to your Junior League and your charity stunts, your proms and Grove parties—to you latest flame. And forget me! Good-bye."

Lynn had strode down the grade from the observation point to where the road forked. He halted below to gaze into the canyon. He heard the hum of the big Lincoln as it passed above him, but he did not look. At that moment his eyes seemed dim. He was saying good-bye to a great deal more than an unsatisfactory sweetheart—to his mother and sister, to a kindly father, to the old life of study and play, of an ephemeral achievement that got him nowhere.

Something burned the dimness from Lynn's sight and left his eyes clear and magnifying. With a deep thrill he fixed them in an eagle sweep upon the scene of this vastness of modern feats of engineering.

The black walls sheered down yawningly in an uneven and perpendicular slant to the far bottom, where the Colorado wound like a mud-colored serpent. Lynn tried to estimate the depth of this lower end of the outlet of the Grand Canyon of Arizona.

46

Three times as deep as the Washington Monument was high! At the bottom it looked no wider than Wilshire Boulevard, which estimate of course was far from accurate, but at the top where he stood the distance to the Arizona rim looked half a mile. This too was the deceit of that rare atmosphere. Nevertheless it was wide. To dam this wedge-shaped project upon which the U.S. government and its engineers and construction companies had set themselves! Right there Lynn received his first mystic conception of the colossal and vain oblations of man pitting himself against the elements of time and nature. He would succeed, too, temporarily, this bull-headed, ingenuous and extraordinary man, this creature who had come down out of the trees only half a million years ago—a span of time nature had required to wear only one little scare in this abysmal rent. But Lynn saw with that mystic sight the day when man and all he had made with tireless hands and ceaseless hopes would have been erased from the lifeless earth.

As Lynn understood the project, from many articles he had read, this turgid yellow river was to be diverted into four great diversion tunnels, two on each side, and the huge V-shaped hole between the walls was to be dammed with a cement block 730 feet long at the bottom, over 1,100 feet high at the top, and wide enough there for a fine road to connect the rival states. Lynn found to his amazement that figures had stuck in his memory, and it gave him a melancholy pleasure. He possessed at least the rudimentary qualifications of an engineer.

The structure would contain 4,500,000 cubic yards of cement —that was to say, a mountain of solidified sand and gravel was to be wedged into the canyon. Nineteen million pounds of reinforcement steel was to be used.

The dam would form a lake of two hundred and twenty-seven square miles. Water held in this reservoir would cover the wide state of Connecticut to a depth of ten feet. The shore line of the lake would be five hundred fifty miles long. And it would extend over one hundred fifteen miles up the canyon.

"Seven years to build!" spoke out Lynn, as if talking to the space

47

that was to be filled. "I'm going to get in on that."

But in the end of that observing acceptance of the dam his calculating faculties gave way before the profound and austere grandeur of the scene. His emotions held sway. This was his first look down into any deep canyon, and even this lower reach was commanding enough to inflame his conception of the Grand Canyon with what its magnificence and sublimity must be. He multiplied Boulder Dam Canyon by five, and he saw the Grand Canyon in all its appalling beauty and unparalleled desolation. The ragged rim of bronze at his feet wound endlessly to the north and south, growing dark in the distance under the mountain peaks above. The opposite slopes were precipitous, rough walls of rusty iron color, and yellow and gray, and far down long blank descents of purple, down to the red sullen-murmuring river. The slopes on Lynn's side were invisible except at the far bends. He felt the heady pull of the depths. One step—but Lynn killed that insidious thought at its birth. He saw indeed what had been invisible to Helen Pritchard—the beauty of this iron-walled rent in the earth and the romance and tragedy of the man-made scheme to improve on nature. He succumbed to both. He was big and strong. He could heave stones as well as footballs. He longed to be a part of this movement and to find in it a surcease of his pitiful complexes.

What with gazing long and with the glorification of feeling Lynn found the canyon taking on more color and light and mystery and depth. He projected his luring thought onto those dead walls. They took on dreamful hieroglyphics of the past, the tracings of the ages, the pictures of what the cliff dwellers had seen upon them. They had secrets that would be revealed to Lynn, if he worked and thought long enough. The step he had imagined he saw faded out of his mind. That had been only his worldly thought—a blot on his fresh and vivid imagination. From that moment Lynn dated the discovery of himself.

At the turn of the road where it took a decided downgrade a burly man came out of a little guardhouse and halted Lynn.

"Where you goin', buddy?"

48

"I don't know just where. But I'm hunting for work," replied Lynn, aware of being studied by keen gray eyes.

"You can't go down without a pass number. Hop on one of these trucks. Get off at the camp an' ask somebody to show you where to go."

"Do you think I can get a job?" Lynn asked hopefully.

"Hell, yes. Flynn would take on a thousand men with shoulders like yours."

The guard halted a huge truck into the back of which Lynn climbed, to find himself among grimy laborers in ragged dusty overalls. Lynn sat down on his grip and lost no time asking questions. He noted that the truck driver could have been favorably compared to Barney Oldfield. Up the grades and round the corners the truck roared. They passed a number of trucks loaded with iron girders, which the men said were for the piers that were being built on the rim. There were to be five lines of electrically propelled cables across the canyon, and these were to swing carriages and tanks to and fro and up and down, laden with iron, cement, lumber and men.

"Gosh, that hadn't occurred to me!" Lynn ejaculated wonderingly. "Do you mean to tell me all materials and workers will be swung over the rim—down into that thousand-foot hole?"

"Not all of them, young feller, but shore a heap. It kinda staggers you first off."

"Well, I guess."

That ride into camp was too short for Lynn. The wide flat where Boulder City was to be built presented a scene which nearly caused Lynn to forget his errand. The open bare bench in the desert resembled an antheap on a colossal scale. Grading, digging, hauling, building—work there made Lynn think of pictures of the army camps. Almost before he realized what was happening he had received a brass number in exchange for his name, and he was hustled into another truck with a score of men, to be whisked away downhill into a broad deep basin surrounded by mountains. Lynn gathered presently that there were other

49

new workers in the car besides himself. By vigilant use of eyes and ears he ascertained that this load of men was being hauled down to the river, where it turned into the canyon which was to be dammed. It was far and downhill all the way. Looking backward Lynn saw the great basin spread and grow, and he pictured in mind the vast lake that was to be formed there.

Railroad construction work was going on down in the basin. This he heard was being built to haul sand and gravel from a point some miles up the river. It was a branch from the railroad already built out from Las Vegas and which ran from Boulder Camp down to the river and along the west bank to the canyon. Prodigious labors had already been achieved, and the real work had not yet begun, according to a loquacious Irishman who was regaling his comrades with gossip about the dam.

The truck landed them at a point above the river bend where a huge rough-board dormitory and mess hall had been built upon the steep slope of the hill. The truck and railroad ran along the level bench, which like them had been man-made. From around the bend came the whistle of an engine, the roar of hedges and at that moment a heavy blast that shook the ground.

"Boys, we're near the front now," one individual said with a faraway look in his faded eyes.

"You said it, buddy. War!" ejaculated another.

Ten out of the load of men were taken into a shack of an office, where a superintendent glanced at their brass numbers and sent them out. To Lynn he gave more than a passing glance.

"Hard labor new to you?"

"No. I've trained for football," replied Lynn.

"You look it. But I meant real work. . . . Got overalls with you?"

"All the clothes I have are on my back," Lynn replied with a grin.

"Humph. That rig won't last a day."

"Well, I'll last."

"Yeah? . . . You get four dollars a day. Eight hours. We provide bed and board, which'll cost you one dollar sixty a day. Pick and

50

shovel squad. Report to McNeale round the bend. . . . I'm Flynn, foreman. Come to me for anything."

"How about my bag?" inquired Lynn.

"Leave it here till you go off duty. What's your name?"

"Weston."

"O.K. Get going."

Lynn caught up with the straggling line of laborers ahead of him; and he did not remember ever running out upon a football field with more of a thrill. But that had been play. That had gone with the rest. This was to work—real work, the foreman had said with a grim smile. Four dollars a day! Lynn had spent his thousands a year, not a dollar of which he had ever earned. There came a lift of his breast, a rush of elation and again that film over his eyes which had blinded him from the rim above.

The broad Colorado, with its mud-red hue and its sullen swirl, turned a bend to enter Black Canyon. The walls sheered up so steeply that Lynn had to crane his neck to see the bank of blue sky above. Bulging bronze walls that leaned forbiddingly over the portal to the canyon! Dust clouds veiled the immediate foreground. A stream of rock-laden trucks rolled out of the dust cloud, and then a locomotive, with whistling shriek, emerged with a freight train of cars.

It became manifest to Lynn that the work going on there consisted of a cutting away of the wall to get room for the road and rails into the site of the dam. What a stupendous task in itself! For the first time Lynn thought of the money involved; and it struck him that this work, like all government work, would go on without regard to expense. Who was going to pay for this in the end? Lynn essayed to dislodge fragments of gossip he had heard or read. For him, as well as for the chief engineer, this Boulder Dam must be right and splendid, the greatest dam in the world, the biggest project for water power and irrigation that had even been undertaken, the mark of progress of the West. For Lynn it held another and intimate significance—the making of a man.

Road and railroad ended somewhat more than a quarter of a mile round the bend. Judging by the overhead cables spanning the canyon below there was still a half mile farther to cut before the dam site was reached. The trucks passed by, following the train; a pall of yellow dust lifted; roar and rattle ceased; shrill yells of men pealed out; the new squad halted to the warning cries and the waving of red flags. Evidently a blast was imminent.

Lynn gazed, all eyes, and waited tinglingly. Suddenly the man-made level of ground under his feet shook violently. Then a burst of smoke billowed up from the box end of the huge cut along the wall. It was accompanied by a terrific boom. Fragments of rock, little and big, went hurtling aloft to whizz across the river and crack on the opposite wall, to fall into the river with hissing, splashing, thudding sounds. A wave of wind staggered Lynn. Then the canyon appeared to rock with thundering echoes from wall to wall, and a yellow darkness obscured the sun.

"That was Big Bertha. Drill ye terriers, drill!" called out a merry voice.

McNeale, the foreman, wore automobile goggles. He was Irish and big enough for the job. He put the new squad to work shoveling dirt and heaving rock into the trucks.

"Them steam shovels are your pacemakers, men," he yelled, "so step lively."

Lynn, without gloves and wearing a business suit, bent to his first job. The only remark he heard during the next hour was a complaint from a fellow worker: "If they're dammin' the river —why can't this rubbish be piled in right here?" he panted.

No one explained to him that the cubic yards excavated were hauled miles from the scene.

Amid dust and heat, and an incessant din, punctuated at inter-vals by a blast, Lynn toiled out the hours of that memorable day. Four hundred and more men went off duty at six o'clock, and not one of them he thought could compare with him for grimy face and sore hands, for sweat-caked filthy clothes, for split shoes. When these workers dropped their tools, left their throttles and wheels, there were other workers to take them up. No time was lost. Lynn divined that a marvelous machine directed all this activity.

Flynn failed to recognize Lynn when he applied for information as to where he could buy clothes.

"Weston? Oh, yes, that young dude. Ha! Ha!"

"Boss, you shure gotta hand it to him," spoke up McNeale, who happened to hear.

"That so? All right. Boulder Dam will hand out what's coming to any man."

"I want to buy clothes to work in," said Lynn.

At the little store he bought overalls, heavy shirts and gloves, hobnailed shoes and underwear. With these and his grip, which he procured from Flynn, he went up the steep steps into the dormitory. It was like a long hall in a hospital and contained hundreds of bunks. Lynn was given one in a corner near a window. He got out a towel and soap and was about to repair to the river for a bath when he was told where to find the shower. He had his turn with brawny, sweaty men and somehow felt the better for such contact. When he was washed and dressed, and went to the mess hall with the throng of workers, his identity vanished, and he was one of them. The food and the way it was served would have done justice to a good hotel. Electric lights and clean beds further attested to the attention paid to the comfort of the workers.

Many as had been Lynn's hard days of training and strenuous games of football he had never been so done up as at the end of this eight-hour job. As he stretched out with a groan on his cot he felt that he would never get up again. He did not have any more thoughts because his eyes went glued shut, and his mind went blank.

If it were possible for Lynn to suffer a hideous nightmare and revel in some strange exultation at one and the same time the succeeding weeks of labor furnished both. But along in the spring his physical misery gradually wore to an end. He had lost twenty pounds; his muscles were hard as iron, his calloused hands as tough as leather.

Nevertheless, despite his unrelenting purpose to stick to this job and the knowledge that he was gaining physical strength and respect for himself due to these things, he soon fell into the evil ways of drinking and gambling. On Saturday nights he would join a truckload of other workers and go to Las Vegas to find relief and pleasure from the brutal grind. However, one habit common to most of the young men Lynn did not sink to, and that was to drift to the dancehall girls. Every Saturday night he drank more than was good for him, usually lost all his wages, and once he got back to camp drunk. But this was the fun, the relaxation, the oblivion a young fellow needed. He never grew deadly serious over roulette or faro, and a little too much liquor made him sick.

Lynn made good on the job. Flynn and McNeale liked him, as did the variously assorted members of his mess table. And none of them suspected he was anything different from all of them. Men from many walks of life were attracted to Boulder Dam.

In the three shifts of that river squad of four hundred laborers under Flynn there were plain workingmen, honest and sober; there were also drunkards, outcasts, outlaws, cowboys, young men from the cities and farms, tough nuts and a few hard-faced, thin-lipped, keen-eyed individuals whose work was probably a blind to other activities. Lynn never made friends of any of his fellow laborers. But he was an agreeable companion and one who got along with everybody.

During the hot summer months, when the heat was almost unbearable down in the canyon, Flynn put Lynn on one of the barges that was used in the building of the upstream cofferdams. He was in the water and then out of it. September he spent working on the cofferdam, and from that job he graduated to a driller in the diversion tunnel. This work paid Lynn six dollars a day. It was fascinating and a terrific job. It required every faculty a mechanic could possess, and particularly nerve. There was peril in that dark tunnel. Workers were killed there by falling rock.

And to hold an electrically driven drill Lynn found harder than it had been to hang on to a football most passionately coveted by eleven young giants on an opposing team. The great diversion tunnels marched under the walls at the rate of twenty-five feet a day. Finished, these tunnels were to be fifty feet high and fifty feet wide. They were to handle the overflow of the Colorado —the volume of river that was not to be utilized for power or irrigation. In the flare of the electric lights, in the dust and heat and the thick air, Lynn carried on day after day, and when he emerged on relief he would be choked, blinded, spent and black as a Negro.

Eight hours of that job took as much out of a man as twice the time at some other labor. It left him very little leisure, especially when he got the midday shift. He would be too tired to go anywhere after hours, and slept until called for his mess.

"Two swell things about this job," Lynn told a comrade, "it annihilates time and you can't spend your money."

Often while he pressed his powerful body against his throbbing drill and held it tight with hands like steel bands he would think of the completed tunnel running full at floodtime, turned by the ingenuity of man from its natural channel. There was romance in that, a work to marvel at, and a thought-provoking conjecture.

Lynn grew to want to have a hand in every phase of this monstrous work. The feeling grew on him in spite of his realization that such an ambition was impossible. He would need the lives of ten men. Day after day as he went to and fro he watched the erecting of a five-story plant where cement was to be mixed and moved by electricity, to the amount of two and a half tons an hour, five hundred and seventy-six a day. One operator on duty for eight hours, three operators for twenty-four—and all each had to do was push buttons! Lynn hungered for that job. Most of all he wanted to see such an incomprehensible plant. Sometimes Lynn did not think he could wait the seven long years it would take to complete the dam. As he worked and thought his toy-playing days came back, and he had run to mechanical toys almost exclusively. Lynn had never kicked a football until his second year in high school. But a plant constructed of open iron-work, with board floors, and endless driving belts to carry sand and gravel in quantities regulated by electric clocks, and tanks to hold only the required amount of each, which spilled their contents on the dot over five hundred times a day and deposited them finally in the huge whirling mixers where cement and water added to the churning roar—all this was too much for Lynn's undeveloped mind, and although he believed and thrilled, he knew he would have to see that plant achieving what only the hands of hundreds of men had done heretofore.

From the completed diversion tunnel Lynn was transferred to the sand and gravel pits twelve miles up the river, where he ran a steam shovel. This job he liked best of all of those he had tried. It was easy work compared to the other and out in the open where he could see distances. The canyon and the tunnel in hot weather were both kin to infernos. Lynn got a taste of Nevada weather in winter, and many a day he felt grateful for the hot fire in the engine box. A nipping wind blew down from the mountains, and before the sun rose high it was bitter cold.

At intervals through the day, when the freight train had to shift along another car length or when it left for the mills, Lynn had opportunity to look about him, at the cold pale river, which lost its red hue in winter, at the Arizona peaks, ragged and wild, with their fringe of cedars, and at the great desert basin which was someday to be a lake. A thin growth of sage and tumbleweed showed on the gravelly ground. Jack rabbits and birds were a rarity; he saw them but infrequently. Deer came down out of the hills to drink. But for the most part this region of sand and gravel was lonely and desolate, a vast layer of earth that ages in the past had been deposited there by a far mightier river. While at work Lynn kept a sharp lookout for a skeleton of some prehistoric monster, like the dinosaur he had seen unearthed in the suburbs of Los Angeles. A mammoth or saber-toothed tiger skeleton would have been much to Lynn's liking. In case of a discovery he meant to shut off his shovel and leap down to rescue a tusk or two, but he had no luck in this regard. There did not appear to be anything but sand and gravel in the world. How many trainloads had the shovels filled! Back at the mills the piles grew as if by magic until they were shining, symmetrical hills waiting to be transported to the cement plant.

On this job Lynn had part of the afternoons off, and he took long walks around the basin. The mill camp where he lived was ten or a dozen miles from Boulder City, and as Lynn had no means of getting there except by truck he did not go often.

"Come to think about it," said Lynn, in his lonely habit of soliloquizing, "Las Vegas and Boulder Dam will someday be the center of a tourists' paradise. And this artificial lake will be a humdinger for fish and ducks."

The idea pleased Lynn. He had cut clippings from newspapers telling about the close proximity of the Grand Canyon, of Death Valley, Goldfield and Zion National Park, the Kaibab Plateau, famous deer hunting forest, and many other places of lesser degree. Lynn calculated that if after a year of labor at the dam he had grown attached to this desert Nevada, what would he feel for it when the work was finished in six more years? Already the nucleus of a plan had formed in his mind, and even if he failed to win his way to a responsible position at the dam he would find a home and living there. It was only by imperceptible degrees or by looking backward could Lynn determine that the desert called to him. He had been born in Los Angeles and had lived there all his life. Westerner as he was he had scarcely known what the desert stars and solitude were like. He was to learn that deep within was hidden some elemental kinship with this region—the flinty wasteland with its canyons and mountains, its alkali flats and plains of greasewood, its sand dunes and rolling sage ridges, its dry arroyos and the red sullen Colorado, the heat and cold, the dust storms and the torrential rains—all the physical aspects of this desert.

57

Chapter 5

One day in early spring Lynn, after being transferred to the mills, bought an old Ford car under peculiar and humorous circumstances. He happened upon a little crowd of workers off duty joshing a fellow worker who could not start his machine. They kidded him along until he was furious.

"All right, *you* start it, some of you saps," he burst out. "Bet you ten to one you can't."

"Take you up," replied Lynn, elbowing in to inspect the old car. One of his few real gifts was an instinctive understanding of engines. He liked a car that was difficult to start. In this instance, as luck or dexterity would have it, he had the fellow's Ford roaring in no time.

"You win, buddy," he exploded in admiration. "What did I bet you?"

"Ten to one, if I recollect."

"Wh-huh. Ten what?" queried the driver, scratching his head.

"You didn't say. But of course I took it for granted you meant dollars," Lynn returned with a smile.

"Sure I did. My middle name is game," declared the owner, and with a fine flourish he handed over a new ten-dollar greenback.

"Would you sell it?" asked Lynn, as he received the money.

"Say, I'd almost pay you to take this gas buggy off my hands."

"Sold. Here's your ten and ten more."

The deal went through, and Lynn in great glee drove off in his own car. It balked in front of other cars, stalled on the railroad tracks and went dead in diverse other places, which uncanny feats endeared it to Lynn. "Old boy, you can't stick me," Lynn said and each time made good his brag.

Through this newly acquired vehicle Lynn resumed his visits to Las Vegas, always once a week on Saturday nights and sometimes on another night if he had any money left over. He edged off the stiff drinks, because he did not care to drive into ditches or rocks out in the dark desert, and went in stronger for the gambling games. During these early spring months he made the acquaintance of friends too numerous to count and gamblers, faro and monte dealers, croupiers at the roulette wheels and other men employed in the gambling halls. The cold passionless visages of more than one notorious bootlegger and racketeer thus became familiar to Lynn.

So that late afternoon in May when Helen Pritchard stood bathed in the sunset glow before his cabin door Lynn's shock was one of relief and joy that he would not have changed the past. It took this young woman's handsome presence to prove that. And a situation which otherwise would have been painful seemed one easy to master.

"Well, if it isn't Helen!" he exclaimed. "Come in. . . . I won't apologize for my home. I'm a common laborer on the dam."

Helen entered with shining eyes and outstretched hands. Lynn omitted to close the door. He shook her hands heartily. A warm color softened her face.

"Biff! . . . You great big wonderful brown giant!" she cried

59

again, and if he had not had hold of her hands she would have precipitated herself upon him.

"Helen, you're not a day older. Handsomer then ever. . . . Well, I really did not know how glad I'd be to see you. . . . It takes an apparition from the past like you to make me realize the change in myself."

"Indeed you have changed, Lynn," she said softly. "You're not the same Biff Weston any more. . . . Aren't you going to kiss me?"

Lynn bent his head, and avoiding the red pouting lips he kissed her cheek. Then he released her hands and pulled forward his old rocker. She did not take it. What penetrating woman's gaze she fixed upon him!

"Lynn, I've good news. Your dad didn't go bankrupt," she said as if to change the subject.

"So Dad pulled—through?" he asked, his voice breaking a little.

"Yes. He lost a million. But there's no danger of your being a poor man's son."

"I'm glad. Not for my sake, at all. Being forced to earn my own living is the best thing that ever happened to me."

"But, Lynn," she rejoined with sweet seriousness, "you can't go on forever earning your living in overalls."

"It's the way for me to work up to a big job."

"That is waiting for you at home."

"I'm sorry if there's anything dependent on me. Because it'll have to wait—for somebody else."

"*Lynn!*" she exclaimed suddenly with a sharp breath. "You'll not go back with me?"

"No."

"You won't—make up—forgive me?"

"Of course I forgive you, Helen. Your showing me the gate helped make a man of me."

"But Lynn . . . I mean the—other."

"Impossible, even if you meant it—which you don't."

"I do mean it, Lynn," she returned earnestly.

"That is deeply to be regretted, Helen. I hope it's just another

60

of your moods. I remember you always wanted what you couldn't get—and soon tired of anything you had."

She had paled, and for the first time took her gaze off him to sweep the cabin. One look would have been sufficient to see that Lynn was not living there alone. But her eyes dilated to pass from one proof to another until they fixed at last upon a pretty flimsy garment not wholly concealed under the pillow on the bed.

Helen rose without dignity. "You've a woman here," she asserted.

"Why yes," he replied with an easy laugh. "I meant to spring it on you presently."

"I might have expected that of you."

"Come to think of it—yes, you might."

"Lynn Weston! . . . You *have* changed indeed. And like a romantic fool I thought . . . This is no place for Helen Pritchard."

"It's not swell, I'll admit," he returned dryly. "But don't miss this, Helen Pritchard. This crude cabin has got a lot of places you've been in skinned to a frazzle."

"For what?" she asserted scornfully.

"Well, for beauty, for the virtue of hard labor, for something you never felt in your life—sacrifice. And lastly for the exact opposite you have in your mind."

"Biff, this hard labor idyll has unhinged your mind. . . . I'll go. I regret my impulse—my faith in you—my hope to make amends. And I'll tell the world—at least the world you've turned your back upon—that the rumor of your climb is unfounded." Helen flashed furiously.

"You're welcome to tell what you like," Lynn returned curtly. "But wait. You certainly want to be able to tell your idle crowd—and my old skirt-chasing friends—that I'm the luckiest fellow on earth. You want to see her, Helen?"

Evidently Lynn's former fiancée stood transfixed in curiosity.

"Anne," called Lynn, raising his voice. "Come in here. I've a visitor who wants to see you."

Light, quick footsteps sounded at the back of the cabin. Then

61

the canvas curtain moved aside to admit Anne. How strange for Lynn never before to have recognized wholly in her what he saw now! She appeared indescribably sweet, fresh, beautiful. At sight of the pale, proud Helen her face took on a scarlet flush that enhanced the lovely contrast. Her sleeves were rolled up over round arms, and her hands, white with flour, plucked at her apron.

"Anne, this is an old friend—my former fiancée—Miss Helen Pritchard. . . . Helen, allow me to present my wife."

"Your wife?" gasped Helen.

"Yes," Lynn replied huskily. The moment stirred him to his depths. If he had ever wanted revenge for the hurt Helen had dealt him he could have reveled in it then.

The shock Anne sustained, which changed her face to pearly white, could easily have been interpreted as a young wife's embarrassment at being suddenly confronted with her husband's former sweetheart.

"How do—you do, Miss—Pritchard," faltered Anne, twisting her hands in the apron. "I'm sorry such a meeting—was unavoidable. . . . Lynn didn't tell you . . . please let me . . ."

"No explanation necessary, Mrs. Weston," interposed Helen, once more herself. "It is all perfectly obvious. I wish you joy. Biff, I certainly have to extend profound congratulations. At your old football trick! You picked this one out of the empyrean. And it explains your quixotic labors at Boulder Dam. . . . Good-bye."

She swept out with her head high, but her haste indicated her realization of defeat and her fury. Lynn stood there until the car sped away down the road. Then it was with an intense curiosity that he turned to Anne. She watched the departing car with an expression no masculine mind could have analyzed.

"Anne, it was a tough break," Lynn said presently. "But somehow I'm tickled pink."

Her gaze came back to Lynn, and it was certain that he drew up sharply. She had no thought of herself.

"Lynn, I—I couldn't help hearing all she said."

"Certainly you couldn't. And it didn't matter to me."

62

"You were—engaged to her?"

"Once upon a time."

"Didn't you love her very much?"

"I thought I did, but now I know I was a sapheaded college boy and didn't love her at all."

"But she is beautiful—and proud."

"Helen has some class, I'll admit."

"But she must love you very dearly."

"She never loved me. Helen couldn't love anyone save herself. She is a swell gold digger, Anne, you take it from me. You heard her tell me my dad had pulled through. Gee, I'm glad about that. Dad is some guy. But it was *that*. Helen's folks never had any too much money. I'll bet they've found it hard sledding. Dad was always in the big money. And if he pulled through it means plenty."

"She called you Biff," Anne went on, wonderingly.

"Yes. A nickname I got in college. I had a bad habit of biffing fellows, as I told you."

"She said you 'picked this one out of the empyrean.' What did she mean?"

"Didn't you get that one, Anne?" Lynn queried with a laugh. "It was a hot one for her, believe me, and a compliment to both of us. When I played football one of the stunts that made me famous was to run and snatch a forward pass out of the air. I guess I had it down pat. . . . Helen meant I had pulled a fast one —that I had made a great run and picked a peach out of the empyrean, which, my dear, is classy for the blue heaven."

"Oh!" Anne exclaimed and showed her first hint of confusion.

"Strikes me Helen discovered that before I did," Lynn went on, more to himself. He closed the door. Anne stood there, her flour-whitened hands still twisted in her apron. "Let's forget it and have some supper."

"No. We can't—*I* can't forget that," she rejoined, her eyes large and dark.

"All right. Get it off your chest, Anne."

"You introduced me to her as—as your wife."

"I'll say I did," retorted Lynn. "I was all ready for her. I put it over, Anne."

"But—but you should not have done that," she protested.

"I'd like to know what else I could have done."

"It was a—a lie."

"Sure, Mike. The biggest lie I ever told. I didn't know I had it in me."

"But—it was wrong."

"Wrong? I don't get you, Anne. How could it be wrong for a gentleman to save a girl's good name in that way? It was the only way."

"Lynn, what might be said about me doesn't matter. I'm nobody, and there is not a person who remembers my name. But you *are* somebody. You have a family—a dad who is some guy, you said. You belong to *her* kind. That is why it was wrong."

"Yeah!" muttered Lynn, who had an inspiration that what was wrong was his stupidity, his slow realization of the fineness of this homeless girl.

"We should have told the truth," Anne went on regretfully.

"You mean the simple truth about how we met, and find ourselves in this predicament now?"

"Yes. The truth is always best."

"It is not. Helen would have laughed in our faces. And she's got a lashing tongue. Do I know? . . . Well, she can't make up any lie, thank heaven. It cut her deep enough to butt—into my wife here. And it cut deeper to find you as pretty as it's possible for a girl to be. Beauty rates highest of all in her set. She worships it. And did she look you over with magnifying glasses!"

"She did look at me. I felt like I wanted the floor to swallow me."

"That needn't have flustered you. It tickled me pink. . . . Anne, haven't you sense enough to realize how you look?"

"Oh dear! I'm beginning to hate how I look," cried Anne. "I used to have pleasure—thinking I was pretty—dreaming silly

64

dreams. But that was vanity. I'm being punished. It never got me anything but trouble. I forgot to tell you. There was a motion picture man who saw me in Mr. Smith's office. He came there every day. He even prevailed upon Mr. Smith to talk to me. But I wouldn't even talk to a man with eyes such as he had."

"Anne, we're getting acquainted," returned Lynn, smiling. "You're confiding in me. Then I'm finding out some things. Believe me I don't regret you're so—so pretty. I'm not going to let *that* get you in any more trouble. Beauty is a joy forever, you know."

"I can't help but like to hear you say such things," replied Anne, blushing. "But they don't get us anywhere. How are you going to correct this—this lie you told Miss Pritchard?"

"Do I have to correct it?"

"Not on my account. But it will hurt you. She hinted of your quixotic work here. Surely you will be going home to your dad sometime. This hard work—your dirty overalls and dusty boots . . ."

"Anne, would you like me better in college-cut clothes, or a tux, or for that matter in my football suit?" he queried, curious.

"Oh, I'd love to see you play, but—but it's not a question of what I like."

"All the same I want to know. I was a good-for-nothing son of a rich man. Here I earn my living by the sweat of my brow. I'm a worker on Boulder Dam. . . . Tell me. Which?"

"I—I . . . You are more to be liked and respected now," she replied, fascinated by the thought he had propounded.

"Thanks. . . . Anne, I'm sticking on this job. I'm going to work up."

"Oh, I'm glad to hear that!"

"Well. If I was clever enough and gentleman enough to think of a lie to protect you—I'm gentleman enough to go through with it."

"What—do you mean?" she whispered, turning pale.

"Why, I'll correct the lie you think it was wrong to tell Helen."

65

Her pale lips formed the word she could not speak. But it was certain she had grasped his meaning.

"Anne, I'll marry you—if you'll have me. That would correct the falsehood. It would make you safe. And God only knows—it might correct what is wrong in me."

"Marry—me?"

"Yes, that's the proposition. If you haven't had that from a lot of men you've sure been hidden somewhere. What do you say?"

"*No!*"

"I had an idea you'd refuse me. But wait. I know I'm not much of a bargain. You could marry a millionaire, or what's better, the best young fellow in the world, if he could only find you. But you're on a tough spot. And I think this is the way out."

"Oh, I—I couldn't. It's good of you to offer to help me that way . . . but I can't. No two wrongs ever made one right."

"Anne, I know you don't love me. I know, too, that in a girl of your kind love is the only thing that'd sanction your giving yourself in marriage. I didn't mean for you to be my real wife. . . . We'd live just as we are now. The only difference would be I'd know I had done something big and fine—and you'd be free of dread."

"Lynn, I thought only that I won't let you ruin yourself to save me."

He set about kindling the fire in the stove, conscious of an emotional disturbance that he had never before experienced. It bore semblance to the troubling symptoms of falling in love, which had come to him at infrequent intervals. But that, he reasoned out, had to do with the physical charm and romantic appeal of some girl. This struck at his intelligence, which Lynn ruefully admitted was not of such a high degree that he could understand his feelings promptly.

Anne stood there watching him while he started the fire. He could tell that she was greatly disturbed and resisted the temptation to look at her. The situation had now assumed different and provoking proportions. By the time Lynn had gotten the fire going and the kettle on he had figured out a few things to his satisfaction. He had been hurt so badly that he had imagined he was off girls for life, but he was dubious about the permanence of such a conviction. Moreover, if he could fall passionately and terribly in love, here while he was toiling on this job, he was doubly sure of developing into a man. Lastly the mood that had intrigued him had been a startling appreciation of the character of this Anne Vandergrift. She loomed so wonderfully that he could not at the moment enumerate her virtues. But they were realities to study out and ponder over and be glad about.

"Well, are you going to stand there and stare at me the rest of the day?" he asked Anne, suddenly facing her.

"I've hurt your feelings," she said impulsively.

"Guess I'm not much good when a white slaver's girl won't marry me."

She cried out at that, an indistinguishable protest.

"That was only fun. I'm sorry," he made haste to add. "Make it a little stenog from L.A."

"I—I told you why I wouldn't marry you."

"Yes, you said something about my ruin. Do you know, that really is something. A girl thinking of saving me for my family! I suppose now that I'll have to fire you out of here before you ruin yourself. Girls sure are funny."

"You won't—let me stay?" she asked haltingly.

"As what?"

"I—I don't know. . . . Just a girl you've been good enough to help."

"That sounds swell, Anne. But I've discovered you're the prettiest and sweetest girl I ever saw. I must have been blind. They used to call me dumb. Helen really discovered you to me. . . . No, I'm afraid I'll have to send you out in the cruel world."

"You're teasing, or hiding the real reason from me."

"Both, I guess."

"Then you're ashamed to let me stay? *I* wouldn't be ashamed. I trust you."

"Ashamed? You bet I'd be ashamed to have Helen or my dad —or even these laborers—find out the truth."

"But the real truth is beautiful, Lynn," she said.

"It is, at that. What has the world come to—that it couldn't believe! ... My dad would, though."

"He must be like . . . Oh, he's nice I know. . . . Lynn, please don't drive me away."

"Drive! Well, you have got me figured, Anne Vandergrift. I don't think . . . I've been kidding you. I wouldn't let you go, that is, leave me altogether, if you wanted to."

Her response to this was a blaze of gladness and gratitude not unmixed with wonder.

"I don't understand you since that—since Miss Pritchard came. But she upset us both."

"Let's forget her and the world in general," he rejoined earnestly. "You hide here until I can find . . . until we think of something better. You can keep house for me. I'll get some boards and build a real partition—move the firewood out and fix a more comfortable place for myself. . . . But understand, Anne. It's sure to be found out. Helen will tell it to the four winds. She's a jealous cat. She'll stop at Boulder in the store and let out some smart crack about Biff Weston and his wife. Oh, it'll come out. And when it does I'm going to lie like hell. I can't conceive of any reason for me to swear to it. My word should be enough."

"Oh, I'm sure there'll not be any more trouble. It's so lonely— this cabin."

"It might get as popular as Aimee's temple—if the tourists get wind of us. . . . There's only one thing, Anne. Swear you'll stand by me—that you won't deny what I may have to say."

Her word evidently did not come easily, and Lynn got the impression that when it was given it would be kept.

"Anne, you can do no less."

"But suppose *she* came again—or some of your college friends —or your dad."

"Don't worry about Dad. I'd tell him. He'd be so flabbergasted

68

to find I'd worked here for over a year, why, he wouldn't be able to say a word. I've an idea he'd fall for you, Anne. . . . As for Helen, and my old friends—they're gone—gone!"

"I'd never forgive myself if this were to hurt you."

"Anne, I fear I'm the one who'll never forgive himself for hurting you. But you refused to be my wife. That's the best I could do."

"It was too much to do. . . . Lynn, I must *not* stay here with you any longer. Get me a place near you—even if I have to stay alone."

"Okay. I'll do that. There's a Mrs. Brown here somewhere who will take you in. I'll go hunt her up."

In June the boss of the mills took Lynn off the shovel job and put him on one of the overhead carriage engines. He went on at four in the morning and got off at noon, with a relief helper for one meal. The work in Boulder Dam did not halt for anything.

It took some time for Lynn to get the hang of this new work. The uncomfortable hours gave him more trouble than the actual handling of a complicated job. Finally he settled down to a custom that suited him best. He slept from nine until three-thirty, then he got breakfast at the mess table and went on duty until twelve.

When he got back to the cabin Anne would have dinner ready. She lived near his shack with Mrs. Brown, wife of the pipe setter. She turned out to be a neat and capable housekeeper. Several nights a week they drove in to the store for supplies. Lynn was looking for work for her.

This new job Lynn grew to like immensely, after he mastered the knack of it. But he liked it particularly because of the afternoons and several evening hours off. He could not get home soon enough from work. He would have been dull indeed if he had not seen how this girl was responding to his presence and what he had done for her. The mills hummed all day and all night; the dust rolled away across the desert; the freight trains left and arrived as regularly as clockwork; the laborers passed to and fro from the tents to the mills. And it seemed that Lynn and Anne were left alone as if by a dispensation of destiny.

At any rate the afternoons passed swiftly. Then when the pleasant weather set in Lynn was no longer satisfied with the walk with Anne in the dusk. There were places to see, and he had the car. It was not so much a relaxation of vigilance as a bold move on Lynn's part. Every day he drifted farther toward a state he refused to face and which he hoped would overwhelm him before he met it. For Anne the development had come unconsciously. With the vanishing of worry and dread she had fallen into the dreamful way which led to enchantment.

Lynn drove the car round to Mrs. Brown's cabin, which was the first inhabited one on the lane. From there only the camp and mills could be seen.

"Hop in and slide down in the seat," he said gaily to Anne, who stood radiant inside the door. "I don't want to advertise you. It's good Mrs. Brown is such a trump. There! Slide down. You're a bigger girl than I thought. . . . It's a shame to cover that curly head. . . . Now we're off. . . . This is great. Why didn't I think of it sooner?"

He drove out upon the desert.

"Can I come up—for air?" Anne called from under the covering.

"Say, I forgot I had a passenger. Yes, I guess it's safe now."

She sat up, her shining hair disheveled, her face like an opal and the light of her eyes, her smile, full upon Lynn.

"Safe for you, anyway," he said plaintively. "It's no use, Biff. You're on the run, blocked out, about to be thrown for a loss."

"Whatever are you saying?" she murmured. "Oh, this is lovely. All so gray and lonely! No, there's a flower—a big white lily. . . . Lynn, I can't be sure this is quite right for you."

"Right or wrong, it's swell."

"Where are you taking me?"

"St. Thomas. It's a little town up the valley that will be submerged when the dam backs the water up. We've got plenty of time. What's the odds if I lose some sleep. . . . There's an ancient

70

pueblo up here, somewhere near St. Thomas. I read about it. The archeologist who discovered it couldn't say whether cliff dwellers, Aztecs or some older race of primitive people once lived there. I've a yen for such ruins. Funny I never knew that until I came to work here. It'll be interesting for me, as an engineer, ahem! to see how these mud and stone buildings were constructed. You can hunt for bits of pottery. Perhaps you'll find a stone pestle."

"What's a pestle?"

"You know—the mortar and pestle idea. It's a stone shaped to grind or crush grain in a depression in the rock. Or you might even find an atlatl, in which case I'll have to reward you. . . . By the way, how does a fellow reward a charming girl these days? I've been out of the world for an age."

"What's an atlatl?" she asked with heightened color.

"Darned if I know exactly. Some kind of dart the aborigines used as a weapon. Oh, I'll know when I see it. . . . Anne, isn't this great?"

Her silence was more of a corroboration than any exclamation could have been.

"I may be a little balmy. But there appears to be richer color on the desert. To be sure I haven't been out on any of these June days. And the dust on the mills hides the desert. . . . You tell me, Anne."

"There's a rich, thick light over all close to us," she replied. "And faraway a bluish haze. The wind smells dry and sweet, a desert scent—bare, hot earth mixed with flowers. . . . How lonely and strange! I've never been out on the desert in my life. It's lovely—yet somehow sad. Oh, I'd like to walk and walk."

He laughed at her voicing his own feeling. But he said, "Did you ever hear that gag about how you knew she was a good girl because she walked home from a ride?"

"Gag? I've heard it. Not so funny," she replied.

"If we should happen to meet a car it's low bridge for you," he advised presently. "What I mean is you are to get down in the car so no passers-by may chance to see your unforgettable face."

"Oh! . . . Am I a fugitive or a criminal?"

71

"You are a darling," he let escape him quite involuntarily.

From then on for a long drive up out of the basin Lynn saw only the contour of her cheek. And she spoke not a word. But there did not seem to be any need of conversation, at least on his part. If he had talked he would have been facetious or exuberant.

At last the road wound into the bronze hills that had beckoned Lynn for months. They had been different every day, and now once attained seemed as elusive as before, great upheavals of rock and flinty earth that had the bulk and dignity of mountains. The sun glinted from innumerable facets of flint, gray ledges cropped out on the slopes, long slides of weathered stone sloped down from high bluffs, dark boulder-choked ravines yawned, and gorges full of the debris of floods worked down toward the river. The road would have been a perilous one to drive in stormy season. This southwest slope of the great canyon depression was now bare and hot, dry as a bleached bone, and its scanty vegetation appeared to struggle for existence.

Across into Arizona the scene grew splendid with its yellow and gray walls of rock rising to rugged peaks. In a few years, Lynn calculated, all this wonderful country of canyon and desert would be under the influence of a great fresh-water lake. It was bound to change, except on the high places, and even there the effect of permanent moisture might cover the slopes with green.

"There's a cave," Anne suddenly spoke up, not without excitement.

Lynn saw a round black hole with a slide of yellow earth leading from it.

"Prospector been digging there," explained Lynn. "You can see such holes all over this desert. . . . 'Thar's gold in them thar hills.' Anne, did you ever hear of a gold digger?"

"I've read all about the forty-niners," she replied with enthusiasm. "It's just dawned on me that I'm here where they dug and fought."

"We're close to it, anyway. I was thinking of another kind of gold digger. The modern kind. . . . Anne, have you read a good deal?"

"Yes. At home I guess I read all the books in the library."

"Did you go through school?"

"High school. They wanted me to become a schoolteacher. I'd have liked that, I think. But it just didn't come about."

"I can get books for you. That's a good idea. You could read until I get you work. Help pass the tedious days."

"Oh, I'd like that. But there haven't been any tedious days yet."

Lynn did not have to drive into St. Thomas to find out the location of the lost city. A crossroad sign directed him, and he soon found the pueblo.

"Here we are, Anne," Lynn announced, waving his hand toward the scene of rock devastation before them. "You'll never become a gold digger, that's certain. But if you want to make a hit with me you'll become an atlatl digger. Do you?"

"I think I'd become anyone you wanted me," she replied.

"Indeed? That's interesting. I might want to make a fortune out of you in the movies. You're as pretty as Jean Harlow and . . . Say we forgot something. Lunch."

"Must you always eat to have a nice time? I won't need any."

Lynn saw at once that the pueblo had been as carefully excavated as its extreme age would permit. The remains of dwellings built of rock and cement gave him a queer, indefinable sensation. The dry odor, a dusty musty smell, increased this effect.

Anne stood gazing with awed face. She seemed to be very sensitive to any suggestion or experience.

"Isn't it wonderful!" she cried. "To think people once lived here! In these little stone houses! . . . Who were they? Where did they come from?"

"Say, you're asking what the archeologists can't discover," replied Lynn. "As I remember the article, the people who lived here flourished probably a thousand years before Christ, or even before that Egyptian pharaoh, Tutankhamen. There are picture writings on the rocks somewhere around here. We'll hunt for them. The scientists have been unable to translate them. The skeletons have been dug out and packed away to museums. But we might find bits of pottery and flint arrowheads. What I'd like most would be one of those atlatls."

"What's it like?"

"It's a prehistoric weapon used by these people before the bow and arrow were invented. The atlatl is a dart fastened to a stick with a feather in the end."

"How was it used?"

"I don't know. . . . Here, use this for a shovel. Dig now, Anne."

"Don't worry, Mr. Weston. This is my idea of good fun, let alone an opportunity of a lifetime."

"Anne, I'm worried about you," he replied dubiously.

That gave her concern, as her wide eyes and mute questioning lips betrayed. Lynn realized he was getting more and more pleasure in her company.

"Don't let it worry *you*. Go dig," he said and forthwith began his investigation of the crude dwellings. The cement, or adobe, or whatever it was that held the structure together, appeared to be harder than the stone. In fact it looked almost indestructible. As an engineer he thought the secret of that cement had perished with the stone dwellers who had originated it. He found the little houses to have been built in a train, no doubt for reason of defense. Lynn sat amid the ruins of this lost city and mused on its origin and destruction. He did not forget Anne. She worked away with her improvised shovel and gradually drew off from the main street of the pueblo. She was vigorous, enthusiastic and engrossed. It amused Lynn and gave him further reason to admire the girl.

Someday there would be many feet of water over where he now sat, pondering on the grave of the stone dwellers. He found more to think of than was usual with him.

The afternoon began to wane. Anne continued to explore and dig as if she had forgotten time. She had worked away to quite a distance. Her hair glinted in the sun. Whatever kind of a girl it could be who delved for hours in the debris of an old ruin Lynn liked her the more for it. He felt a protective and chivalrous interest in her. Poor kid! She had no home—no people—no friends.

She was a hunted fugitive. Her beauty was a fatal dower. Lynn wondered if that had always been true, clear back to the life of this lost race. It had been so in the day of Helen of Troy and Semiramis. Lynn had a difficult task to link the Greek and Babylonian worship of beauty of the ancient past to the present when white slavers could sell a girl for a fabulous sum. But he succeeded in satisfying himself that it was true and all owing to the power of female beauty over the passion of men.

His musing was cut short by a call from Anne. She waved something at him and ran to meet him.

"Lynn. See! I've found a whole one—and this piece," she trilled before he got near her. They met and she thrust into his hands two thin arrowlike sticks.

"By Jove!" he ejaculated. "It's an atlatl, or I'm a born fool. . . . There's the queer-fashioned dart—the long straight shank—the feathered end. . . . But no notch."

"Look there in the middle," Anne said, indicating a worn uneven place on the shaft. "This thing has been thrown with a limber stick, like the boys throw apples. I've seen them. Only the apple is on the end, and when they swing it slips off. So! You should see how far. . . . This must have been stuck in the end of a split stick."

"I'd never guessed that, because I never threw apples with a stick. . . . Anne, I've never been a boy. . . . You have found one for me. An atlatl! It's a most precious souvenir. How did you find it?"

"Oh, I could always find things," she replied proudly. "I could beat the boys all hollow. Four-leaf clovers by the hundreds. Once I found a perfect six-leaf clover. If anything was lost I could always find it. My Dad used to say I could find a needle in a haystack."

"Anne, I wonder if you're not going to find something for me," he rejoined ponderingly.

"What? Your fortune? A gold mine? . . . Oh, I wish I could."

"I meant something precious—I don't know just what."

Chapter 6

Days flew by so swiftly that Lynn took no count of them. His fears for Anne's safety were lulled. The companionship of this girl was the sweetest thing that had ever touched him. What it would lead to seemed inevitable, but he refused to face it. The marvelous truth was enough—Anne loved him, but she did not know it.

Midsummer came, hotter than the preceding one. A shift of laborers occurred at the sand and gravel mills. Lynn was ordered to report at the upper cofferdam on the following morning. That was a blow, but not crushing until it developed he had to move his quarters along with other laborers to Boulder City. Hurrying back to find Anne he imparted the news to her.

"Don't look like that," he said. "I'm not going to let it faze me. I certainly won't desert you even if it costs me my job."

"I'll not let you quit," she rejoined spiritedly, awakening to his side of the situation.

"It's been swell here. Almost like that picture *Seventh Heaven*. And you're something like that Janet Gaynor. . . . Gee, I hate to leave. But we'd have to someday. So we might as well go now."

"Where will you—we—go?"

"Boulder City. I'll take you along of course. . . . Anne, you're thinking—now right here promise me—swear you'll not run off from me to save me trouble. I read that thought in your eyes."

She dropped her eyes, while a telltale blush spread over her face.

"You'd hurt me more by leaving than any possible thing which might come up."

"How could that be?" she asked with lowered eyes.

"Well, I was going haywire when you came along. Drinking, gambling. You steadied me. The responsibility of you on my hands made me stay here. It's a fifty-fifty proposition."

"Lynn, you're just telling me that."

"Yes, you know I'm telling you. Before we go any further you swear you won't ever run off from me."

"All right . . . I swear."

"Good. That's that. Now let's eat and pack all our stuff in the Ford and beat it for Boulder. We're in for an adventure."

"It's all been adventure. Only I had forgotten."

To Lynn's great relief he found that the Browns were also to be transferred.

In less than an hour they were on their way to Boulder City. Dusk had fallen, and the hot air was moving up out on the basin. Once started Lynn grew gay, and his excitement was communicated to Anne.

Lynn had driven regularly to Boulder City, at least once and sometimes twice a week, but he had not seen the place by daylight since early spring.

"Drive down Main Street to the end and turn left," the agent at the office told them. "You'll run into the cabin section. Single and double, hundreds of them. You rent from the Six Companies. Cheap for good houses, light, water, etcetera."

Presently Lynn found his car parked before a neat little frame house at the end of a long row of similar houses. Brown's was next door. The attendant led Lynn indoors and switched on the lights. In contrast to his old cabin this little house was luxurious. If it was not completely furnished Lynn could not at the moment see what was lacking. It had two rooms, the smaller of which was a kitchen.

Thanking his guide Lynn hurried out to the car. "Spiffy is the word. I won't know how to act here after living in that dump. A lot of my junk we won't need. Hope I can find some place to stow it." Lynn carried most of his effects in one load. He ran back for the rest. Just then a knock outside the open door interrupted him. Lynn stepped to the door. The light showed Anne and a stout pleasant-faced woman on the landing.

"How do you like this?" she asked. "Can we do anythin' for you?"

"Oh, it's swell, Mrs. Brown," replied Lynn.

"You haven't met my husband yet. He's an ironworker. Never home! I'm glad to have such nice young people as you to be friends with. There's all kinds of people on this job."

"I'll tell the world," rejoined Lynn with a laugh.

"I came over to ask you to board with me," continued Mrs. Brown. "I get awful lonely. My husband has bad hours. I'd like you to."

"And would I like to? You bet," laughed Lynn. Anne's lack of composure appeared to fit in somehow. It certainly was charming to look at. Mrs. Brown told them to come presently to supper, whereupon Lynn closed the door.

"We're lucky to fall in with a plain honest woman like that," said Lynn. . . . "What's the matter, Anne? You look sort of queer."

"Do I have to—to—tell you?"

"Well, I guess you do. I can't read your mind."

"I'll be scared here. So many people. It'll bring *that* back . . ." She broke off.

"I am a sap. That hadn't occurred to me. . . . Let me see. . . . Really I don't think it's so serious now, Anne."

"But it *is*," she replied. "Here they could find me."

Lynn earnestly sought to allay her roused fears.

She shook her head tragically and gazed up at him with dark eyes of unconscious worship. There was no use for Lynn to try not to see that. For her he was a champion, a knight. He decided he would like to be what she thought him and that he would never again seek to destroy her exaggerated opinion of him.

"We were hidden down there," she said. "It was so lonely. I loved it. Something will happen here."

"I suppose it will," Lynn replied practically. "We can't change life, you know, or stop the succession of events. Besides I want to get you a job. In the office, perhaps."

"Then—he'll surely find me again."

"Who? . . . Oh, that white slaver, Bellew. Anything is possible, Anne, so we must be careful. Perhaps you'd better hide here just the same. We can walk out at night. My new job is from eight to four."

"I might cut my hair and paint my face black," Anne said mournfully.

"You will not!"

"But I'd be just the same."

"Well, you wouldn't look it. And I'm telling you that I get a lot of joy, courage, inspiration and Lord only knows what else out of just looking at you."

"Lynn, this isn't serious for you." Her eyes were wet with tears, and she was trembling visibly. A wave of pity swept over Lynn. He was only a man and pretty thickheaded. He could only divine the feeling that possessed her. He took her in his arms, the first time that he had ever laid a hand on her deliberately. "Listen, you poor kid. I am serious. I offered to marry. What more could I do? . . . Well, it's natural this change would upset you—rouse your old dread. But don't give up to it. Maybe we are borrowing trouble. It's a thousand to one that you'd be discovered here even if you keep your lovely face and bright head hidden. . . . Anne, I'll take care of you—fight for you."

79

She had suddenly relaxed in his arms, with her head on his shoulder. Her fragrant hair brushed Lynn's cheek. All he thought of at the moment was that he wanted her there.

"I know you will. I'm all right now," she whispered and drew away from him. Her eyes glistened under long downcast lashes. "I felt sick and weak. It seems so—so different here."

"Really it needn't be. Soon as you get used to it. Go back to Mrs. Brown's, I'll be over in a moment or two. . . . I forgot to ask that fellow where the bathroom was, if there is such a thing. Of course there is—the way these fellows build things. Here's another door." Lynn discovered a tiny bathroom next to the kitchen. "All they forgot is the radio and phone. Ha! Ha! Go on, Anne. I'll come right over."

She was standing there pale and dark of eye. He led her out and closed the door. Then when she left he sat down on the kitchen steps, more concerned about his own sensations than her agitation. The cool desert breeze fanned his wet brow. And Lynn thought how he had been unwise to take Anne in his arms that way. He swore to himself that he had wanted only to comfort her, somehow reassure her. But the tender act, whatever its motive, had loosed a hundred strange and clamorous and imperious desires. At his touch Anne had just sunk limply upon his breast. He acquitted her of the slightest approach to any such feelings as had possessed him. He would have staked his life on the conviction that such an embrace was as new to her as it had been stingingly provocative to him. It had precipitated another and more drastic test. All in a flash it seemed he had graduated from a kindly, brotherly pity and protective regard to a strong compelling physical desire for her. All in a moment he had fallen in love with this homeless Anne Vandergrift. It was not the first time. And his last love affair, the unsatisfying and humiliating one with Helen Pritchard, had hurt him in some indefinable way. So he distrusted this sudden passion for the girl who had fallen under his protection. It seemed natural and inevitable and did not occasion him any shame. Up to this hour he had done creditably by Anne. But now he faced an entirely different problem.

"I'm put on the spot," Lynn pondered almost audibly. "My Boulder Dam job wasn't enough. . . . My God, what'd I ever do to be stood up like this?"

The answer seemed to breathe down to him from the black desert heights. In his creed, which was the creed of the average college man, there was nothing wrong in yielding to love. It was the exception not to do so, though that had been far from Lynn's own experience. He had been neither flirt nor philanderer. Probably if he had not been faithful to the strict training and abstinence imperative for football men he might have passed from one light affair to another, up until his engagement to Helen, which came in his third year in college. Here he had to do with a singularly perplexing proposition. Lynn cudgeled his brains to think right. There was vastly more in this whole Boulder Dam adventure than had appeared at its inception.

"I'm in love with Anne," he admitted remorselessly. "Who wouldn't be? But is it as big and fine a thing as my work? Wouldn't I just be slipping back into the old Biff Weston self? . . . What kind of a guy am I going to turn out? It's a cinch—if I think of this girl's sweetness, her beauty—what it'd be to kiss her—have her. . . . I'll fall like a ton of bricks! And that's that. But if I think of this queer angle my life has taken—that this homeless girl who loves me might have been thrown in my way to prove me—then I feel something that just chokes me. . . . I must keep that ever before my consciousness."

Lynn went to bed wholly conscious of the splendid part he might play and of his very probable lack of strength to grasp it. Before he went to sleep, however, he induced an old spirit that had been his mainstay, the secret of his great success on the athletic field, and that was to work up an anger against the idea of failure. That mood solely had enabled him to battle against his inferiority complex. It had sustained him through the first agonizing weeks of toil there at the dam. Could it be great enough to sustain him in a far more complex fight—one not against the pangs of aching bones and muscles, but against a tremendous and staggering elemental instinct?

At seven-thirty next morning Lynn reported to the bus station as he had been ordered. He had to laugh when he saw the huge triple-decked bus that looked like one of the dormitories on wheels. And he had his old thought about how these Six Companies, who were building the dam, could spend the government's money. He found a seat in that bus among one hundred and fifty men, a representative group of laborers, the diversity of type and character of which it would have been useless to estimate.

The driver did not take the road down into the basin, as Lynn had expected, but went out the main highway toward the rim of Boulder Canyon. Lynn had not been on that road since the day Helen Pritchard's chauffeur had driven out there, now seemingly so long ago. A new branch of the railroad ran out this way. Lynn could not see very well from the inside of the closed bus, and that only at a backward glance. They passed an enormous building made of galvanized sheet iron. As they turned a bend in the road Lynn had a glimpse of one of the steel towers on the rim. There were to be five of these and were to anchor the cables that crossed the canyon with their running carriages. No detail of the dam structure interested Lynn more than these.

The new road had been cut down into Boulder Canyon below the dam site and extended along the left side. They crossed a wooden bridge from under which rose a roar of sullen rushing water. Then Lynn realized that the Colorado River had been turned into the diversion tunnels. It excited him so that he pounded the man next to him and raved.

"Keep yore shirt on, young feller," replied this good-natured laborer. "Sure the river is diverted. She's raisin' too, an' the bosses are afraid of a flood. It'd be a backset if she washed out thet up-river cofferdam."

"When did they turn the river into the tunnels?"

"Some days ago. It's the raise thet's causin' alarm. You see this quick flood caught the engineers with their pants down an' only one diversion tunnel ready."

"Whew!" whistled Lynn and felt the roots of his hair burn. He had come to an appreciation of the colossal and almost impossible task of these engineers. He knew that they had not planned and constructed with any consideration of luck. They had to meet all obstacles and be prepared for the unexpected.

Finally the big bus ground to a halt, and the laborers streamed out like bees from a hive.

Lynn heard the strange sucking roar of furious waters before he saw the river. Then his keen gaze caught the muddy torrent swirling round the bend above. He followed the river in a sweeping survey to where it met the cofferdam across the canyon, and in a curve, angry, swirling, boiling, it appeared in a great black hole in the cliff.

Fascinated, Lynn watched that point as if his eyes were deceiving him. All of the Colorado River was running down into a tunnel fifty feet wide and fifty feet high, and still it failed to fill the hole. There was a black arch of tunnel visible above the seething current. It gathered speed just before the entrance and slid with a hollow howl out of sight. Bits of driftwood and brush appeared to sweep toward the center where a visible swell ran higher than on either side.

Then Lynn tried to grasp the physical features with his engineer's capacity. The truck road ended there on the cofferdam, which was still forty feet above the river—a solid obstacle of lumber and sandbags. It hid the half mile of construction work downstream where the pit for the foundation was being dug. But the volume of sound attested to the concentrated labors of two thousand men, who with their equipment were at work. All along each slope and high up, five hundred feet above Lynn's head, higher than the Soldiers' Monument in Washington, hung men on cables like spiders on their webs.

"That's what I want to tackle!" burst out Lynn. "I'm telling you."

"Hello, Weston. You're telling me what?" called a big voice behind him, audible above the din. Flynn's brown visage wore a grin.

"Morning, boss. Oh, I was just kidding myself that I'd like to try their job."

"Drillers, huh? Don't blame you. That's a kick. I'll put you on there later. They'll be months on the walls. . . . Weston, I like your enthusiasm. First off I took you for one of those dudes on a lark or a jag. I'm going to recommend you. . . . Today I want a bunch of a hundred active young fellows. You pick them out for me and take charge. I'll be comin' and goin' all day."

"Thank you, sir. What's the work?" Lynn rejoined eagerly.

"We're leery about the river. It's come up twenty feet since yesterday. Snow meltin' in the mountains. Of course it wouldn't do a hell of a lot of damage below if it did spill over. I've got a gang clearin' the way. A forty-foot raise, which is the highest ever recorded here, wouldn't budge the cofferdam. But it'd give Carewe and his corps the jitters."

"I shouldn't wonder. . . . Shall I pick out these younger men and report to you?"

"Yes. Your job will be handlin' materials fast. Trucks will be comin' upriver to unload here. And there'll be a trainload comin' down on the other side. That stuff has to be unloaded over there and floated across on a barge. It'll be a wet job attended with some risk. Ask each man if he can swim in that muck. If he's uncertain don't take him. . . . Say, I took it for granted you could swim. You've got such a build."

"Flynn, I'm second cousin to a fish. Used to be a lifeguard at Redondo Beach."

"Hop to it, Weston. Let's see if you stack up in gray matter as well as you do in shape."

Elated and thrilled Lynn turned to the several hundred waiting men. He had only to glance at each one to make certain deductions; and then a crisp question or two settled the selection. In a quarter of an hour he had his gang picked out, when he reported to the busy boss.

"Hurry across the dam an' up where that barge is landin'. Have the stuff packed up on the dam. Lumber can be floated down, if you're careful. Use your eyes first, then your head. An' look out for your men."

Lynn ran off at the head of his gang to begin what he knew would be the most strenuous and exciting day he had ever spent on the job. He felt keen, forceful, capable. His exhilaration and enthusiasm recalled the first day he had made the varsity squad. He had fallen short of the pinnacle of success owing to the gray matter that Flynn had stressed. That old football game had been play, this was labor and the stern business of life. He tackled it grimly.

The big barge, heavily loaded, was drifting across on a cable. There were men on it yelling to the few on shore at the landing. Lynn grasped that many hands and quick action could solve the problem.

"Too big a load," yelled Lynn to his men. "The cable will hold, but the ropes or pulleys might break. Whoever loaded her over there didn't figure the current on this side. . . . Grab the ropes they sling ashore. Rest of you stand ready to wade and hang on to her."

"Wade hell, boss! It's a mile deep right off shore," shouted one of the men.

"Swim then. She must be swung in out of the current and made fast."

That proved to be no slight task. If Lynn had not arrived in the nick of time the barge would have broken away and gone down the river with its enormous load. The three men on board jumped and made shore. They lost no time doing this after they had thrown the ropes. It took all Lynn's gang to hold the barge long enough to make fast.

"River has come up three feet since we began loading," said one of the men who had ridden over on board.

"She was loaded too heavy for this rigging," replied Lynn.

"Are you the boss of this crew?" came the query.

"Yes."

"Budd, the foreman across where the train dumped all this

stuff, said he'd advise no more trips today."

"Budd? Has he more authority than Flynn?"

"No. Flynn has charge of all these upriver men."

Lynn made a mental reservation that he would not even suggest to Flynn an inadvisability of more trips. He knew what answer the boss would make to that.

"Some of you on board," Lynn yelled and leaped up on the barge. "Rest of you pack this truck up to the level. . . . Run out a plank."

Then Lynn's first experience along the river above the dam there had been a launch to run men across and tow barges. This demand for more materials had evidently been a hurried one because there was no launch to be used. Without asking questions Lynn figured out that the barge had to be towed up the river, like a canal boat, and then either drifted across or run on a cable.

Flynn came over just as Lynn's crew were finishing unloading.

"Good work. I need these bags bad. We've sprung a leak over there. . . . Weston, I see you can handle men."

"Thank you, boss. It's duck soup if you set a pace yourself," Lynn replied and thought with melancholy pride of the day when his qualifications for leadership of the varsity had been recognized, but had failed because he could not play politics.

"Pull the barge upriver to the landin' above. Then shoot her across for another load. Keep up your snap."

By noon hour, when the squad stopped for lunch, Lynn had brought over another bargeload. During this respite Lynn had time to look about him. The river continued to rise. Flynn had three gangs of men at work on the other end of the cofferdam where the brunt of the current struck heaviest and then surged along to narrow into the funnel-like curve in the cliff and pour frothy and turbulent into the diversion tunnel.

Lynn's engineering faculties went into eclipse. He had a few minutes off duty, and after all the great project held more romance for him than reality. The sun stood straight overhead in the blue gap between the canyon rims above. From that vantage point it looked like a big white ball suspended in a deep blue. High and black above the rims the cable towers stood silhouetted, like the turrets of a battleship. At one place five swinging cables like threads stretched across the canyon. From where Lynn sat he could see the west wall of the grand V-shaped canyon, and it presented a spectacle which taxed his credulity. He imagined a feeble and miniature contrast by visualizing a clay bank dotted with innumerable spiders hanging by shiny cobwebs. With less similarity he thought of mud wasps at work or a flock of cliff swallows perched at their holes. These human toilers were so faraway and so high that the consciousness had difficulty in accepting them as atoms of humanity. Lynn was reminded of church steeple painters, who swung at a dizzy height. The iron-workers on skyscrapers went higher in the air and farther on the climb toward perilous adventure. But these drillers suspended between heaven and earth, each as he sat on his little board, holding an electric drill pressed by hands and body against the rock, these men seemed magnificent and superhuman to Lynn Weston. Side by side they descended the bronze wall drilling holes close together and some feet deep. Their hours were short. But the strain on nerve and ear and eye, on both the physical and mental, must have been excessive. What a spitting, crackling, rattling roar the hundreds of drills made! It rose above the many other sounds of labor down the canyon. The shovels, the hoists, the trucks, the inclined scaffolds, the engines, all were incessantly adding to the din. Then shrill yells of men came faintly to Lynn's ears. Whistles pierced the air at intervals. Suddenly the solid rock under Lynn shook hard enough to make his feet quiver. A wave of air smote Lynn in the face. Then followed a heavy blast and detonating echoes. Billows of yellow dust rose from behind the cofferdam.

The elemental proximity of this master toil of modern times, the fact of its reality, the tremendous sights and sounds almost uprooted Lynn's strange and old-fashioned conviction of the supremacy of nature. Was not the mind of modern man, heir of all the ages, the most marvelous of all developments? Was not

Carewe, the chief engineer on this seven-year job, a mathematical and constructive genius who made the firmament his playground? How must the primal gods of geology and evolution succumb to this earth-riving prodigy of their own creating! Man had been primitive, but he had become mental. Man, the thinker, the reasoner, the destroyer and builder! But man had spirit. And over against this unconquerable soul nature had only one weapon—and that was Time. The ages! But even there Lynn wavered in his allegiance to the forces of the earth. What was this spirit, this soul, this mind of man?

It was something that must have come down out of the trees with the arboreal ape man some half a million years ago. It had its origin in mystery and therefore must have been omniscient and eternal—that was to say, an attribute of God. For no intelligent man could deny its inception and growth. Lynn thought of the Cro-Magnon cave man when his awakening mind conceived the flint arrowhead. He thought of Christ the Nazarene and whence had come his power. Christopher Columbus had had a glimpse of the infinite which was blind to all other men. What had been Emerson's thought when gazing up at the myriad of bright stars in the heavens he shook his head sadly? Irvine, in his conquest of Mt. Everest—on the summit of which his great heart cracked and he disappeared forever, to leave his race to wonder and revere—had he not proved the supremacy of mind over matter? Was not Lindbergh a classic example of the unlimited possibilities of mind, of the heroic spirituality of man, of the endless growth toward perfection, or whatever the inscrutable thing life meant for its highest creation? Lynn got farther along and more deeply involved in his pondering this eventful day than ever before. He himself might be a proof of the very thing he doubted. At that he was not so sure of what his doubts consisted. One thing emerged clearly, however, and that was the process of change in himself, the probing and disturbing of his own mind. The meaning of much that he had studied and read began to bear fruit under the stimulus of Boulder Dam.

He went back to work with his gang. He had ferried the third bargeload across at the upper landing, from where it was floated down close to shore out of the swifter current of the rising river. As they moored the barge at the end of this trip Lynn saw that the sharp-eyed Flynn had not missed the innovation. Flynn's red face flashed among his laborers on the dam. He waved a commending hand at Lynn.

Several workmen had ridden across on the barge, one of whom Lynn had seen before, a lean, brown fellow carrying a heavy bag of tools. Its weight made scrambling over the irregular surface of the loaded barge awkward and, as Lynn saw, a rather dangerous task. With fifty active men throwing and swinging off bags and planks every man had to look out for himself. This lean individual with the bag got in the way of a plank. He went down like a ten-pin, but if he had not clung to his bag he might have saved himself, unless the blow had been too severe.

As it was he went overboard into the swirling current.

"Man overboard!" Lynn yelled lustily and leaped over the obstructions. "Stand by with ropes."

Hoarse cries rang out.

"He went under like lead!"

"No! There he is. He's drowning!"

"It's Ben Brown, the ironworker!" Lynn recognized the name of his neighbor.

Ropes were thrown, planks were thrust out, but the unfortunate man could not avail himself of them. The current caught him, bore him along toward the end of the barge. If he were a strong swimmer it was not apparent. He rolled heavily. But he was conscious.

Lynn ran beyond the yelling workmen and dove into the river. His momentum carried him to the man upon whom he laid powerful hold. Then he whirled to face the shore. His men were running along the dam shouting and gesticulating. Several had ropes. One threw a coil which straightened out and fell short.

"*Help! Help!*" Lynn cried piercingly. The instant the silt-laden

89

river seized him in its strange heavy clutch Lynn recognized his peril. He was an exceedingly strong swimmer, but for all his desperate efforts, burdened as he was, the current took him farther out. It carried him, floated him along. But making headway against it seemed impossible. Changing his tactics Lynn took to an angle that would win him the lower end of the dam. Then going with the current and redoubling his struggles he gained toward his objective.

All the workers, several hundred in number, now saw Lynn with his helpless burden. The man had become unconscious. Lynn had no trouble holding him. But to gain shoreward with him was the hardest job Lynn had ever set his muscles to. The river had a leaden clutch. It felt thick as mud. And the swirls were as hard to swim against as the weight. A fiend seemed to have hold of Lynn's legs. He realized that he had been tackled by a rapacious and irresistible river.

Lynn's keen judgment of movement and distance told him that he would never get within reach of help from the lower end of the cofferdam.

The workers on the dam had ceased to run and yell. Their red visages flashed in the sunlight. Flynn stood on the extreme point, hatless, his hair up like the mane of a lion. He cupped his hands to his lips and bawled in stentorian voice:

"*Let him go! Save yourself!*"

Lynn pealed out with all the force of a sudden bitter passion: "*Tell it to the coach!*"

Next instant the accelerated current caught him as it swept in narrowing slant toward the tunnel. One instant longer he saw the great gap of black walls, the cofferdam with its motionless men, the burly Flynn standing with arms aloft, and then he whirled around in the current. He calculated that he had a moment to gain the exact middle of the river. By God, thought Lynn, I helped dig this tunnel, and I can run it!

Chapter 7

With a hollow gurgling roar the constricted river swept Lynn under the arch of the diversion tunnel. He rode the crest of the current, holding the man's head above the buffeting waves. There appeared to be fifteen feet of space above his head in the center of the tunnel. In front a yellow gloom began to darken; behind him the current slanted perceptibly up to a level line where the river took the plunge under the dark arch of rock. He saw the figures of men on the dam vanish, then the sunlit wall of the canyon. He faced forward into a dusk that swiftly went black.

Lynn did not submit to the horrible sense of catastrophe that came with his plunge into the man-made cave under the canyon wall. The grim anger that had assailed him got the best of fright. Action always liberated latent forces within him. The life of a helpless comrade depended on his strength. For himself alone in this Homeric mood the accident of being washed into the tunnel would have been an adventure, unique, stinging with peril, something to beat out. These few flashing thoughts succeeded to grip his mind on getting through. He had been famed for getting through a tortuous, blocked, apparently impossible field.

It became pitch black. The bellowing roar of the constricted chafing current appeared to be receding to the rear. The swift thick water still upheld him, but he had to swim to keep from being sucked down. Pieces of driftwood bumped against him, and a plank struck the man. He shoved it away. His great peril consisted in running into an obstacle. Trees with branches had drifted into the tunnel, and pieces of lumber. He also ran a risk of striking his head on the low curve of the arch. The current had slowed; there was no crest in the center; bulging eddies dragged at him. But he swam on, husbanding his strength implacably.

Lynn's elemental physical senses dominated his mind. But as the ride in the current grew interminable, the awful blackness seemed to compress his skull, the demonical laugh and suck and scream of rushing waters split his eardrums, the suckholes whirled him easier and deeper as his legs began to fail as from terrific weight. His burden weighed a ton.

On Lynn drifted through the impenetrable blackness. The moment came when it was pierced by a pinpoint of light. It grew. It took on the shape of a shiny disc cut black across the bottom. He was gradually settling down when he recognized this as the mouth of the tunnel. That shot him through and through with galvanized life. He saw the sunlight again. The old might came back to his muscles. And as clearly as he saw that widening brightened half circle he felt renewal of unquenchable spirit.

Lynn realized he would make it with something to spare. Only then did the somber, terrible, nameless clutch at his cold vitals lose its sickening power.

He felt the current quicken for the grade at the outlet and an accompanying impetus to his drifting. The great tunnel was only half full of water at that end. He saw the trestle of the bridge he had crossed that very morning. Beyond it where the river widened again he saw men in boats rowing hard up the current. He would drift out of the tunnel, under the bridge, and be picked

92

up. It was nothing now to keep his charge afloat, to swim power-fully, to repel the leaden tentacles of the octopus of these sand-laden waters.

He drifted on more swiftly. This last hundred or more feet was like a rapids in a river. The gleaming half circle of tunnel en-larged and brightened. Then the gap of the canyon far down the river suddenly filled with blue sky. The rugged river shone gold. On the bridge below and on the shore opposite men were running, congregating, excited by something across from them. Lynn knew then that Flynn and his gangs of workmen had run the half mile of road down the canyon to the outlet of the tunnel.

The constricted river, roaring out of the huge hole, vomited Lynn and his burden out into the wide light, the open, the great pool below the dam site, relinquishing them with sullen murmur and flash of unsatisfied malignance.

Lynn drifted between the piles of the trestle bridge, into a slow-ing current, to the foremost of several skiffs.

"Thar, me lad!" a burly oarsman shouted, as he clutched Lynn with hand of iron. No human voice had ever sounded so sweet in Lynn's ears, no touch so ineffable in its meaning as that of this brawny worker. "Row ashore, Bill. I'll tow them."

Shrill shouts pealed out over the river. The squeak of oars propelled by vigorous arms sounded like music to Lynn. He lay on his back, dragged behind the boat. He gazed up into a bronzed visage of the Irishman who held him.

"Begorra, an' it was the ———— ————est stunt yet on Boulder!"

Above the honest sweaty visage, high up the yellow walls to the sunlit rims of the canyon, Lynn saw the iron turrets silhou-etted against the blue and the black shiny cables swinging with their weights. Death and life seemed only a short step away, but the work on Boulder Dam went on.

Crowds of dusty, grimy laborers lined the rock ledge along the river shore where Lynn was towed. He felt solid substance under his leaden feet, and he waded ashore in a din of shouts. But before he got out of the water he sat down abruptly on the bank.

Many hands dragged the unconscious man ashore. A bloody gash in his pale face gave him a ghastly look. Lynn hoped he was not dead. They carried the man up to a level. Slaps on Lynn's back and shouts in his ears attested to the fervor of the workers. They were comrades. All in a day's toil! But for Lynn the moment was incalculably big and far-reaching. He stood up on half-paralyzed legs and, assisted by eager hands, got up to the level. The man he had rescued lay in the rocks, his head under a coat, his eyes open. Someone was wiping the blood from his head. A hum of voices encircled this little space, into which Flynn elbowed a vigorous way.

"*Weston*! For the luv of Gawd if you didn't do it!" he boomed, and he almost hugged Lynn. Then he bent over the man on the ground.

"Ben Brown! An' alive, by gosh!"

"He's not bad hurt, boss. Nothin' but this bump on his dome," said a kneeling worker.

"Brown, you lucky duffer!" ejaculated Flynn. "The hospital an' a week off with pay for yours. . . . An' to think I yelled for Weston to let you go. But, man, you'd been knocked out, an' I figured if Weston let you go he might save himself."

"I heard you—boss," Brown replied huskily.

"What? Don't kid me. You'd been knocked senseless."

"No siree! I knew everythin' that happened."

"Boss, he must have," announced the kneeling man.

"Shure an' he niver was oot of his sinces at tall," spoke up the Irish oarsman. "Fer if he wuz how'n hell could he have held on to this bag of tools."

"For cripes' sake! Don't try to tell me that!" exclaimed the incredulous Flynn.

"Boss, I didn't want to lose—my tools," explained Brown.

Lynn bent over eagerly. "Say, neighbor Brown, do you mean to tell me you had that bag of iron hanging on to you? All the time!"

"I couldn't let go," Brown replied with a faint grin.

"No wonder you weighed a ton!" ejaculated Lynn, marveling at

94

the man and at his own achievement. "But if I'd known it I'd have clipped you one—worse than that."

"Put him in a bus and send him to the hospital," ordered Flynn. "Back on the job, you loafers. What you think this is—a picnic or circus?"

"Boss, I reckon we all forgot the job. You did."

"I should smile. But we had the flood licked. . . . Weston, how in the hell did you pull this stunt?"

"It was duck soup," Lynn replied with a smile.

"Yeah?" The boss's big eyes held a warm gleam in their depths. "Well, if you give me your recipe I'll have our cook dish out a lot of such soup. . . . But Weston, you can't get away with it like that. Listen. This Boulder job is big and it's hell, as you and I know. We've got all kinds of men. And things happen every day. It's life in the raw, young fellow. And we take what comes. But this stunt of yours today is the biggest I've known to be pulled off yet. Do you get that?"

"Yes, I guess so. Thanks, boss."

"Oh, I almost forgot. For the love of Pete, what'd you mean by that crack you yelled back at me when I ordered you to save yourself?"

"What'd I say?"

"I yelled let him go. And you came back at me, '*Tell that to the coach!*'"

"Did I say that? Well! . . . Boss, I was a football player, and I trained under a real coach, believe me. One of the foundations of his great training was this. If you get hold of the ball or a man —*never let go.*"

"Weston," Flynn returned earnestly, as he gripped his hand, "when the big things come along—say a change in a man for the better and love an' opportunity—an' success—you hold on like that. . . . You will hear from this stunt. Let's go back to work."

"I just can't get over that man hanging on to his tools," said Lynn, speaking his thought aloud.

"Ha! 'Most as wonderful as your hanging on to *him*," retorted

95

Flynn. "But wasn't that just the ——— ——— funniest stunt you ever heard of?"

"Funny! Yes. About as funny as death! . . . Maybe the extra weight gave me the queer feeling I had."

"No. That was the old Colorado. It's not like any other river. The sand in the water acts like a compressor. All over your body. . . . Brown is an expert mechanic on iron. He's on the cable job. And all you gotta do to get a slant on *that* job is to look up there."

"I'd like to see in his bag."

"Easy enough. It'll go wherever he goes. Lot of superfine tools in that bag. Why, Brown can hang in air, a thousand feet above the river, and cut one of those cables. And are they steel? I'm telling you."

By the time Lynn got back to the cofferdam his clothes were dry. It was hot down in the canyon. The same old rattling, cracking din filled the air.

"Carewe will hear of your ride through the tunnel," the boss went on. "You're the only man who ever rode the river under that wall. And it's a cinch no other man will ever go through alive. Some distinction, my lad. These big engineers will want to know what it looks like down there when the river is on the rampage."

"Shall I unload the barge?"

"Sure. We'll leave it there till the river drops. Pack the material up on the cofferdam. Report to me at eight tomorrow. I like the way you get work out a crew of men."

"Flynn, get me a job on that swinging drill crew."

"Son, unless you're a trapeze performer you'll be courting death on that job. It doesn't pay any more."

"But it's such wonderful work."

"I've got you, Weston. You're some millionaire kid getting a kick out of Boulder."

"No, Flynn. If you want to get me right. I'm poor and on my own. I'm here to work. I'll do anything to work up. But these successive jobs, all different, have given me a harder kick each time."

"I see, Weston. *You* are building Boulder Dam. Fine! . . . All right, you go on the wall presently. They'll be a year on that job. Incredible? Sure. But they will. For the present, however, you handle a crew down here for me. The men get cranky and sore during the hot summer. The engineers are excavating deep under the river bed. This old dam will be anchored two hundred and fifty feet below bedrock. There'll be a blast in a few days now that will rock the foundations of the earth."

On the way back to Boulder City in the bus Lynn remembered Anne. He pondered over the possibility of her hearing about his ride through the tunnel. It would be the talk of the camp. The laborers had a pride in such a thing as that. Mrs. Brown? She would hear it. Lynn thought he would give her a tip not to tell Anne.

"Say—that guy's name is Ben Brown," soliloquized Lynn. "And my neighbor. Gosh, anything could happen to me. . . . That stunt would scare Anne."

He got off at the station and made a merry getaway from the men who wanted to shake his hand and hurried toward the store.

It was approaching sunset when Lynn, laden with bundles, reached the end of the street of small homes. Mrs. Brown's door was open. He saw clear through to the back door, which was also open. Lynn listened. There did not appear to be anyone at home. No doubt she had been called to the hospital. That thought occasioned Lynn relief and satisfaction. He could tell Anne first and make the incident appear trivial. He went round to the back of his house and opened the door into the kitchen and stamped in. He heard a suppressed little cry. Then Anne appeared from somewhere like an apparition to fly at him.

Some of Lynn's bundles fell to the floor, the others on the table.

"*Anne!* . . . What's wrong?" he asked quickly.

Her eyes had been wide and dark gulfs in a dead-white, anguished face, and now they were tight shut as she blindly reached for him. Lynn did not help her find him. He divined she had heard of his rescue of Brown—that Brown of course was his neighbor—that the story had been grossly exaggerated and had done something terrible to the poor girl. When her shaking, reaching hands found him and with a gasp she enveloped him—and appeared to incorporate with his her palpitating straining body —then Lynn sustained the exquisite shock of his life. She clasped him convulsively. He had not dreamed she could be so strong.

"My goodness, Anne!" he ejaculated in a thick voice. "What the hell's got into you? . . . I'm all right. Can't you open your eyes and see me? . . . I suppose you've heard some cock-and-bull story about Brown. Why, I'm okay. It was duck soup. Just a nice ride in the dark. Wet, of course. But honest, it wasn't anything. . . . Don't carry on like . . ."

Suddenly her blind frenzy and strain ceased. She would have fallen if he had not upheld her. Whereupon Lynn carried her into the living room and sat her down. Then he held her as she burst into a storm of weeping such as his limited experience had not known. It was an uncontrollable relaxation from a devastating fear. Lynn made no effort to stop her. It shocked him to see and feel her so broken over what could only have been a possibility in her mind. He might have been lost. You bet he might, thought Lynn grimly! And after that came succeeding thoughts, surely sweeter, more kindly and wonderful ones than any that had ever evolved in his mind. The culmination of them was a conviction that he must be hopelessly in love with this amazingly strange and lovely girl. Those few moments, holding her in his arms as she wore out her grief, seemed marked with a singular moment of subjection for Lynn; and he did not know whether or not it was her irresistible attraction, or the damnable fascination of his predicament, or his growing distrust of himself.

"Anne, this will never do," he began presently, as her sobs spent their strength. "A great big girl like you—scared out of her wits! Why, any day something really *might* happen to me. I might fall off a cliff, or have a leg blown off, or something."

"That's just—it," she said with a catch in her breath.

"But I'm pretty quick and sure on my feet, Anne. And I've got eyes trained to snatch a football out of the air or follow it in a tangled mess of legs and bodies. I'm a good bet, even if I do say it myself."

"They—they told Mrs. Brown—you—you'd been taken to the hospital. . . . And I didn't dare go. . . . It nearly drove me mad."

"Oh, so that was it? Damn their wagging tongues! . . . Tough on you, Anne! . . . I understand. But, honey, it just didn't happen that way. See, here I am."

The term of endearment that escaped him, accompanied by a little shake that could have been taken for a hug, evidently brought Anne to a realization of where she was. She drew herself out of his arms, rather hastily and with lowered eyes and flushed cheeks.

"I—I guess my nerve's gone. It was silly of me—to be so—so scared. . . . I was reading when the car came for Mrs. Brown. I heard her scream—then run out talking wild. When they knocked I grew scared. But I opened the door. A young man stood there. He said Weston went through the diversion tunnel with Brown. He's being brought to the hospital! I nearly fainted. But I managed to ask if you were injured. He said he hadn't heard, but supposed you were. I told them I'd go presently. . . . I was fighting myself—to know what to do—when you came in."

"I sure spilled the beans, didn't I?" Lynn laughed and set to picking up the bundles he had spilled on the kitchen floor. She helped him, while he rambled over the large list he had bought. But he was thinking hard and tinglingly conscious of his own sensations. The blunt information given Anne, the vagueness of which could have been construed in any way, had shocked her terribly. And her halting story, her averted eyes and, now, her confusion and awkwardness, attested to her desire to hide it. Lynn slammed the last bundle on the table with an energy imparted by a fierce resistance to his longing to take Anne in his arms and tell her what she was trying to hide and what he could hide no longer.

"I forgot something Mrs. Brown wanted—fruit, wasn't it?" he said and bolted out the door.

"No, here's some. Feels like oranges," she called after him.

But Lynn pretended not to hear and strode swiftly down the street. Before he got back from that errand he had cursed himself into an armistice which he hoped would give him time to meet this problem like the man Anne believed he was. He found her in Mrs. Brown's kitchen, helping to get supper and woman enough to have collected her wits. But there was an alluring change in her. He could not define it on such short notice. Then Lynn, throwing aside his whirling thoughts, went back to his home for the supplies he had bought.

After dark Lynn took Anne for a walk around Boulder City, avoiding the bright-fronted stores and the corners where workers congregated. Still he could not wholly avoid being seen, and in his present mood he did not care. Anne reacted subtly to his boldness. That hour gave Lynn an awakening desire to take Anne to the many places where he had been in California. There was not a girl he could recall who could hold a candle to her, even without the modish gowns.

Lynn bracketed Boulder Dam and Anne together.

But what a fall there was for him, when they returned home with a couple of hours to spend before bedtime, to be ambushed again by the tiger in him! Lynn had not yet thought it out—this natural and strong instinct in him, and the spell of it, and what his final reaction must imperatively be. It bothered him. He was not only ashamed to face the facts, but afraid. His career in college had not been a building up of character calculated to rise superior to a temptation like this. The effect upon Anne of his perilous ride through the tunnel had altered the situation in a way he could not define. But he felt on the crest of a current far more mysterious and dangerous than that of the Rio Colorado. Anne's gratitude must not be mistaken for anything deeper.

"You're tired," Anne said solicitously, as he sat pondering on the porch.

"I guess so. Do you know, Anne, that damned idiot Brown held on to his bag of tools—a canvas bag full of iron tools! All the way through the tunnel! If that doesn't get my goat! You see I

100

didn't know that until they fished us out. I came so near drowning I hate to think of it."

"Lynn, didn't you think of letting him go?" she asked softly, her gray eyes darkly rapt upon him.

"Never entered my head! I'd have held on and drowned with him. . . . Anne, I'm an awful sap."

"*I* think you are wonderful."

"Yeah? . . . I'm afraid your experience of life doesn't qualify you to be a good judge."

"Indeed it does. Just set a nineteen-year-old girl adrift in Los Angeles to find work!"

"Don't omit to say a perfectly stunning girl."

"Lynn! You'll have me believing such—such nonsense yet," she remonstrated. "I'm only human. I love to hear you say nice things."

"I haven't started yet."

"You're a little flighty, aren't you?" she asked with a hint of archness that seemed another promise hidden in her. "No wonder. I should think you'd have lost your mind altogether."

"Don't kid me, Anne Vandergrift," he retorted. "I'll get back at you."

"But you are not just the same."

"As what?"

"As this morning."

"Well, are you?"

As she sat there in the light from Brown's cabin Lynn could see a slow painful wave of deep scarlet suffuse her face. She dropped it and covered it with her hands.

"Haven't *you* changed, Anne?" he queried, thrilled into remorse-lessness.

"Not changed. Just—wiser and sadder."

"How come? Wise is okay, but sad—I'm not for that. What do you mean?"

"I've found out—something."

"Will you tell me what?"

"No. . . . And please—please don't ask," she returned.

101

"All right—if it's that upsetting. But I'm darn curious. . . . Anne, where in the world are we getting? We can't go out to dinner and to the movies. I want to dance with you."

"Oh, Lynn, that would be nice. But, I fear, impossible."

"Of course you can dance?"

"Yes, indeed I can."

"Did you ever read *Alice in Wonderland?*"

"Yes. I loved it. And *Little Women,* too. I used to haunt the library in our town."

"*Robinson Crusoe?*" he ventured.

"I knew that by heart."

"I think I'll have to surrender," he concluded thoughtfully. He did not answer her wide, questioning eyes, but bade her good night and sent her home.

From that hour Lynn walked on the verge of a precipice, reveled in it, played a game with fate and defiantly subjected himself to all the tests possible. Day by day he traveled farther on this sweet and perilous road. While at work he thought of Anne continually, so that the hours passed as naught. His energy, his cheerfulness, his example, earned more plaudits from the blunt Flynn. But for the time being Lynn's ambition to climb played second fiddle to his love affair.

At breakfast one morning he told Anne that he soon was going on the cliff drillers' squad. And he had to explain.

"Wonderful!" she exclaimed. "But isn't that dangerous, too?"

"No more than some of the other jobs I've been on."

"Oh, I'm such a coward. If I were a boy I'd want to do as you do. But I can only feel—and worry."

"Don't worry, Anne. I'm going to beat this whole dam. And when he caught up his hat he turned suddenly with that devil of torment working in him.

"It just occurred to me. You can kiss me good-bye."

"Lynn! . . . But you—you're not serious," she protested.

"I am. You will kiss me, won't you?"

"Yes . . . if I—if you . . ." And she did kiss him, with eyes closing and the red fading from her face.

"Thanks—Anne," Lynn replied thickly and left the cabin with conflicting emotions. He was playing with fire. He was unjust with Anne. In the big bus, with its nearly one hundred men, smoking, talking, laughing on the way to work, he felt alone. And all day long, through the dust and heat and the din of labor, he thought of his return to Anne.

When he got back and tossed his cap and his dinner pail aside and called her over he thought of what had been in his mind all day.

She too must have been disturbed by the memory. She tried to speak, to laugh, to hide her confusion. She failed utterly to hide something that must have been fear. Pale, with parted lips and veiled eyes, she appeared to be afraid he had misunderstood her. Lynn thought if it had not been the end for him before, it surely was then. And all his pondering and brooding and analyzing and doubting came back again. Anne regarded him only as a protector, a brother.

Even this trouble, and the midsummer labor, with its heat prostration for many workers, failed to affect his zest for his job. Flynn gave him prodigious tasks. He ate them up. "Summer practice. Be sure you give me some work in the fall," he told the boss.

And during all these days his mind revolved around the personal, intimate problem with Anne. The moonlight hour came one August night, when he and Anne were out on the desert, that settled forever the fact that he had found the one girl in all the world for him. But she did not love him. All he could do was to take care of her and hope.

At last with September well on and the great cliff driller job at hand Lynn almost persuaded himself that he had been big enough to meet the test chance had imposed upon him. It seemed incredible that he had lived for months in intimate seclusion with an innocent, homeless and singularly beautiful girl without having transgressed in deed or thought the chivalry he owed her and something he imagined he owed himself. Perhaps he was only sentimental and bullheaded. But the girl herself and the wholly

103

unprecedented and tormenting situation had inspired this thing. He had been a failure in and out of college. Boulder Dam had struck unsuspected depths in him and Anne Vandergrift had called to the unusual, the noble, the magnificent that was not impossible of attainment. No one else would ever know how he had paid for the bitter past and burned its shame away.

Yet in his obsession he kept on tempting himself and deriving immeasurable misery out of the things he said to Anne.

One night after supper he remarked casually, "Well, you may lose your big brother tomorrow."

"Oh! . . . Lynn! How? . . . What?"

"I'm going on the cliff driller job. It's very dangerous. They let you down over the wall from the rim. On a little swinging seat. Down and down. Two hundred feet down now. With more than a thousand feet underneath. You have an electric drill with which you drill holes into the stones. They tell me it's a hell of a job. You have to press the drill with your body. I'll bet it's coming to me."

"It's coming to *me*—you mean," she said tragically. "Suppose I lose my—my big brother? I don't understand you any more —unless you're just teasing me."

"I'm just a plain matter-of-fact worker on the dam. I eat up hard work. They don't call me Biff Weston down there. Hell-rattling Weston! What do you know about that? . . . I'm not teasing. Just telling you! You must come out and see me on the wall. Say at a certain hour. I'll wave a handkerchief so you'll be able to see me among all the other drillers."

"You're growing more careless every day," she protested. "You're forgetting another kind of danger. To me! Bellew will never stop hunting for me. I feel it."

"Yeah? Well, young lady, I feel if he ever approaches you again that I'm going to break every bone in his body."

"My God! Lynn! Those men kill! Murder is in their hearts. They think nothing of taking anyone for a ride. . . . Bellew would *kill* you."

104

Chapter 8

Lynn went to the Boulder Dam hospital to see a friend he had made and had almost forgotten. He was a cowboy from across the river, and he regarded broken bones much as Lynn did his injuries—all in the game. His name was Curtis—Whitey Curtis he had frankly confessed, owing to his tow-colored hair.

"Wal, so they call you Biff?" he queried, eager to talk. "I read it in the papers, an' then I heah these big blokes talkin'—Biff, huh? What they call you thet for? I'll bet I can guess."

"Go to it, Whitey," Lynn replied good-naturedly.

"'Cause you're as much of a socker as a kicker."

"Not that good, Whitey," laughed Lynn.

"Wal, if you don't mind I'll dodge 'em both. Say, Biff, ever since I heahed you'd run the diversion tunnel I been itchin' to tell you somethin'. . . . Set over so I won't have to talk so loud."

Lynn sat down on the cot and leaned toward the cowboy.

"Weston, if there's any occasion for you to mention what I tell you keep mum aboot my name, will you?"

"Mum as an oyster, Whitey," replied Lynn.

"Talk aboot rackets, this heah Boulder Dam place beats hell oot of Chicago. Listen to this one. I'm sorta ashamed to give way what a damned sucker I am. But all the same I want your angle on this deal, 'specially on what I heahed more'n what was done to me. Nobody knows that I owe this busted laig to the rotgut booze I soaked up at thet speak down by Rankin's. But I know it, an' I shore hated to heah my boss blame thet truck driver."

"How'd you break your leg?"

"I hadn't got over the effect of thet knockoot stuff I drank down there. I walked in front of the truck when I thought I was backin' away from it."

"You must have been ory-eyed."

"No. I was just dotty. It comes over me every once in a while —thet spell to my haid. . . . Wal, last month I saved all my wages, an' like a jackass I flashed my roll heah in the store more'n oncet. Biff, do you know there air a lot of workers on this job thet are scouts, spies, pimps, for some gang or other."

"It's new to me, put that way, Curtis," returned Lynn, much interested.

"Wal, I know. My roll is gone, an' I have this busted laig to show for it. In my shift there was a chap named Bink Moore, young, likable, always makin' friendly. He cottoned to me right off. I'd never been off the range in my life. Don't know nothin' but cow-punchin'. But I'd looked on red likker. Last weekend Bink an' me drifted down to Rankin's. It was too swell an' fast in there for us to do more'n look on. Bink said he'd heahed of just the place for us to go. An' he took me. It was over beyond the pass. Thet diggins is shore populated now. You'd never guess it from the road. You gotta go back in the hills. There's every kind of a joint, an' some gangs thet'd do credit to the old Hash Knife ootfit of Arizonie. But I didn't know thet then.

"Bink 'peared to be acquainted, all right, a fact I took little notice of at the time. I reckon this place he took me wasn't a speakeasy. It was a camp. A haidquarters of the gang Bink belonged to. He wanted me to set in a game of poker. But I was shy of thet. An' a couple of drinks was enough for the moment. Then he introduced me to a black-eyed girl that I fell for like a steer when his pins air yanked oot from under him. She was pretty, an' she took to me more'n Bink calculated on, I'll bet. But she got me to drink an' right there my lights went oot pronto."

Curtis wagged his tow-colored head as if the recollection staggered his belief in his own sanity.

"When I come to I was lyin' oot on the ground. My haid was splittin', and my belly felt like a dawg's thet has swallered a dawg poison. But I wasn't so sick that I couldn't heah. Some man was cussin' some other man because I hadn't been packed away an' dumped in the road for a car to run over. An' the man who was gettin' cussed said Bess wouldn't stand for it. Bess was the name of the black-eyed girl I'd fallen for. It 'peared I was layin' half under a board platform with a tent over it. Anyway thet was Bess's tent, an' she sneaked me into it. I'd died shore if she hadn't got medicine to give me. As it was I was turrible sick. Bess hid me in her tent for nearly twenty-four hours. When I was able to walk she got me oot to the highway. Thet was late at night some time. I told her I was comin' after her an' take her oot of thet rotten hole. She cried an' begged me not to think of such a thing. I said, would you leave—an' go across the river with me to my home on a ranch? An' she said she wish'd to Gawd she could. . . . Wal, soon as I'm on my feet I'll pack a forty-five over there an' show them hombres what an Arizona cowboy is. An' I'll pack Bess oot, if she'll go. . . . I rode in on a car an' next day started to work, when I was hit."

"And that was that racket?" Lynn inquired thoughtfully.

"I didn't have a dime left of my hundred an' sixty pesos. . . . When I was hidin' in Bess's tent I heahed a lot of talk not meant for my ears, you bet. I'm not so dumb as I look. What little I got oot of Bess dovetailed in with the rest. She'd fallen in with an ootfit from Montana. A two-bit ootfit, I'd call it. Their racket was to get the wages of the workers like me. I'll bet they did a pretty big business. No fellow is gonna give himself away, even if he does get hit with a truck."

"I'll say he won't. It means his job. Whitey, I had my lesson. I used to hit up the bottle and buck the tiger aplenty last year. No more for little Willie! I hope this will be a lesson to you."

"Biff, you must know a lot aboot girls?"

"Ha! Ha! Are you asking me? . . . Whitey, I'm the dumbest cluck who ever thought he knew it all."

"Aw, you cain't bamboozle me. What'd you think of this girl Bess?"

"Pretty decent and risky of her, if it's as you figure."

"Wouldn't you say she must have liked me a heap to do that?"

"She must have, Whitey. Girls are queer, no matter where they're placed."

"Wonderful, I call it. Wal, I'm gonna go back for Bess when I get on my feet. I'd shore like to have you with me, Biff."

"I'll be darned if I wouldn't like to go. . . . But see here, cowboy, I've got the swellest, loveliest . . ."

"Shore, you would, Biff," interrupted Curtis. "But you wouldn't run any risk. I'd have some cowpunchers with me. An' mebbe Logan, the Las Vegas . . ."

"Say, do you know Logan?" Lynn interrupted in turn.

"He's my cousin. My mother is from Texas, a blood relative of Logan's. I can get him."

"By gosh, it's something to think of. Only I shouldn't—I can't. . . . But Whitey, what was that you heard while you were sewed up over there?"

"I was comin' to that." Curtis looked around warily and again lowered his voice. "It was late in the afternoon of thet day Bess hid me in her tent. She had gone oot. I was layin' on her cot, still sick, but a lot better. I heahed voices close by her tent, an' I figgered they came from the cabin next door. I peeped through a tiny hole in the canvas, an' I seen three men settin' on the back doorstep of the cabin. They was mebbe ten feet away, an' though they talked low I could heah distinctly. I could see them good.

But thet hole was too small, an' I was afraid I'd move the canvas. They were well-dressed, though, an' shore no common crooks. One of them looked like one of them radical guys. The others must have been what these two-bit hombres call big-shot racketeers. The very first crack thet I paid attention to made me forget I was a sick man an' robbed of my dough. Heah it is: 'There's a hundred grand in it.' One of them said: 'Pooh! That wouldn't be loose change for this job.' An' the third man spoke up: 'We'd nail this Six Companies for five hundred grand. Mebbe get it. We'd shore rake in two hundred an' fifty. . . . If we can get the iron-worker, the pipe fitter who can pull the job. . . .' 'I've got him sold,' replied the first man. 'I've engineered this job an' let you men in to help me pull it. We need months to lay our plans. An' when we spring it we want the cement to be runnin'.' 'We'll give the engineers just enough time to save the dam—to save all their work an' the millions it cost the government—provided they pony up the coin to find oot where the great fault is.' The third man —the radical guy—said the money would be okay. But he wanted the dam ruined. . . . They all sat quiet for a minute, an' I could heah their hard breathin'. . . . 'Let's sleep on it,' said one. 'An' plan to satisfy us all.' Then they left, an' the last I heahed was they'd have a drink."

"My word!" ejaculated Lynn. "How extraordinary! Why, Curtis, I don't know what the hell to think. . . . Graft, blackmail, Communism, on a tremendous scale."

"Them's high-soundin' words, Weston. I call it just plain rustlin'. An' shore as easy as cattle stealin' when there's no riders standin' guard."

"Oh, wasn't it just baloney?" ejaculated Lynn, trying to convince himself he had a nightmare. "We've had these agitators operating among us. But they never seemed to get far with well-paid American laborers. I don't know what the hell to make of it."

"Baloney? Wal, mebbe. I was of the same idee. An' I wanted yours. But there might be somethin' in it."

"Ruin the dam—make useless all the labor, the materials, the

109

millions—and the sweat and blood—the lives of men who have died for it? . . . Oh, improbable, unthinkable! What a ghastly thing! There couldn't be men such dastards."

"Is thet so? Wal, there *are*. An' what's more, hombres who spell thet name with a capital *B*. . . . An' in my way of thinkin' they'd be Sunday-school teachers compared to some of these ootfits heah."

"Right! I'm a white-livered, softhearted sap," retorted Lynn. "All the same I think the idea we get out of what you heard to be impossible of execution. It just couldn't be done."

"How do you know? Air you an engineer?"

"Yes, I am," Lynn replied stoutly.

"All right. If thet's so we needn't bother our haids. An' I'm darned glad."

"*But* . . ." The thing stuck in Lynn's craw. "Whitey, could you recognize those men—or any one of them?"

"No, I reckon not."

"Don't you remember some feature—some look—some distinguishing mark? Everyone has something. Look at your white hair. Why, you're a brother to our beautiful platinum blond movie queen. Look at me—at *these!*" And Lynn held up his great brown hands that certainly showed their contact with Boulder Dam.

"Doggone it! If I only had some memory. But I'm a dumbhaid. . . . Hold on. One of them hombres, the nearest to me, had a mole as big as a dime on his upper lip, near the corner. He wore one of them little doodad mustaches—like the movie actors have—just a dark line. It was your crack aboot the platinum blond movie queen that made me remember. . . . Yes, I'd shore recognize him."

"Keep this under your hat, Whitey," Lynn concluded somberly. "I want to think. It might turn out that I'll take the plot seriously. But in any case I'll help you get the girl Bess away from there, if you find you really want her, mean to help her."

"I'd be most damn obliged to you, Weston. But I reckon it's a forlorn hope, with my laig busted an' my pocketbook wuss!"

"Your leg will mend. And I've a little dough to blow in a good cause. . . . Here comes the doctor. Remember, Whitey, mum's the word."

"I'll make no more noise than a buck hidin' in the brush."

Lynn left to ponder over the amazing story told by the cowboy. It was ridiculous, yet it intrigued him. And he bent all his energy of mind toward a possibility of such a gigantic plot. He decided after no small mental conflict that such a plot could be possible. Very well, then—if it was possible—then would not the execution of it be so? In the wildest flight of his imagination he could not conceive it.

That conviction prevented Lynn from making a fool of himself, and jeopardizing his chances in the future, by rushing to Flynn, to take him to the officials and tell the story. That would betray to them how poor an engineer he really was.

Nevertheless Lynn could not brush the thing aside as one of the innumerable plots concocted by crooked men to make money out of the construction of the dam. There must be a thousand ways to succeed in that, where there was only one way to fail. And could not the magnitude of this plot be something born of the great work itself. The daring of it took his breath.

Suppose it were true! Suppose radicals and racketeers had really planned this villainy? Then how would he act? It seemed to him there was no way to circumvent the working out of such a plot. Even if the engineers heard of it and were convinced it might prove dangerous, what could they do? How could they pick out the traitors from a thousand workmen? It would be impossible to hire a guard to watch every man.

Then Lynn began to ponder on what these conspirators had in mind. An ironworker whom they had bought. And whatever he was to do had its significant relation to the running of the cement. Lynn puzzled over this relation. Whatever were the machinations of such grafters they must be bought off before the cement began to run. That was to say, by that crucial time the damage would be irreparable.

Lynn bewailed his ignorance of the construction of the dam.

111

He was learning much, but he needed to see the blueprints, to read the specifications, to know all about everything that went into the dam. After hours of reflection, during which he was irritated by interruptions to his thought, he made a discovery which struck him like a flash. This plot, whether fictitious or real, was going to be the cause of his more intimate study of the building of Boulder Dam. How strange that was! Lynn had to take it seriously, to place it beside things which one after another had built up step by step the cardinally important structure he must call his experience. There was fate behind it. That night, while awake for hours, and in his dreams, this thing dominated his conscious thought, almost to the exclusion of Anne.

Bold as Lynn felt himself to be, he quailed momentarily as he gazed down into the stupendous abyss from the east rim, at the point where he had to go on his new job as a cliff driller.

Flynn had been mysterious of late. It was Lynn's guess that the gang boss had been boosting him to the engineers and had something swell to spring on him when he got ready. He was friendlier than ever, more solicitous as the days slipped by, and he kept Lynn at small jobs two weeks longer than Lynn thought was needful. But anxious as Lynn was to get back to a big job he did not make an strenuous kick, and he spent his daytime hours thinking of Anne, dreaming dreams and wondering how in the world he could win her.

If Helen had been catty and gossipy his family and friends and everybody would think his relation to Anne queer and significant.

Lynn had his first ride across the canyon on one of the cable carriers, and it was an experience not to be forgotten. The big car carried men, tools, steel and lumber to the weight of tons, yet it scarcely sagged the black, glistening cables. The wheels of the car ran smoothly and noiselessly. There was a perceptible swaying from side to side. The cable towers stood up high above the rims—steel structures anchored in huge blocks of cement. But the thrill of the ride prevailed over Lynn's technical curiosity and admiration.

From the middle of the canyon the depth appeared magnified! The great walls yawned down to a throat of indescribable confusion—a red and yellow obstruction in the river, trestles and bridges, dams and banks, the diversion tunnels belching red streams, piles of debris, lumber, iron, slopes of talus, huge muddy holes in the river bed, trucks winding along the threads of roads. All of which appeared to make a hideous monstrosity imposed upon the sublimity of nature by thousands of workmen who resembled crawling ants.

It was early morning, with the sun a couple of hours high, and the canyon rims wandered away to north and south, rugged and shining.

Lynn arrived in time to see the cliff drillers come up over the rims for the shift. Every one of them was caked with dust on his overalls, silent, grim, exhausted. Some of them staggered dizzily. These drillers had short hours, but manifestly they were long enough.

The shift to take their places compared favorably in Lynn's eyes with any squad of lithe, powerful, bronze-faced and fearless-eyed football players he had even seen. He felt at home among them, despite a surprising qualm over the nature of this particular job.

"Over you go, men," called out the division foreman. "Slow, and keep even."

"Drill, ye terriers, drill!" sang out a lusty-lunged Irishman.

Lynn took a peep over the rim, and that was enough for him. He sustained a sensation as of floating, like falling from a height in a dream. It blanched and tightened his cheek. He had thought long and often about this job, but not at all about the actual peril. There was only one job more perilous than this—that of the scalers, who came last to scale off the loose slabs and fragments of rock left by the dynamiters who blew the holes of the drillers.

"Baird, here's a new man, Weston. . . . Yes, *that* guy, I'm glad to say," introduced the foreman, indicating Lynn. "Show him the ropes, and put him next to you."

113

Lynn felt the grip of a rough, iron hand and the keen scrutiny of a real man. He replied with a coolness that was simulated. Baird showed him how to get into the seat and the procedures through which he would be lowered over the rim. With the heavy drill on his lap and hanging on in spite of himself Lynn went down beside Baird. For a moment his tongue clove to the roof of his mouth, his hair rose stiff under his cap and a cold sweat oozed out of his skin. He felt Baird close beside him on the lift and another driller close on his right. There was help in their communal risk. But Lynn did not see anything except the yellow wall, the smooth ropes, the slender dusty cable that had the potentiality of a snake. It seemed alive.

Down and down they went, and while Lynn spat cotton or swallowed hard and kept his appalled eyes glued to the wall, his fellow workmen talked and laughed all along the even-swinging line. Lynn gritted his teeth and fought for the old reckless, unconquerable spirit. But it did not come at will. Once he thought of Anne and imagined that if he kept her in mind he would fall.

Little black holes in the wall, like the holes swallows dug in the clay banks for their nests, began to pass Lynn, a line of them, regular and cut far apart. These were the holes already drilled and not yet shot.

A call, merry yet somehow sharp, ran along the line of descending drillers. It was the call to halt. Lynn complied with nervous, awkward hands. Once more the wall of rock appeared bare of holes.

"Drill, ye terriers, drill," sang out the Irishman and went on with his song of the workers.

"Weston, you know these drills?" asked Baird, leaning over to Lynn.

"Yes. I drilled through one of the diversion tunnels," replied Lynn.

"Yep, an' you swam through one, too," said Baird. "You got it on us. . . . But for this job you watch me till you catch on. It feels harder'n hell at first. Don't look down an' don't forget you're

114

hangin' between heaven an' hell. Way up here with us fellers the bottom of this hole is sure hell. Roar, smoke, dust, heat, all come up. You'll think you heard nothin', or felt strangled, or sweat blood before. . . . Watch me. Go to it—an' hang on!"

"Hang on? . . . Ought to be—duck soup for me!"

But Lynn found that hanging on was alone the hardest trick he had ever tried. The seat was unstable. It swung easily. It never rested. He tried to hold it steady with his knees and feet, while he watched Baird start.

A rattling, cracking roar ran along the line. Puffs of dust shot out from the wall. Talk and song became as if they had never been.

Lynn switched his drill into operation and began his task. It required both hands to hold the infernal machine and to direct the drill. Had he not braced himself with spread, powerful legs he would have been knocked off the seat. The drill leaped away from the wall. He found hanging in mid-air, trying to drill a hole with a machine as jumpy as a struggling animal, vastly different from drilling with his feet on solid ground. He kept knocking himself away from the wall. He could not keep the drill in the hole. He was mortally afraid he would lose his balance. The din was in his eardrums. He should have stuffed his ears with cotton. The fiery stinging bits of stone, the dust flying out like hot steam, struck him in the face. He had forgotten his dust glasses. But neither Baird on his left nor the man on his right wore glasses, nor did they bend away from the rattling drill. They took it on the chin, Lynn saw; and he realized in desperation that that was what he had to do.

Neither fear nor failure had entered his calculations about this job. But he had now to contend with them. It took all the old fighting spirit and then some to forget them. Then he had to think to get the knack of the work. Only by pressing the drill against his abdomen could Lynn acquire a sense of stability. This steadied the damned drill. But what would stabilize him? He was not a ropewalker nor a trapeze performer. He realized that he was a

115

big lout who had gotten stuck on his football prowess and who now had been put on the spot by his overweening vanity to tackle a job that was simply terrible.

Here was a predicament, a racking task, where roused anger proved to be a bad asset. He had to be clear-eyed, coolheaded, a thinker and a balancer. This fact came to him, but its attainment seemed futile.

Then, at the instant when this change of mentality worked havoc in Lynn's sense of balance and muscular coordination, the infernal drill bounded back from the wall and almost knocked Lynn off his seat. He recovered his equilibrium to discover that Baird had a vicelike clutch on his shoulder.

"Careful! Don't ease up—don't forget!" his comrade yelled hoarsely in his ear.

"What'd I—forget?" yelled back Lynn.

"To hold on!"

"My God!" Lynn, realizing, whispered to himself. Of all things for Biff Weston to forget! But he would not have fallen. He might have lost hold of the drill, but not of the rope. Nevertheless the accident, with its possibility of fatality, was, after the first ghastly shock, what Lynn needed. And the succeeding thought of Anne brought a cool stern courage and intelligence into play.

He went back at the job, and relentlessly intent upon it and what it took to accomplish it he finished his first hole five minutes behind Baird, who had waited for him.

"Yeah, you've got it," he shouted. "Now hang on to that."

"This job's all hang on," Lynn shouted grimly.

"I'll say it is."

They lowered themselves a few feet, down to the line of drillers again. And by dint of all that was in him Lynn found himself equal to the job.

He applied all his faculties to the task of hanging on to seat, to rope, to drill, to wall. And he kept up with Baird.

Lynn had no conception of how many holes he drilled, of how many feet he went down with the line. He concentrated on the

116

one essential, which he grasped as the secret of this aerial job. No doubt experience and time would make it automatic, as his fellow workers appeared to react. But he strove to exclude any thought that deviated from the few essentials of the work.

So obsessed had he become that when the screaming rattle of the drills ceased to let the roar below once more fill his deadened ears he could not believe the shift hour had arrived.

"Come on," called Baird. "We're off. Up you go—and hang on!"

"What! Are we—through?" Lynn gasped incredulously. He saw indeed that they were. On the ascent, again the swaying, bumping, unstable seat appalled Lynn. Once he had crawled over the rim he made no effort to get to his feet. He seemed overcome by a multiplicity of sensations, paramount among which was the strange one that the bottom had dropped out of his stomach.

"Weston, you did fine," Baird said heartily, slapping Lynn on the back. "For a green hand on this hell-rattlin' job! I didn't tell you these drillers had some practice before going down."

"No—you didn't. . . . It wouldn't have helped any. . . . Do I look—like you?"

"I can't see myself. But if I'm shiny an' black, then you do."

Lynn sat there while the next shift of clean, lean-visaged young men took the places of the toil-blackened, dragging atoms of humanity who might have come out of war trenches. Lynn marveled anew. The work on Boulder Dam never ceased. How little the world knew of this monumental work—of its strife and agony! What was one dam more or less? But Lynn was one of the builders. He got to his feet spent and sagging, with almost a totally deadened muscular sense. He turned to watch that shift go down over the rim. He lost the feeling of relationship to them. He scarcely included himself in a band of toilers who proved beyond doubt that heroism had not forsaken a modern world, that courage and sacrifice were as great as they had ever been, that labor of hands and body were the hope, the salvation, the progress of a race.

Spent as Lynn was, he walked as far as he was able to before getting on a bus. His muscles seemed to be tied in knots. Upon arriving at his cabin he bathed and put on clean clothes, then went to supper. Anne was curious, but respected his mood. He felt unashamed of eating enough for two hungry men.

After supper he dragged himself to the store, where he bought new overalls and shirts. He thought he never would make it back to his cabin. And he attributed this unusual collapse to the depletion of blood and vitality incident to a day's job that beat two football games.

"By gosh, I'd never admit that job could beat me—like this," he panted, as he threw off coat and removed his shoes. Then he fell asleep. And he slept from four that afternoon till seven the next morning.

"Am I dead—or what?" he asked, wonderingly. He decided in favor of the latter. Upon discovering that he had not undressed he felt shame and chagrin.

Five days passed without Lynn knowing where they went. They just vanished, leaving behind a chaos of impressions—a swinging seat over a frightful chasm—an infernal jolting, thumping, steel fiend—dust and heat, a blank wall before his sore eyes and a hideous, incessant, rattling racket.

At last he managed to give more time to Anne, explaining his neglect by saying that he had tackled a job which made all his other labors seem tame and easy.

The cliff driller job had seized upon him with a many-sided fascination. It was something to beat and infinitely harder than anything he had ever attempted. It frightened him as nothing else ever had. It was more than excessively difficult, hazardous toil. It grew to have an indefinable meaning for Lynn. It called to the last ounce of physical stamina. It took all the courage and intelligence he could muster. He had not been born for such a job, that was certain. His comrades were better men than he was.

In time Lynn conquered. The romance and wonder of the work made up for his loss of pride in his physical prowess. That too returned in fuller measure. In time he hardened to the pounding drill and to the swinging on a board seat five hundred feet from the jagged rocks below. He protected his eyes like a race driver, and all the rest that had been so sickeningly unendurable came along in the day's work.

For hours at the stretch he was a cliff dweller. He grew as free as a canyon swallow—the strange black-shining little birds that sped by him with silken, rushing wings. He could gaze down like an eagle from his lonely crag. He could gaze up at the black rim seven hundred feet above and not feel dizzy. He gained an inordinate pride in becoming one of these drillers in the stone wall, swinging halfway between heaven and earth. And sometimes the thought would come to him that the place where he drilled would soon be a wedge for the concrete dam, an anchor to hold the enormous man-made rock against the floods of a rapacious river.

How long would this contraption fostered by the government and built by toilers under the direction of engineers last against the forces of nature? The pyramids in Egypt, the Sphinx, the Appian Way—these constructions of man had lasted thousands of years beyond the lives of those who sought service out of them. But what was a few thousand years to nature? Not a grain of sand on the desert! Boulder Dam would outlast the need of man—Lynn felt sure of that. Nevertheless, he was strangely curious about the fate of this dam that he had come to love.

One afternoon as he alighted from the bus he was accosted by a young man leaning on a crutch. The clean-cut youthful face, somewhat drawn and minus the brown so characteristic of workers there, the blue eyes with intent direct gaze, these flashed into Lynn's mind as another proof of what the cliff driller job had done to him.

"Whitey Curtis!" he ejaculated. "You cowboy son of a gun! Up on the bum leg, eh? Gee! I'm glad, Whitey. How are you?"

"Aw, I could fork a hawse, if the Doc would let me," replied Curtis, with his frank grin. "Biff, I'd never recognized you but fer them shoulders."

"I'm on the wall, Whitey, drilling to beat hell. It's a honey of

119

a job, I'll tell the world. . . . Wait for me here, Whitey. I'll run down, wash and change. Be back in a jiffy."

"I'll be heah, Biff. I shore got somethin' to tell you."

"Yeah," returned Lynn, suddenly recalling Curtis' story. "All right. I'll cut the corners running back."

His hobnailed boots rang on the pavement. And in his mind revolved the plot to blackmail the engineers and destroy the dam. How had he ever forgotten that, Lynn soliloquized? He could not have taken it seriously. No one could go out there on the job, such a job as he had, and believe anything could injure or retard the movement of that great work.

He hurried back to meet Curtis.

Whitey's glad smile dispelled Lynn's perplexity. Plainly this Arizona cowboy had taken a fancy to him.

"Too early for mess, cowboy. Where'll we go?"

"Reckoned you might fetch your car."

"Didn't think of that. Anyway, we haven't time enough for a drive. Wonder how my old calliope is, anyway? . . . How far can you walk, Whitey?"

"Aw, I don't need this third laig. Look heah." And Curtis showed that he could walk without his crutch.

"Fine and dandy. Whitey, I've had bad legs. All well now. But when I ran down to my cabin just now the muscles felt tied in a knot. It hurt, too. Hope there isn't anything wrong inside. We fellows can't afford to get in front of trucks and bullets."

"Biff, every bone in me, almost, has been busted. Cowpunchers don't think nothin' of thet."

"Football players break a leg occasionally. But they are never so good after that. I never had a real bad hurt."

"It'd take a truck to bust you, Biff. . . . Let's go to the park an' set down on a bench."

The green park was only half a block away.

"Whitey, are you still nuts over the girl—Bess, I think you called her?" Lynn queried as they found a seat.

"Wuss, Biff," replied the cowboy soberly. "Got it turrible bad.

Reckon I've been piled in a heap once an' for all. . . . Biff, she came to see me at the hospital."

Lynn's heart quickened to the warmth of his comrade's voice. "What? You don't say? How'd she get away from that—what was his name?"

"Bink Moore, the guy who played part to me. I'll bet he got my roll. Wal, I'll get even by rustlin' his girl."

"Whitey, it's kind of risky," said Lynn, shaking his head. "These gangsters haven't one single human feeling."

"Wal, they cain't have nine lives like a cat," the cowboy replied darkly.

"No. But that one they have is sure tough. . . . I wonder, did Bellew leave Vegas?"

"No. Bess told me his ootfit was known to hers!"

"By gosh! Still hanging around. I wonder!"

"Bess's ootfit heahs all the underworld dope. But they don't belong to the underworld, so called."

"Now, Whitey, what's your idea about this girl Bess?"

"I don't know. Except I shore want to get her oot of thet life."

"Marry her?"

"I would—so help me Gawd! But I never told her thet."

"It was swell of you. I like you better for it. So would she, if she's worth a damn. But why didn't you tell her?"

"Guess I was kinda shy aboot thet. You see I played bein' a sport. Rich rancher's son on a lark! Wish I hadn't. 'Cause I shore cain't keep such a bluff up for long. If I had a little dough an' could get Bess away! She'd be lost in Arizonie. An' she'd like ranch life."

"Let me meet Bess, will you?"

"I shore want you to. An' I will soon's I can. She promised to write me. If she keeps the promise I'll know shore she likes me. . . . But this aboot Bess wasn't the main thing I wanted to tell you, Biff."

"It wasn't. What then?"

"Yesterday I seen the hawk-faced guy with the little doodad of

121

a mustache thet didn't hide the mole on his lip."

"You did! Where?" flashed Lynn, suddenly galvanized.

"Heah in Boulder. It was just after supper, not yet dark. I was standin' on the corner, a block down there, in front of thet store. He was walkin' with a workman. I was so keen to make shore I recognized the hombre that I didn't see what the workman looked like. They turned down the street. I'm tellin' you thet hombre had a hell of a lot on his mind."

"Whitey, I'd 'most forgotten. Now you bring that up again. . . . Cowboy, I'm afraid you're full of baloney."

"Shore, if baloney is the same as hunch. Biff, I don't know what a cowboy's got thet every man hasn't. But it's somethin'. Livin' ootdoors, mebbe, makes him sharp."

"You didn't strike me so darned smart, Whitey. That was a dumb stunt you pulled."

"When I'm sober, I mean, Biff," the cowboy replied humbly. "I'm gonna lay for thet hombre. An' if I see him again I'll foller him."

"It might be a good idea, if only to find we're both full of baloney. . . . That reminds me of my empty belly. Come eat with me. . . . After supper I'll show you how to find my house."

Lynn did not see his friend again very soon, and in the press of his trying labor, and the need of rest during his off hours, he forgot the cowboy. The plot against the builders of the dam, however, did not wholly fade out of his mind, though as the short days passed swiftly by, lengthening into weeks, the poignancy of the fear and conviction gradually lessened. To Lynn the great engineer Carewe was supreme. He would complete Boulder Dam. Only nature and a hundred thousand years could destroy that work.

The dynamiters went on the job. Their work was easy compared to that of the drillers and scarcely to be mentioned in the same breath with the exceedingly perilous and cardinally important toil they left to the scalers.

Lynn had often heard the blowing out of the holes made by

the drillers, and the rattle and crash of falling rocks and the concatenation of echoes. Even at a distance it was disturbing enough to halt any workman for a listening and gazing moment. For this phase of the work more than any other had a semblance to war.

At the end of the last shift for Lynn he waited for the shooting. He had a desire to see and hear the thousand and more holes he had drilled, and those of his comrades, blow out in fire and smoke and resounding crash. Always behind Lynn's passion for the construction of Boulder Dam were two forces that vied with each other for supremacy. One was elemental, sensorial, and the other intellectual and constructive. The latter grew as his months of contact and thought passed by, but always the stronger was the sheer physical joy of sweat and blood, the thunder and boom, the conquest of muscle over granite.

The afternoon waxed hotter and hotter up on the rim. There was no shade, no breeze. Nothing but the empire of the desert sun! But Lynn stuck it out, surely the only man of his shift who cared to see that their labors were not effaced forever from the cliff walls.

Work directly under the wall to be shot ceased for the time being, but upriver and downriver it went on monotonously, as hard and fast as foreman-driven squads could go.

Lynn leaned over the wall to watch and listen. As he was close, so close that once a watchman cautioned him vainly, he clapped his hands over his ears. Then he stood tranced and stiffened at a sight and sound for which he had no name, except to call it the barrage of the cliff workers. Lynn had read of the great German barrage during World War I, and a greater one later by the A.E.F., but if either had it over this grand and continuous salvo of the dynamiters Lynn thought he would not have wanted to be there.

Long after the cracking, bursting shots ceased and their echoes had died away the heavier detonation of sliding, rolling, crashing rocks filled the canyon. That section disappeared in smoke and

123

dust. Then roar subsided, and finally the roll and thud of splintered rock.

"Pack that load out, you racing-truckers!" Lynn called over the rim of the sulphurous, smoky abyss. And then as he drew back, his face and hands dripping grime, he added with a steely ring, "Me for the scaler's job!"

He caught a truck and had a hot dusty ride back to Boulder City. Dusk had fallen over the Nevada desert when he reached his home. His quick eye caught a bright line under the window shade. Had he left the light turned on and the blind down? He could not remember, but such absentmindedness was frequent with him of late.

Chapter 9

Lynn in his day had viewed with critical eye perhaps half a hundred squads of athletes. And during his long job on the dam he had seen as many more, notable among whom were the drillers. These last had, as he would never forget, filled him with a despair of emulation. But none of them could equal the veteran scalers.

This squad whom Lynn joined did not number as many members as the others. They made him think of a bunch of rodeo cowboys. But the best comparison he could find was a group of professional baseball players he had watched train on the field at Catalina. The cowboys appeared merely boys; the baseball players were older; and the scalers were men.

Physique and condition were paramount in Lynn's critical eye. This squad of scalers whom he was about to join appeared magnificently fit for what was claimed to be the most hazardous and strenuous job known to contractors. They had been recruited, as Lynn had learned, from the ranks of steeple climbers, tower painters, ironworkers on the construction of skyscrapers; and from other unusual walks of labor that required remarkable nerve, agility and strength. Lynn scraped acquaintance with an engineer who had run the Twentieth Century Limited on the Grand Central Railroad for the allotted years these men were limited to. "I used to run into the next block while the signal was still red," this worthy said with a smile. "Had to do it to make the time. Ninety miles per."

There was a quiet, leonine man of middle age, the kind of man Lynn would have liked beside him in a battle; and this fellow had helped paint the cables on the Brooklyn Bridge and the upraised arm of the Statue of Liberty. A mountaineer from Colorado caught Lynn's fancy. There was a hardy sailor whose nose had been flattened, probably by a belaying pin, and he had the build of a gorilla. No doubt he could hang on to a yardarm with one hand and reef with the other, while the ship was performing didos with the big seas.

If there were drinkers in the body of scalers no casual observer could have noted it. And Lynn, keen as he was, could not catch any evidence of the baneful bottle. Altogether this aggregation of wall-scalers, among whom Lynn was proud to be numbered, was unique and admirable. He felt somewhat like he had when he first joined the varsity squad.

When Lynn met the foreman, Regan, he grasped a clearer conception of this squad of scalers. Regan had the frame of Jack Dempsey and an eye like Babe Ruth.

"Howdy, Weston," was his greeting, with a handclasp that cracked bones. "Flynn told me about you. But I'd heard before. There ain't nothin' to this job for you. I'll put you next to me. An' you do what I do. Thet's all."

"I'm tickled pink. I've been stuck on this scaler job," Lynn replied heartily.

"Yeah? So am I, an' I can't get off it. . . . Flynn says he has you slated for higher up."

"So he told me. I hope I make good."

"Shure you will. Weston, I don't need to tell you thet we have no minor injuries on this job. Get me?"

126

"I think so," Lynn replied dubiously. "But you do have major ones?"

"Yes, if you can call death a major injury," Regan returned dryly. "I ain't worryin' none about you, Weston. Only you watch me!"

"Okay, boss," Lynn said with cool and easy assurance. To work beside this man would be more than a privilege. It would be adventure first and achievement afterward.

The scaler used a crowbar. His work was to go over the rim and pry or break off loose slabs of rock that had been cracked by the dynamite. Lynn was so glad to have the iron bar in his hands, instead of that jolting infernal drill, that he could have whooped. He went over the rim with Regan and obeyed instructions implicitly. Lynn had a genius for grasping the essentials of work that required nerve, strength, agility and a perfect coordination between eye, brain and muscle.

The job was a peach, he thought. He was not jammed up close to a worker on each side of him. He was not nailed to one spot for long stretches. He had space to work in. The scalers had to keep out of each other's way. There was no telling how far a crack in the rock extended, how large a slab might loosen under the crowbar and break grindingly off the wall. Herein lay the main hazard, and Lynn grimly appreciated it. But he had supreme confidence. He felt at home on the swinging seat. He could walk along the wall like a huge spider, and when he stuck his crowbar under a slab something had to give way.

Down and down Lynn went, and from side to side, keeping even with Regan. The workman on Lynn's left was sometimes above them a little, never below. The foreman set a swift pace. He kept calling to his squad, usually cheery spurs to keep up, but sometimes profane. The exigency of this job was that it should be performed as by one man. The speed called for owed its need to the demand from below. Trucks and laborers had to be utilized during the scaling. This had to dovetail. There was no loss of momentum, no slackening up, no rest on Boulder Dam.

The few hours that it took for the scalers to clean off the thousand-foot section of wall passed so swiftly for Lynn that he was astounded by the call to quit. He had gotten the hang of the work to his satisfaction and was reveling in it, deep in his old fancy that he was building the great dam, and sometimes wishing Anne was up in the rampart to see him, when the scale for that day ended.

"Buddy, I'll say you don't need no wings," Regan said when they pulled out on the rim again.

"Swell!" beamed Lynn. "Makes a hit with me. . . . Short hours and big wages!"

"Wal, we earn them, take it from me."

Lynn hurried home, and while he was in the bathtub, removing the stains of honest toil, he left the living room door ajar and regaled himself by a recital to Anne of his day's adventure on the new job. He hardly meant to make it seem dangerous, but he could not keep it from being dramatic. And when he dressed and came out to Anne he reproached himself. Pale of cheek and dark of eye she appeared the loveliest, sweetest, most precious thing in all the world. He would then have to retrench and modify and make her see that the work of a scaler was no more than football practice. She would be persuaded, reassured and comforted.

"Anne, let's celebrate," he said gaily, having brought back the roses to her cheeks.

"What? You're always celebrating," she pouted. "Biff, you spend so much money. You must save."

"Well, as to money, Anne, I have spent some. Not much. Every time I buy you a doodad or an ice cream soda you throw a fit."

"Oh, Lynn. That's not so. I mean the foolish things you buy me."

Summer passed, and with the fall days labor at Boulder Dam lost its heat if not its dust. Also the drilling and scaling of the canyon walls neared the end. Coincident with this had been the great event of the actual running of cement. The great two-hundred-and-fifty-foot hole below bedrock had been filled. The foundation of the dam had been laid. Thereafter no letup in the pouring of cement could be allowed until the whole vast concrete dam was done.

Lynn, from his lofty eyrie on his swinging seat, would often gaze down at the long irregular patchwork of cement squares. It resembled a colossal checkerboard with its dark and light squares. He would watch the two-ton buckets swing out over the dam, on their thousand-foot spider-web cables, and dump their precious contents down into one of the squares. And at such moments he would rejoice that evidently the plot to ruin the dam had failed. There it was, growing daily in his sight, an incredible thing. He would never know, nor would anybody else, if the blackmail money had been collected. Like as not, reflected Lynn! And then he would recall the cowboy, Whitey Curtis, and his girl Bess, to wonder what had become of them. Even to this day Lynn had not forgotten to keep a sharp eye alert for the man with the mole on his lip.

With the end of the scaling job in sight Lynn began to think about his next move—what would be his next contribution to the building of Boulder Dam. It could never be finished without him. When he interrogated Flynn on the subject he encountered more mystery. Lynn grew afraid he was in line for promotion. That was swell, but he was not yet ready to go into the office, as he had a hunch Flynn's influence had him headed.

The next time he met the red-faced boss he had a happy inspiration.

"Flynn, let me have a crack at the cement mill."

"Wha—at? That sand an' cement mixer! Why, you'd do nothin' but push electric buttons. That's no job for you."

"Neither is pushing a pen. Please, boss, just for a while. I'll bet that mill is a marvelous place."

"Weston, I'll see if I can place you there. But the next time you go up."

"Up! That'll be swell. Up in one of the cable turrets, running the cable engines. I could do that."

Flynn laughed and held aloft his grimy hands. Lynn thrilled to realize how solid he stood with the boss of bosses. Yet how simple to understand now! His heart had been in his job. Wages, time out to play and gamble, holding back on energy, these had not been in his mind. Lynn had applied his passionate enthusiasm for football to the sterner call of work. Flynn would never know the bitterness behind Lynn's struggle, nor would anyone else. But the incentive was Lynn's own business, his secret. At last he had a mental grip on what would lead to success in life.

The V-shaped canyon walls had assumed proportions almost to please the engineers on a tour of inspection. One of these was the chief, Carewe. They consulted blueprints and held a brief discussion. Whatever they said to Regan did not set happily upon that worthy's mind. "What the hell!" Lynn heard him growl as he turned away with blue fire in his eye. "It'll all be the same in a million years!"

Lynn agreed with whatever the foreman meant by that. And in his own mind there was a picture slowly being etched by the sight of the canyon day by day and the thought of how nature would revenge itself in future ages for this violation.

The scalers did not work that day. Deeper drill holes in the bulge of wall below and stronger blasts had been the order. A shallow blasting minimized the danger to the scalers and the reverse magnified it.

Lynn spent the day with Anne. They took another long drive. Lynn celebrated that by giving Anne her first lesson in driving. She proved to be less quick and adept than he had expected she would be. Anne told him that he made a very handsome teacher, but not an effective one.

"Besides," she concluded, "I don't think a woman's place is to be a mechanic."

"Where should it be?" he asked.

"At home, with housekeeping . . . and babies."

"Oh, Lord! In this day and age? . . . Anne, you are a hark-back to the prehistoric age of home, love, family, happiness."

"Biff, you're old-fashioned yourself," she retorted.

"Not a chance! Kid, your dope on me is all wrong."

When Lynn reported next day for work the canyon was full of smoke and the smell of brimstone. It was a cool fall day. Regan's squad had orders to rest a half hour to allow the smoke and noxious fumes to drift away.

When Regan did order his squad over the rim he was not in his usual cheery humor. He took occasion to give his men an extra admonition to keep spread out.

They descended several hundred feet before they came to the section of wall that had been drilled the day before, loaded during the night and shot that morning. Lynn found his work cut out for him, and he would not have cared to tackle that job without all his apprenticeship. Deeper drill holes and stronger blasts had left strenuous toil for the scalers. Slowly they worked down to the seven hundred foot level from the rim. This was at a point a little downriver from the dam and above the diversion tunnels on the Arizona side. The need for all that drilling and blasting on this side was not clear to Lynn. He knew the electrical plants had to be built somewhere just below the dam.

At that level, where the bulge of wall had to be blown off, the scalers encountered the hardest work in months.

Lynn, always alert and on edge, as in a hard game, saw scalers on each side of him take chances that betrayed a wearing of strength and fraying of nerves. Lynn for himself felt nothing of that. But if he had been captain he would have called time out and sent for reserves.

Regan was all over the wall, equal to two scalers. Something had rubbed the Irishman the wrong way, perhaps the imposition of more labor to be done in the same shift. But enduring and agile as Regan was, and goaded by anger to Homeric efforts, he too began to show the strain. Smitty, a bridge painter on Lynn's right, appeared to be in good shape. He was an unusually careful scaler, somehow getting his work done without waste of energy. Doddridge, on Smitty's right, kept the pace, yet he appeared about done. Others along the line betrayed that they had almost reached their limit.

Lynn grasped the critical time for that shift had come. It was like the end of a game which had been all fast and furious with the climax in sight. His faculties received the added spur of this premonition. When the edging along the wall brought him close to Smitty again he said: "Smitty, look out for Doddridge." And the sweat-blackened Smitty replied: "Righto. But somebody ought to cuss Regan."

Thereafter, what vigilance Lynn could spare from his own efforts he applied to the boss. But even so he could not continually keep an eye on Regan. And at last, darkly intent on finding his end of the blasted wall, Lynn did not look up until an ominous sound above shocked him out of his own absorption.

At that moment, to his amazement, he saw Regan twenty feet up and almost in line with him. But that did not shock him as much as the boss's singularly rigid doubled posture. Regan had his crowbar in a crack that he had evidently widened. His rigidity was not that of prying with his iron tool. It was a holding of a scale of rock in place.

"*Regan!*" yelled Lynn.

"*Spread below!*" Regan rang out, piercingly.

Again that low ominous sound—like a grind of rock teeth! Regan thought of the men beneath, not of himself. In a flash Lynn saw that if or when the loosened scale of rock let go it would cut Regan's cable or knock him off the seat. A sharp call came from Smitty.

Lynn flexed his knees and gathered his muscular force for a spring out from the wall.

"*Boss! Let go—bounce out!*" yelled Lynn.

Regan groaned, either with a dreadful fear or an expenditure of the last ounce of strength. It seemed to be answered by a like sound—the sound of rock against rock. With a clanging ring Regan's crowbar went hurtling through the air. The man let out a hoarse cry. Not an awful cry at his own doom but of dread for the scalers below! The scale of wall loosened, cracked free, started to slide.

It knocked Regan out of his seat. The board split and dropped in two pieces. Regan appeared to fall and catch, dangling in distorted black silhouette against the sky.

Lynn timed the slide perfectly. His flexed knees straightened with tremendous power. Out from the wall he catapulted. The sliding scale shot down. Lynn swung back to catch the wall with feet and legs that gave just right to prevent rebound.

Then right above him appeared Regan, sideways along the wall, one hand spread and trying to grip the rock, the other slipping on the broken tackle. He lost power to hold on. He slipped till he hung head downward, a yard to Lynn's right.

Lynn edged over and leaned far at the same instant. His great clutching hand as if to snatch a football out of the air! The cut rope snapped. Regan fell.

That brown hand flashed. It caught Regan by the left ankle. Nailed it to the wall! Lynn braced for the shock, held his seat and also Regan.

There was a precarious instant when all went red in Lynn's sight. He swung violently while still he leaned to hold Regan. Then he steadied in his seat. He crushed Regan's foot to the wall.

"*Help! Help!*" he rasped, through teeth hard to unclench.

"Hang on, Westie, I'm comin'," Smitty shouted and then let out a trenchant call for Doddridge.

"Careful!" advised Lynn, cool and hard.

"Can you—hold him?" panted Smitty, striding sideways as on seven-league boots.

"Duck soup! . . . Never let go—in my life!"

Smitty reached him and laid brawny hands on Regan's leg. "By Gawd, Westie! . . . If you ain't some guy! . . . There! I got a good grip. . . . Regan, you ——— ——— Irish mick, we're gonna save your life!"

"Careful, Dodd!" yelled Lynn to the second scaler, who was coming with might and main.

"Have you got him?" Doddridge called excitedly. "There comes Roberts—on your side. . . . Just a minute more, fellers."

133

In less than that four more strong hands laid hold of Regan. That enabled Lynn to release his terrific grip. His hand was cramped.

"Now—what'n hell?" queried Smitty.

"Listen, men. It's a cinch," said Lynn, released from his physical and mental lock. "We'll pull him up—get him straight—back to the wall. . . . Easy now . . . there! It's duck soup—I told you. . . . Stick his left leg inside Smitty's rope—the other inside mine. . . . Aha! We've got him!"

"He's groggy. We gotta hold him," said Smitty.

"Looks like he was out," added Doddridge.

"Blood gone to his head—that's all," chimed in Lynn.

"Westie, we can't hold him on an' raise ourselves, with him too," complained Smitty.

"We'll go down. It's shorter," Lynn replied tersely. "But wait. He's coming around. . . . Regan!"

"Okay, thanks—to you," the boss said in a husky whisper. "I'm dizzy. But I can hold on."

"Good! Let's give him another minute, Smitty. . . . You other fellows work down now."

Presently Lynn saw that he could trust Regan to cling to the two ropes while they were descending.

"Now, Smitty, let's have some teamwork," said Lynn.

Cautiously they began the descent, facing the wall while Regan faced the canyon, and with concentrated care and effort they went down safely to the tunnel ledge, some fifty feet above the river bed. Here a number of scalers and other workmen caught them with eager hands. A babel of voices rose.

Regan, when lifted out of the two seats, appeared unable to stand without support. They set him down back against the wall. Both water and coffee were offered him.

"Whisky," said the scaler boss.

When he had taken a stiff pull at a flask the ashen hue of his face retreated to admit a return of healthier color. But the bronze did not come back at once.

134

"Are you all right, boss?" Lynn asked with a smile.

"Am I? . . . Don't seem to hurt anywhere except here." Regan rubbed his left ankle with a shaky hand.

They removed his hobnailed boot and heavy sock, to disclose the fact that it was swelling rapidly and was already black and blue. On the inside were bloody contusions.

"What did thet?" he queried. "I don't remember the rope round here. . . . An' thet damned crowbar missed me."

"Boss, this is where I nailed you. Oh, boy, but I almost missed you."

"Nailed me? You grabbed me—*here*?"

"No place else, boss. And I pressed your foot against the wall. There was a little protuberance of rock that helped, believe me."

"Lemme see your mitt," Regan rejoined brusquely.

Lynn held out his right hand. It had always been a big powerful member, but a year and a half on Boulder Dam had made it less a thing of beauty and more a magnificent thing of calloused brawn.

"For the luv of Mike!" burst out Regan. "S'pose I'd fallen feet first? You'd scalped me—or broke my neck!"

That was all the encomium the accident and rescue wrung from the boss of the scaler squad. Lynn took it as compliment and thanks enough.

In due time the excitement subsided. Only an incident of Boulder Dam work! So the workers took it. Regan, at the head of his scalers, walked through the tunnel, and eventually they got to the river. Here it was Lynn's good or bad luck to run plump into Flynn. And then Lynn, making a move to run, got nailed himself by a hand as big and powerful as his own.

"No you don't, buddy. I saw that mess up on the cliff, and I heard the damnedest yelling. What's it all about?"

"Boss, I pulled a boner," replied Regan. "But I'm layin' the blame where it belongs. Higher up! An' they'll hear from me. . . . Weston saved my life, Flynn. But for his sharp eye an' steel hand —well, there'd been a bloody mess under the scaled wall."

135

That was all Flynn could elicit from Regan, and Lynn refused to talk. But Smitty took it as an occasion to blossom forth as a narrator. Lynn's ears began to tingle and he shifted uneasily under Flynn's staying hand. . . . "My heart was chokin' me, boss," went on Smitty, "an' I was scared to death. But I could see. Might as well have had a telescope. . . . As I was sayin', Regan's crowbar went spinnin', the scale busted his seat an' left him hangin' an' slidin'. The big scale of rock slid down on Weston. He swung out far. Let it go by. Then when he swung back Regan had fallen head down. Weston pounced on him like a tiger. Caught his foot. Stopped him—held him against the wall, by Gawd! . . . Talk about your trapeze performers! . . . Thet was the ——— ———est, thrillingest sight I ever seen. But I ain't hankerin' to see it again. . . . I yelled to Weston—asked him if he could hold on. He called back, 'Duck soup!' an' said he'd never let go of nothin'. . . . Wal, I got to him an' . . ."

Lynn slipped like an eel out of Flynn's grasp and fled. He crossed the bridge and walked up the winding road out of the canyon, where by that time he had regained composure. He let two buses go back and finally hailed a truck. At Boulder City he stopped at the store. When he bought supplies on his own account Anne always scolded, and he thought it would be wise for him upon this occasion to take home a load and thus escape her interrogation.

But when he got home with an armful he escaped the scolding but not Anne's perception.

"Lynn! What's happened?" she cried, the instant she saw him, letting her sewing fall to the floor as she sprang up, her wonderful eyes dilating.

"Hello, can't I come home early with a lot of stuff same as any other day? Where's Mrs. Brown? We'll have . . ."

"You are pale under your tan. Your eyes . . . Lynn, have you been biffing anyone?"

"Ha! Ha! That's a good one. No, I haven't biffed anyone. Fact is I'm growing soft. I don't get sore any more. Something has transformed me, I guess. Nothing much happened today. We had our biggest scaling job. I overworked. It's a strain, though, that job. I'm glad it's almost over."

"Raspberries!" retorted this gray-eyed girl.

Lynn howled in mirth. He did not, however, give Anne any satisfaction at the moment, thinking he had better wait awhile. Anne regarded him doubtfully and shook her pretty head. Lynn went for his daily bath and change, about which he took a good deal more time than usual. After that he presented himself in the living room, feeling equal to the occasion. But Anne did not ask him any more embarrassing questions. Lynn read a newspaper he had gotten at the store. Altogether several hours had passed, and it was midafternoon when a messenger brought a note from headquarters. It was marked urgent. It required his immediate presence at the office of the Six Companies, and was signed Carewe.

"Holy Mackerel! Now I'm in for it!" he declared, jumping up.

Anne snatched up the note, which Lynn had dropped, and scanning it she cried out: "Oh, Lynn, I knew you had done something terrible."

"Anne, don't look like that," he made haste to reply, soberly. "I only saved a man's life. I hoped it'd not get to headquarters. But it has—damn Flynn! By gosh, I know what I'll do. I'll take you with me."

Instead of exclaiming strongly against that Anne surprised Lynn by saying: "I'd love to go."

"Oh yeah? Well, put on your best duds—the blue one—and we'll beard the lions in their den. If I know men by this time none of them would look at me twice if I had you along. Hurry now."

Lynn went to get the car and to adjust something he had neglected. In a very short time, it seemed, Anne came tripping out, her face having that opal glow and her eyes the dark, intense loveliness emotion always lent them.

"Am I a wise guy, showing you off to these officials—to *any* men?" he queried dubiously, shaking his head.

137

"Nonsense. They're likely to think more of you with a—a girl friend."

"Sure. But that wouldn't keep them from wanting you. My dear, now and then in this mortal world of ours, there's a woman comes along whom all men want. It isn't beauty or charm or sex, altogether. It isn't It, as the movie guys call it. Just something beyond words."

"Lynn, are you sure that's all? . . . You must have done something very bad. I hope to goodness you won't lose your job."

"Say, little lady, I'll bet you they'll want to make me a big shot in the company."

Lynn drove to the big office building in the green park and took Anne in. What a lot of offices the doorman escorted them by! Lynn did not feel at all the cool and easy person he posed as. There was a tingling in his nerves, a swelling of his veins, a suppression in his breast. Finally he and Anne were ushered into a big well-lighted office. The two occupants therein rose to greet Lynn. He knew them both, though he had never seen Mr. Halsey, president of the California Company, the largest of the Six Companies banded together on the construction work. The other was Carewe, whom Lynn had seen often, a tall, pale-faced man, with deep fine eyes and a broad, thoughtful brow. At close range Lynn had an instant impression of the intellectual capacity of this great engineer.

"Well, hello, Weston. I'm glad finally to meet you face to face," he said, with a quick and bright smile, as he extended his hand. "This is my colleague, Mr. Halsey, head of the California branch of our Six Companies."

"Mr. Carewe, I've known you a long time by sight," burst out Lynn, forgetting his cool poise. "I'm happy indeed to meet you— and you, too, Mr. Halsey. It's an honor I appreciate greatly. . . . This is my friend, Miss Vandergrift."

Both officials greeted Anne warmly. And Mr. Carewe placed a chair for her. "This is a delightful opportunity, Weston. I imagine you were afraid to come to see me alone. Well, more proof you're

138

the most fortunate young fellow in the world. And to square matters you are to be congratulated on a realistic fact, as well, no doubt, as possible romance."

Anne's blushing acknowledgment of the introduction scarcely detracted from the eloquent concern her lovely face betrayed.

"Mr. Carewe," she concluded, "what *has* he done now?"

"Hasn't he told you yet?" asked Carewe, gravely kind.

"No. He never tells me what happens at the dam."

"I never heard that he was so singularly modest," replied the chief, his eyes twinkling. "But this Boulder Dam takes the conceit out of all of us. . . . Miss Vandergrift, I'll leave it to someone else to tell you what he did today. Suffice it for me to say that it was the most wonderful act of nerve and strength that I ever heard of."

"Yes, it was," chimed in Mr. Halsey, "entirely apart from our work here on the dam. It was like Lindbergh's stunt—a world epic. It is proof of the comradeship of man. That our race is still young and full of heroism."

"*Oh!*" cried Anne, growing white as alabaster as she turned to Lynn with great, horror-stricken eyes. "I knew—it must be—terrible."

"To you and us, yes," Carewe said hastily. "But not to him. It was what he called it, no doubt. 'Duck soup!'"

"I declare, that is the strangest, the funniest, thing ever said by a man in peril," added Mr. Halsey. "But let us not distress Miss Vandergrift further by dwelling on the accident."

"I'm sure she would be happy to hear that such dangerous jobs for Weston are over," said Carewe.

Anne gazed at him with mute lips and spellbound eyes, in which the dark dread had begun to lighten and glow.

"Flynn!" Lynn ejaculated with rueful resignation.

"Yes, he was here with fire bells on," laughed Carewe. "He has promised to fetch you to see me. But it seems there was always a new outside job that appealed to you. And to tell the truth Flynn liked to see you tackle them. That was your forte, he said, tackling tough ones. So I sent for you on my own hook."

139

"I'm sure I'm tickled pink—and scared stiff," Lynn said with a gulp.

"No need for the latter. By the way, before we get down to brass tacks let me ask you something. Do you remember Stan Ewell?"

"Stan Ewell! That Oregon State right tackle?" burst out Lynn.

"He's the boy. I saw that Oregon game, at Portland three years ago, in which you put Stan out of the running. He was not so good after that collision."

"But, Mr. Carewe," expostulated Lynn, feeling his face sting red, "I didn't do that intentionally. I just ran my damnedest—made no effort to dodge Stan. I was sore, yes, because he clipped me. Stan had one bad habit. He would clip you."

"Stan is my nephew, and he's a good sport," went on Carewe, evidently desirous of alleviating Lynn's concern. "He blamed himself for that unwise tackle. And incidentally he admitted he clipped you—that you never clipped any player. He said no really great football player ever used the clip."

"That's true. But my word! How many times did I want to!"

"Well, I've had that in mind to tell you," Carewe went on genially. "Just so we wouldn't seem strangers. Stan had as great an admiration for your football as I have for your Boulder Dam work. Now for the brass tacks. Your intention in college was to major in engineering?"

"Yes—sir," Lynn replied haltingly.

"You left in your senior year?"

"Yes, sir. To my regret."

"How about that gossip of fraternity politics—that you were framed out of the captaincy and All-American honors?"

"Just—gossip, Mr. Carewe," choked out Lynn, feeling that he was on the spot with himself and that he had to be loyal to the college which had not been wholly loyal to him.

"Just gossip, eh?" repeated Carewe, as he turned his pencil up and down in long nervous expressive fingers. "There was big publicity at the time. I've forgotten much of it. Still I recall . . .

140

It was ridiculous—that rumor of an injury to your spine?"

"Mr. Carewe," Lynn spoke up frankly, sure of himself now. "There was never anything wrong with any of my bones except my bonehead."

"Biff, I have great doubts of your having a bonehead," responded the chief. The use of the nickname on the lips of this great engineer quite overcame Lynn.

"Don't you, Miss Vandergrift?" asked Carewe, turning to Anne.

"Lynn a bonehead!" exclaimed that young lady with a disdainful lift of her head. "It's not true. Lynn has the clearest, quickest thinking head of any young man in the world. If he were thick-headed or boneheaded how could he have saved the lives of your workmen?"

"That's settled even if I hadn't settled it before you." Carewe smiled and turned to Lynn again. "Weston, you've been nearly two years on the job?"

"Yes, sir."

"Flynn says you've done everything from heaving rocks and handling a shovel up to this toughest job on the dam—the scalers."

"I guess I have, sir."

"Your idea, of course, could have only one interpretation—which I have given it. Learning construction work from the ground up. Fitting yourself to be a great engineer."

Lynn could not answer this. He felt tongue-tied. To be sure his dreams for a year had had such an inception as Carewe imagined. But Lynn knew he had not come to Boulder Dam to learn to be an engineer.

"Only in dreams, sir, did I ever think—that way," he confessed.

"De Lesseps was a dreamer. So was Geolett, who built the Panama Canal where De Lesseps failed. Edison was a dreamer. So am I. Whoever built the pyramids of Egypt had dreams before he learned how to displace a single cubic yard."

To be included in such a band of dreamers robbed Lynn of any more inclination to confess inferiority. He was only human. He

141

divined what was coming. Strangely he forced his fascinated gaze from the smiling official to Anne. She had caught it even before Lynn. And he vowed to carry forever in his memory the soul of gladness on her face.

"I like your idea," concluded Carewe. "I had the same. I worked up. Stick at it as long as you can learn. Flynn has orders to put you on any work you want to study. Your raise in salary is a matter for me to consider. I will do so. My only other suggestion is that when the time comes you study very carefully the cooling system —and the pipe fitters. The success of our great dam depends solely upon them."

"Cooling system—pipe fitters!" echoed Lynn, and it seemed a flash of lightning illumined a dark place in his mind.

"Yes. Neither the world, nor the government, nor the mass of workers on the dam realize that," Carewe answered earnestly, his big eyes gleaming with the fires within. "But we engineers know it. You must learn it. . . . The settling of cement on such a colossal scale as must be in our dam would ordinarily take seventy-five or a hundred years—*if it ever settled solid.* We must make it set by artificial means, that is to say, an intricate and elaborate system of pipes that will carry cold water—keep the cement cool until it sets quickly. . . . There, Weston, we confide in you our greatest worry and dread."

Carewe rose to his feet and looked at his wristwatch. "By that time—I hope—you will come into the office here as my assistant. We may never have another layout like Boulder, but there will be other big dams, aqueducts, canals and what not to build. Selah!"

And he held out that long, shapely, speaking hand. Lynn leaped up to grasp it, forgetting his strength, losing his voice.

"Wow! Let go of *that*—you iron man," cried Carewe, extricating the valuable member before it was too late. Then, rubbing it carefully, he turned to Anne.

"I'd like you and Biff to come to dinner at my house tonight at seven o'clock. Mr. Halsey will be there with his wife. No one else besides my family. We'll have a nice little party. I daresay you'll

142

hear a minimum of talk about Biff's latest stunt."

"We'll be happy—to come," murmured Anne.

Lynn went out in a kind of daze. Once out in the open, seeing the western sky all ablaze with gold and rose, he drew a deep long breath. He located their car and helped Anne in. Then he leaped over the wheel, longing to express what seemed a bursting something too expansive and painful for his breast. Anne's eyes shone upon him, exquisitely soft and humid, their slate-gray depths translucent through tears.

"Angel face," he said, a little husky. "Did you say raspberries?"

"Lynn! . . . Once in your life—live up to your name. Be serious. Oh, boy, be grateful!"

"I am—honest to heaven. Grateful? . . . But, Anne, when it comes time to celebrate *this*—once in *your* life you are going to get spiflicated with me on champagne. Nothing else will do."

"Pooh! I'm spiflicated now!"

Chapter 10

Lynn's eleventh job on the dam was foreman of the electric cement-mixing mill. His shift was the most desirable one, from eight until four. His force consisted of an electrician, and a laborer whose main duty appeared to be that of watchman. There were a thousand gadgets to go wrong, but nothing ever went wrong. Night and day the mill mixed cement, two tons every two and a half minutes, twenty-four tons an hour, five hundred and seventy-six each day. The cement for Boulder Dam was running. It must run for years. And for Lynn Weston, that five-story structure, open and light as a factory, large as a Los Angeles department store, was a veritable wonderland.

It stood on the man-made level above the river, around the corner just outside the entrance to Boulder Canyon. Lynn recalled that place as the never-to-be-forgotten scene of his first labors. As much had happened to his mental building as this incredible cement mixer had magically done for the dam.

His work, compared to what he had accomplished before, was little less than a joke. He had to be there, and that was about all. But for the perennial source of delight and awe and mystery he found in the mill he thought he would have died of inertia. For a man constituted as Lynn was, whose physical nature called for action, the lack of manual labor caused him great discomfort and even distress. But he conquered these by creating exercise for his need and by study and thought on the lines of future engineering work.

Many times a day Lynn went the rounds of the mill. His favorite habit was to go downstairs and out on the level bank to the end of the long incline where materials were loaded upon the runway. Three railroad tracks passed that point, and there never was a time when one of them was unoccupied by a freight train.

Sand, gravel and cement rode up that steep runway to the top floor. Here they spilled onto endless belts that carried each to a great metal tank, cone-shaped and inverted, which operated by electricity under the mastery of clocks and meters. When a tank had received the measure of material due, a clock clicked, and the tank closed for two minutes and a half, during which time it performed part of its miraculous sifting task. At the end of that time the bottom of the tank opened to spill its contents down into the next floor, where it was received on another endless driving belt which took it to another tank, which in turn worked some mysterious alchemy and then spilled its contents down to the third floor, where larger tanks received sand and gravel and cement together, and mixing them thoroughly, let the correct mixture down upon another and broader endless driving belt which carried it to the great iron mill that operated on cogwheels. This last tank hung from the second floor over the railroad track. It whirled and churned and rasped with its two-ton load. It slushed with the addition of water. And the sound of the mixing changed every few seconds as the ingredients became thoroughly incorporated with each other. Then in precisely two minutes and a half the huge cube-shaped tank turned over to empty its yellow wet cement into a huge bucket that waited below on the flatcar.

The engine that hauled this flatcar and its precious load had just two minutes to run down to the dam, where a cable carrier lifted the bucket off the car and ran back to the mill again. Minute after minute, hour after hour, day after day, this marvelous precision went on.

Lynn's big job here, he realized, was to learn the mathematics and mechanism of this cement mill. It seemed a hopeless task at first. But he studied, he watched, he persevered, until he began to get glimmerings of what it was all about.

The probable cost of that electric plant had staggered him at first, and like other things at the dam, had roused his resentment. But it did not take long for him to grasp the great saving of time and labor. The dam had to be fed. It was a dragon with an insatiate hunger.

From his chair on the second floor Lynn could look down the canyon to see the colossal yellow wall of cement rising, sheer and blank-faced, staggering to the imagination. Already it had arisen a hundred and fifty feet above the river level. The trestles and bridges below had passed from sight, and the river appeared to have vanished.

Far aloft, like black threads across the sky, the cables stretched and swung with their queer many-wheeled engine carriages as they ran to and fro, lifting and swinging the great buckets on their thousand-foot cables.

Lynn never tired of that sight, nor of the strange, low, seething, rattling hum of the cement mill. It was a beehive of the mechanical gods.

In his office, which was a corner of the second floor and opened right upon the rattling iron cog-wheeled monster, there was a chair, a desk, a telephone, a few colored electric pushbuttons. No more! One of these buttons, a red one, could stop the mill, the mixing of cement, the building of Boulder Dam. Lynn could scarcely believe that. He had grown used to the idea of Boulder Dam being perpetual motion. He had an itch to push that red button, and he had a premonition he would some day. What would Anne say to that? What would Carewe say? Biff Weston

146

had not only been the one man to go through the diversion tunnel, but he had also actually halted the construction work!

But the cement mill, engrossing as it was, did not wholly absorb Lynn's thought and activity. Every day he came an hour early and stayed an hour after his shift. He spent this time walking to and fro, watching the work, watching the men, watching the tourists and sightseers. He had never forgotten Carewe's strong and significant statement about the cooling system. He saw the miles of pipe go into the dam, an intricate, baffling system. But right there lay the secret of Boulder Dam's vulnerability. Lynn trusted no plumber, no ironworker, no watchman, no curious sightseer. He had queer fancies that he would not divulge even to Anne. He was living the dream of his boyhood. He was the great builder.

At the cement plant, when he was on duty, he made himself courteous and obliging to all visitors. Usually he escorted them up and down the plant, explaining the puzzling works.

One afternoon, toward the end of his shift, Lynn was surprised and pleased to encounter his cowboy friend Curtis and a dark-eyed, pale-faced girl.

"Howdy, Biff," said Whitey, with lean hand eagerly outstretched. "Been a long time aboot lookin' you up. But I'm heah at last. . . . Meet my wife, Bess."

"Oh, I'm glad to see you, Whitey," burst out Lynn, seizing the cowboy's hand, to make him double like a jackknife. "Mrs. Curtis. . . . Bess! I know about you. Whitey confided in me. Indeed I'm happy to congratulate you."

She was frank without being bold, quite striking with her pale face, in which sadness and havoc appeared to be warming out, and her graceful figure was modestly and stylishly clad. Lynn liked her direct look into his eyes. She was used to men, but not many like Curtis or himself. It was plain that love and gratitude were transforming.

Lynn showed them over the plant, and when he had explained everything the day shift ended.

147

"Fine. I'm off. I'll walk out with you. Do you want to look over the dam?"

"Naw thanks, Biff. I've had aboot all of this damn dam thet I want. Your cement buzzer is shore a humdinger of a place, though."

"How's your leg? You're working, of course."

"Yes, steady since last fall. My laig is okay. I reckon I can fork a hawse as good as ever. My old man passed on, Biff. An' I'm gonna run the ranch over in Arizona."

"Aw! Sorry, Whitey. I've an old man, too. That thing happens. . . . Where was it—your range?"

"Across the river. Up on the desert near Ashfork. I went home for my father's funeral. Mother an' kids there. The ranch is bad run-down. But there's the makin's of a good cattle business. I've got a thousand or more haid left."

"And you, Bess, how will you like living on a ranch?" asked Lynn, turning to the girl.

"Oh, I'll love it. I never had any outdoors to speak of. But I'll be an awful tenderfoot."

"Whitey, I'm tickled pink for you. How long have you been married?"

"Guess," grinned Curtis.

"Not very long. You both look sort of honeymoonish, if you get what I mean."

"Less'n a week. But thet was Bink Moore's fault. Bess finally persuaded him to give her up."

"Bink Moore! . . . Persuaded?" ejaculated Lynn, his memory reaching out.

"Shore. I reckon he was fond of Bess."

"Bink needed me in his racket," Bess interposed frankly. "Whitey had told you what that was. Bink has gotten thick with some big shots. He offered to let me go if I'd leave Nevada. And he made the condition that Whitey marry me. Which was all a bluff. What Bink wanted was to get me out of the way. I know too much."

148

"Ah! So that was it? Very fortunate for you and Whitey, I'd call that," Lynn replied thoughtfully.

"Shore was. Bess an' me will make a go of it. . . . Biff, she married me broke as I was."

"Broke? You said you'd been working?"

"Wal, I was in debt. An' I had just enough left to pay that Greta Green gazabo in Vegas."

"Oh boy!" exclaimed Lynn, laughing with Bess at the cowboy's sally. "You can't start married life being broke."

"Can't we? By golly, we're gonna."

They reached the place where Curtis had parked his car. It reminded Lynn of his old Ford. The couple got in.

"Hate to say good-bye so pronto, Biff," said the cowboy.

"You're not going to. I'm taking you and Bess to dinner. Wait till you see *my* girl, folks!"

"Oh, can I meet her?" asked Bess.

"I'll say you can. Let's see. It's four-thirty. I must go back to the dam. But I'll meet you at six o'clock. Corner Main Street. Get me, cowpuncher?"

"You bet. But Biff, if you're not in a hurry let me spill somethin' you might not want yore girl to heah."

"Go ahead, pardner."

"Bink Moore has a new racket. But Bess, slick as she is, couldn't get a line on what thet racket was. No more two-bit stuff, believe you me!"

"Well, what kind of racket?" Lynn queried sharply.

"Biff, thar's a thousand rackets heah. No telling what Bink has on now. But what matter? The dope I want to give you is thet he is thick with Sproul."

"Sproul? I don't recall that name. Who is he?"

"He's the guy I seen thet time through the hole in the tent? Remember? He had a dinky little mustache, white on the upper lip. White hairs on a white mole."

"That guy? . . . Oh!" whispered Lynn, suddenly vibrant and strung. "That guy who had a plot to blackmail the officials. Who

149

had an ironworker on his staff? . . . A scheme to scare the daylights out of the bosses—when the cement began to run—to cash in on that or ruin the dam."

"Yore memory is perfect, pard. Thet's the ticket. Only there's more. Sproul is in with his racketeers for the money. But he's a Communist. That's my hunch. He means to destroy the dam! . . . An' you can lay to this. Thet's Sproul's plot. It worked slow because the cement had to be runnin'."

"But the cement *has* been running! The dam is over one hundred and fifty feet high!"

"No matter. It wasn't time. I don't get it clear. But that's the idea."

"By—God!" Lynn gasped as a startling idea flashed into his consciousness.

"Mr. Weston," Bess interposed earnestly. "Bink caught me listening in on him once. He slapped me over. He was furious. But I swore I hadn't heard anything. I lied. I heard a lot."

"Give me details."

"They have an ironworker named Brown . . ."

"*Brown!*" rang out Lynn.

"Yes. Ben Brown, a skilled worker—and a Communist. Sproul had him fixed. But they needed another arrow for their bow. A dynamite bomb dropped in your cement mill—that was one of them."

"Pard," broke out Curtis, his face grave. "Thet was what made me curious to see yore plant. Jest reckon oot what'd be the cost if them crooks blew up yore mill."

"Heavens! . . . It cost a million. But that's nothing. They couldn't replace the mill in six months. . . . The work would have to stop! . . . *Unthinkable!*"

"Like hell it is! Them crooks think big things an' do them."

"Mr. Weston, I seemed to get the cement mill idea as a last resource," added Bess. "They have something very much bigger than that up their sleeves."

"Pard, it's up to you to find oot," said Curtis.

150

"Whitey—Bess! I'll never be able to thank you enough," rejoined Lynn, thick-voiced in his agitation. "But I'll tell you what I'll do. If there's anything in this talk—and I feel there is—I'll buy a half interest in your cattle ranch the very day I get rich enough."

"Whoopee!" shouted Curtis.

"That's that. See you at six, corner Main," Lynn replied and turned away to stride back toward the canyon, his mind whirling.

Days passed by. Lynn had detected nothing, discovered nothing. But that did not lull his suspicions. He divined that every single day brought him closer to catastrophe. Nevertheless, as he had no proofs he grew more and more reluctant to confess his fears and forebodings to anyone. He did not even confide in Flynn.

At length his brooding worried Anne so much that Lynn had to let her into the secret. To his relief Anne took it seriously. She had seen and heard these racketeers, and she believed they were capable of unheard-of evils.

Lynn had tried to cultivate his neighbor Brown. It developed that the man who had been so friendly and grateful, who owed his life to Lynn, had grown morose and unapproachable. He drank. He avoided Lynn. He had a night shift, the one laborers hated most. He slept all day, so Mrs. Brown said, and she dared not awaken him. Lynn had Anne watch Brown's house during the daytime. No one ever came. Then a significant and perplexing thing happened. Brown left his home and wife. Mrs. Brown seemed to take that as a matter of course. Lynn could not find out where he ate. Struck by this peculiar circumstance Lynn approached Flynn.

"Say, boss, what's become of that ironworker I swam with through the diversion tunnel?"

"Brown. Ben Brown? He's on the job, an' it's sure a big job now with all that piping. Queer chap, Brown, as you know. Packs his tool bag everywhere. Ha! Ha!"

151

"That tool bag wasn't funny. . . . What's his shift, Flynn?"

"He likes to work at night. Says he sleeps best during the daytime. His shift is from eight to four. We haven't any third shift from four in the morning on."

"What's Brown working on now?"

"Pipes. That cooling system. It's a corker. Have you been down lately—through that hole in the dam?"

"Not lately. I'll go."

"Better go soon. You won't have many more days that you can walk through."

"Why so?" queried Lynn, trying to appear casual.

" 'Cause we're going to fill that hole with cement."

"Pipes and all?"

"Sure. Why, pipes big and little run through the cement like arteries and veins in your body. I don't savvy the darn job. But it's so important they keep secret just when they'll finish the piping and run the cement."

"Will they fill it quick?"

"I'll say they will. Matter of about two hours. All the cable buckets will go on the job."

"How'll they ever run cement through that long hole?"

"Search me, Weston. But I imagine it'll be a gravity flow from the upriver end."

Lynn went his way, feeling like a sleuthhound on a hot trail. It was all he could do to keep from telling Flynn. Sooner or later if he did not uncover the plot or circumvent it he would be compelled to tell, and he decided Carewe would be the one. Lynn dared not take the risk of indefinitely keeping the possibilities to himself.

It was then late afternoon. Lynn went home to pore over his blueprint of the cooling system of pipes for the dam, some of which had been laid and more were to follow. He racked his brain to grasp the intricacy of that labyrinthine system. The best he could do was to get a mental picture of the network of pipes in his mind—to conceive how they might appear without the cement.

152

"Lynn, Mrs. Brown called you twice," Anne said plaintively. "Supper is ready. And she is very nervous and irritable these days. She is worried about her husband."

"I'm coming, Anne." But he still hung over the table.

"You've lost your appetite," added Anne.

Lynn howled in mirth, made for her and rushed her over to Mrs. Brown's, where he ate such a meal as would have convinced anyone of his rapacity.

Next morning Lynn was on his way to the dam bright and early. December had come and with it frost on the high slopes. Gullies and ravines on the mountain slopes showed the bright hues that came in late autumn. The air was crisp and nipping. The desert basin, which was nearer by two years from the day Lynn saw it first to that in which it would be inundated, showed green after the first winter rain. Lynn felt an exhilaration that could not be wholly due to the fine day with its colors and smells or the desert with its deceiving purple distance, its mountains of porphyry and lava. A ruddy light shone on the Arizona peaks above which the sun had not yet risen. The turgid river wound out of its red canyon, gleaming pale as it flowed by with sullen swiftness.

It was seven o'clock by Lynn's watch when he parked his car and started down the canyon. An empty freight train passed him, from the engine cab of which the engineer waved a gloved hand. Round the bend another train was unloading materials for the mill.

All the machinery in the mill, down to the minutest thing, had been installed in duplicate. It was the upriver half of the mill that was in operation at this hour. When Lynn went on at eight he shut that side off and started the downriver side.

Sight of the dark frothy hole of the diversion tunnel, where the river bellowed its constriction, gave Lynn the creeps. He had never crossed the footbridge without thinking of Brown. These days he had not needed the roar and sight of the river to remind him of that questionable pipe- and ironworker.

Lynn crossed the cofferdam and worked his way over the

rocks around the holes in the denuded river bed, across the piles of debris to the rude stairway leading up to the square hole in the mass of concrete. That sheer perpendicular wall appeared enormously high and almost straight up. Pipes and ropes and girders, a queer elevator that ran upside down, and a zigzag stairway defaced the beauty of the wall. It had a perceptible curve toward each side of the canyon.

Drawing a sharp breath, conscious of something nameless and potent, Lynn entered the oblong door of the tunnel. It appeared to be about seven feet high and nearly that wide. It was a long, dark, dripping hole, seven hundred and fifty feet through to the downriver side of the dam. On the left side, as Lynn slowly walked along, extended an enormous pipe over a foot in diameter and three feet from the floor. It seemed to have a potential and inscrutable force hidden within its black body. Drops of water dripped upon Lynn. They oozed through the concrete. He laid a sensitive hand upon it, then his cheek. It felt solid and cold. But he knew it was neither. And there was fully a hundred feet of concrete over his head.

At the downriver opening of this tunnel the great pipe made bends to join branches that ran in different directions. Lynn had to straddle the main pipe to get over to the platform outside. This end of the dam was vastly different from the upriver end. Step by step, block by block, the irregular squares of concrete had been formed, some with sides still encased in partitions of lumber, others yellow and ragged, all dripping muddy water. The whole ugly and immense face of this lower side of the dam showed a prevalence of water. It ran off the roof of the squares in miniature waterfalls, it seeped out of the blocks, it lay in pools on every hard, rough level.

Water in great abundance came from somewhere, as important to this bewildering structure as the concrete itself. Lynn had grasped that fact.

He climbed the ladders from one block to another. This method of surmounting the dam recalled pictures of Indian pueblos, one

154

house of mud built above another, all slanting toward a pinnacle. The top of the dam, nearly two hundred feet now above the river, lost its checkerboard conformity at close range. It was a huge area of squares, dark, light, yellow, up and down, fenced with ends of boards, some of it solid, much of it soft and all of it muddy and wet.

Lynn spied only three men on top besides himself. There were paths of boards laid here and there. Lynn traversed them and went toward the west side of the dam, where the buckets were emptying cement. A man with a red flag waved and yelled Lynn back. He took one more survey of the hideous monstrosity, then went back to the ladders and descended to the lower platform.

This was far above the black ragged hole excavated below the river bed. It was full of water here and broken rock there. Across it rose a ridge that extended from wall to wall. Along these walls and upon the flat and beyond was concentrated the labor of thousands of workmen, of steam shovels and trucks, in endless and apparently violent confusion. But there was order there; only it was too big and complicated to grasp with the eye.

For a moment, Lynn, surveying it all, lost his sense of the dreadful that weighed upon him and again, for the thousandth time, reveled in the tremendousness of the scene, its action, its fury of sound, its drab and variegated hues, its smells of smoke and dust and brimstone, its whole terrific significance, all clear and perceptible under the bright blue sky and shining sun. Then he turned to the cooling system again, to the numberless pipes running everywhere, to the mystery that baffled him, to the impending disaster.

Three days of intensive watchfulness and vigilance passed by. On the morning of the fourth day, when Lynn arrived at the mill he found an extra force of men unloading a double amount of materials at the landing of the incline runway.

The sight gave him a start. A rush of hot blood raced through his veins. His emotion overran his thoughts. This was the crucial

155

day. But his relief did not equal his perturbation. He did not halt to ask why there were six freight cars loaded with sand, gravel and cement when before there had always been but three. He left his lunch bucket in the accustomed place on a rafter beside the stairway. This morning the familiar rattling, swishing roar of the big iron cement mixer sounded like an inarticulate voice. The silky seething hum of the electric plant whispered as inarticulately. But for Lynn there was something sinister in the sound, in the air, in the sullen river, in the red sunrise.

He had an hour before his shift came on. And he made swiftly for the dam. Laborers were working with heavy timbers and planks in front of the central tunnel through the dam. It looked as if a shaft was to be raised to the opening. Before Lynn got anywhere near a guard ordered him back.

"Yeah? What's doing?" queried Lynn.

"Orders. Scram!"

Lynn scrammed, but back to the east wall, to the terminus of the railroad, where he mounted a scaffold, at considerable risk, and reached the top of the dam. At that moment one of the great iron buckets, huge at first hand, swung out over him. Lynn made his way down over the irregular squares to the lower side and there got down the ladders. On the platform before the tunnel Lynn spied a pile of heavy planking, which he deduced was to be used to close the opening. Everywhere planks were used to stop the spread of cement. Platform and entrance were vacant of workmen at the moment.

Lynn entered the tunnel. At the far end, through the gloomy lane, he saw and heard men working. He walked halfway through, then returned. He could not see anything different. But he knew this was the place for catastrophe. It fascinated him. He had dreamed in the night, something strange and vital that had left an oppression on his breast. But he could neither remember nor interpret the dream. He halted for a last survey just inside the entrance.

The great bend in the big pipe, the elbows of other adjoining pipes, came in for a most intent scrutiny. But Lynn was not a plumber. Underneath the pipes and all around that confined space he found footsteps in the thin mud on the cement. Every footprint was identical with the other. A single workman had left these tracks there. They had been made early that morning.

Lynn got down low to scrutinize tracks and mud. He found a fine powdered steel, scarcely visible, underneath the great bend of the major pipe. That puzzled him. But it meant a sharp tool of some kind, a saw or a file, had been used there since his last visit late the afternoon before.

He searched and felt for a long while. But he could not detect the slightest cut or abrasion on the big round, cold, black pipe. Yet if ever an inanimate object had tried to convey meaning to human consciousness this thing seemed to do so. Lynn consulted his watch time and again. How the tense minutes sped!

Baffled, defeated, chagrined, Lynn left the tunnel and hurried back over the dam, across the trestle and up the track to the cement mill.

His shift would go on in a few minutes. Adams, the foreman, hailed Lynn with relief.

"Worried me, your not showin' up," he added.

"Been down to the dam. Any orders?"

"I'll say. You're to expect an important phone call."

"When?"

"Didn't say. The order was 'Expect,' with a capital E."

"Yeah. Big doings, presently."

"I'll tell the world. You'll be running both mills. That never happened before."

"It'll be great."

"If you ask me I'll say I'm damn glad the responsibility isn't mine. Those in the know look kind of tense. Flynn was here at six o'clock, surlier'n hell. Black as a thundercloud . . . Ten seconds to eight, Weston. Beat it!"

Lynn did not need that much time to reach his corner. Miraculously the rattling roar and rustling hum ceased from the duplicate mill he had just left. How compelling the sudden silence! Then Lynn pushed a button and instantly his mill responded like an awakening volcano.

The work went on without perceptible cessation in the mixing and removal of cement. Lynn sat down to wait. Then he got up to pace the floor of his little open office. He could see down through the wide cracks between the floor boards—the ground, the iron rails, the freight car coming along, the big muddy bucket.

He paced to and fro. He watched from the windows. He listened for that telephone call. The minutes seemed to drag. But when Lynn consulted his watch he found that they flew by.

Visitors as usual, only more of them, began to arrive, some without guides. For once Lynn left them to do their own sight-seeing. Yet never had he watched with keener eyes. These tourists came and went, only a few of them bothering him.

The mill hummed on. Every moment Lynn expected the call to put the duplicate mill into action. Evidently the engineer of the cement-hauling train had received his orders, for he had two cars and two great buckets to push and haul with his engine. But every two and a half minutes he departed with only one bucket full. The extra force of men waited out at the end of the inclined runway. The regular force were loading materials as usual.

When would word come? Never had Lynn waited the whistle for play with such conflicting tides of feeling. He paced and waited. Thought of Anne helped to pass the interminable moments. Soon it would be lunch time, and he would be hunting for the sweet things she always hid in his bucket.

Then the telephone rang, tinglingly vibrant amid the humming rattle and roar. Lynn ran to jerk up the receiver.

"Hello. Weston. Cement mill," he called eagerly.

"Hello," came after a slow moment, in a voice Lynn did not recognize.

"Who's calling?" queried Lynn.

"Jones, of the Chicago *Tribune*," followed the suave reply. "I'm at Boulder City. I have inside information that the pipe tunnel is

158

to be filled with cement this morning. . . . Are you running both mills?"

"No," Lynn replied shortly.

"When will you start?" The voice had a sibilant hint of intense eagerness.

"I don't know. . . . And wouldn't tell if I did," Lynn ended and jammed down the receiver with a forceful hand. "By thunder!" he muttered, darkly pondering. "That was a bluff—a fake! Jones of the Chicago *Tribune*? . . . Bunk! That was a feeler. That was the opening of one of these racketeers. They're on the job. . . . So help me God! I've got the hunch. But what—*what* can I do?"

He cursed his helplessness. Should he call Flynn? No! Better Carewe and confide his fears? He pondered. Would a break like that jeopardize his future, his splendid record and standing with Carewe and the Six Companies?

"To hell with my future!" he ejaculated. "I'm rich anyhow. I'd save the dam at any cost."

But the shrill ring of the telephone made him jump. He leaped as before.

"Hello. Weston. Cement Mill."

"Hello, Biff," came the reply, in a voice that tingled up Lynn's spine. "Carewe talking."

"Yes, sir. . . . I knew you, Chief," Lynn replied huskily.

"How about you there for the double run?"

"All set, sir. Waiting for the whistle."

"Kick her out of the lot, Biff."

"Mr. Carewe I—I get you. . . . But . . ."

"Weston, run double until further orders," came the sharp, interrupting command.

"My God—it's—up to me!" whispered Lynn. Then he ran the few intervening steps, across the open-boarded floor to the little office identical with his own.

His big finger shook as he pushed the button. Dynamic power clicked all through that side of the building. The seething, silken

159

hum, the rattling, metallic roar, the vibration of the plant, merely doubled.

Lynn stood there in a kind of trance. The rumble of the two huge mixers seemed to fill his ears with thunder. In exactly two minutes and a half, with jolt and jar, the great tanks turned over to spill their muddy contents into two yawning buckets below. The train of cars and engine moved out from under the floor. The double run was on. The success or ruin of the dam was in the lap of the gods.

Lynn went back to his office, to his chair. Then he spied his lunch bucket. He was not hungry, but he opened it, and absent-mindedly ate the contents, ending with a double cut of a most delicious apple pie.

At the bottom of the bucket he spied a note, and a flood of emotion relieved the tension in his breast.

He opened it to read:

Dear Lynn:
Mind you eat all of this lunch. And especially the apple pie. My first! Oh, I hope I have remembered how.
Lynn, you have been strange lately. Restless at night—gloomy by day. I suspect you are worried over your responsibilities. Don't worry, Lynn. All will work out right. You are honest, faithful. These always win in the end. Your beloved Boulder Dam will not be wrecked. If your fears are well-founded something will happen to wreck the evil-doers. Believe this, Lynn. Trust it. Think right. There is something greater than we are.
I feel that today. I shall think of you every single minute.
Come home quickly.

Anne.

Lynn closed the note and replaced it in its envelope, uplifted for the moment.

"After all, love and life are the greatest things," he mused, feeling the truth of Anne's words. "What do I care whether or not a mountain of mud hardens!"

Nevertheless he did care. In the resurging of thought he dropped Anne's note. It slipped through a crack between the

160

boards and fluttered to the ground below.

"Gosh, I'm getting goofy," he muttered and got up to go out by the head of the great rumbling mixer, along the endless driving belt, to the outside stairway and down. He found his note, wiped the mud off it and placed it inside his jacket.

At that juncture he felt the presence of others. He turned. Two men approaching saw Lynn and halted, though apparently casually.

Lynn recognized Bink Moore from the description Curtis had given him. The other man, slight of build, well-dressed, with wide-brimmed slouch hat pulled down, wore a slight tdianghe of a mustache, at the left of which showed a white mole.

All Lynn's internal mechanism corollated the scintillating explosion in his mind. But he moved on as if he had not even seen the two men. Down the road several sightseers appeared. And at that moment the train with its two cars and empty buckets backed into place under the mill.

Lynn picked desperately at his leaping thoughts. He caught one. That he had Sproul and Moore between him and the dam. They could not get by without passing him, which he swore would be never. Out of the corner of his eye he saw the two men cross the track in front of the bucket train and go up the outside stairway on that side, leisurely like any other sightseers.

Suddenly a marvelous coolness and clearness transformed Lynn. As if black letters had been silhouetted against a flash of lightning he saw the facts, passing as in a cinema across his mind —the cowboy—his story—the timely meeting following—Bess's revelation—his own persistent brooding fears—his ceaseless vigilance and search—the footsteps and steel dust under the big pipe —the fake call and the genuine one—the humming of both mills in duplicate—Anne's prophetic note—and lastly Sproul and Moore there—there in the cement plant!

Lynn's training from youth to manhood had been to think swiftly, to decide swiftly and to act swiftly. He could take one swift look down a forming, changing field of players and see the one way through.

This game had all been mapped out for him. Fate! With a grim muttering, "Duck soup!" he ran up the outside stairway on the upriver side of the mill and entered. Just then the two huge inverted cone mixers rumbled and vomited their heavy cataract of muddy mixture in the buckets below.

Lynn did not see the two men until he got to the dusty corridor between the mixers. Then he spied them beyond the running belt on that side. Like any other sightseers, apparently! No doubt they were intensely interested. Moore had on workmen's garb—overalls and jumper. Under his arm he carried a bundle of clothes, rather a large bundle, held securely. Lynn suspected that it might contain something unsupportably fatal to Boulder Dam.

What gall—what effrontery—what astounding brazen nerves these Communists had! But on the other hand no mental capacities allotted to crime would suspect destiny itself. In that long gaze at them Lynn had the play figured. Sproul and Moore would hardly visit the cement mill from altruistic curiosity. They had a mission they would not trust to anyone else. And while they were there, their accomplice racketeers were blackmailing the officials. It was Saturday. A payday! If they got only the week's wages of the laborers it would amount to something close to ten hundred thousand dollars. A slick, clever, modern racket, worthy of the big shot racketeers. Only it would never work!

Lynn went around the left side and come upon the men at a point between the stairway and the big mixer. Moore pointed down into the churning tank.

"Hell of a hole to fall in!" he said to his companion.

"Say, my good man," Sproul began blandly as Lynn came up. "Would you mind explaining . . ."

He cut that query short. No doubt a swift glance at Lynn would have strangled false speech in any crook's throat. Sproul had little steely eyes, boring as gimlets. In one flash they measured Lynn. They verified what the man's quick sense grasped.

"Sproul—Bink Moore—what are you up to here?" demanded Lynn, loud above the hum and roar. He had placed himself just opposite the two men, within reach, between the stairway and the open gateway to the rumbling mixer.

Moore's keen young face turned a ghastly rue. He was not up to the caliber of this racket. He betrayed guilt and cowardice. Quick as a cat he darted away to have his legs kicked out from under him by Lynn. He fell headlong, and the flying bundle gave forth a sodden thud. Moore scrambled up and ran like a deer to the stairway.

Lynn let him go. Sproul was the man Lynn wanted.

"What's your game?" yelled Lynn, cold and hardy.

"What's it worth to you?" queried Sproul, unmasked.

"All the dough you crooks think you'll get wouldn't buy me. . . . Sproul, your life isn't worth a dime."

Lynn saw Sproul's nervous hand slip toward his pocket. He anticipated it, as if he had no more need than the terrible eyes of this ghoul. But Sproul's action was slow. Lynn clipped him on the jaw.

Sproul fell with a thump, and he slid by the mixer into the corridor opening into Lynn's office. Stunned but not unconscious, he did not move until Lynn pounced upon him. Then roused by the jerk he sustained he struggled. But he was a pigmy in the hands of a giant. Lynn took the gun away from him, jerked him up, and spun him round into the office, where in another instant he was a rat in a trap. The green of terror for his life paled appallingly in his face. Strangely all of it took the hue of the mole on his lip—the ineradicable, distinguishing mark that had betrayed him.

"Steel doesn't go bad in cement," rang out Lynn, and he tossed the gun into the yawning churn. "Sproul, talk or I'll toss you in, too!"

Still the racketeer or Communist, whichever he was, though panic-stricken, did not recognize the inevitable.

"Talk! What? I don't know anything to tell."

"Time is flying, man! I'll shut off this mill. The cement will stop running. Your vile plot has failed."

Lynn sprang at the wary, slinking man and tripped him up so that his feet shot almost as high as his head had been. Lynn seized a leg and swung the man off the floor. He let him down so that his head dragged. Then he swung him with both hands over the yawning mouth of the mixer. Sproul's body sagged limp. He might have fainted. But next instant Lynn felt the convulsive stretch of muscles. The man was conscious. His arms flung wildly, as muddy water and flying gravel struck his face.

Lynn swung him up and onto the floor of the corridor.

"God—Almighty!" gasped Sproul, getting to his knees.

"Don't call on God! Talk now! If you don't I swear—in there you go!"

The huge grinding vat yawned there, wheeling with its loose and rattling load. Sproul surely saw it as the mouth of hell.

"I'll—talk. . . . Man, you're not—human. . . . What do you want to—know?"

"The game—what's your game? Your racket?"

"I'm not the—main squeeze. . . . I'm in on it—but not for money. No racket for me. My pards—big coin—from the big shots. . . . Brown fixed the pipe—so it'd break with the—pressure of cement. . . . Moore had a time-clock bomb—to drop in here. We meant to double-cross our accomplices. They thought it was all to force Carewe—to pay—to find out the dope—in time to save the pipe. But we meant to . . ."

Then Lynn clipped Sproul and laid him out flat and limp as a sack.

Lynn leaped up to press the red button over his desk. His ears rang so with his throbbing blood that he scarcely heard the subsidence of the left-hand mill. He rushed pell-mell into the other office—to push the duplicate red button there.

The electric cement plant became like a sepulcher. Lynn stared at the red button, strangely aware of the sudden silence.

"Oh-h! I knew I'd push you someday! . . . By God—the cement has stopped!"

164

It took Lynn a moment longer to lift the telephone receiver and another to find voice to call the head office of the Six Companies. Line busy! *Carewe in conference.*

"Listen, girl," Lynn pealed into the receiver. "This is Biff Weston talking. Get that? Biff Weston! You know me. . . . Call Carewe again and again till you get him. Say it's Weston—tell him to look out for bandits—matter of life and death!"

A pregnant moment succeeded that imperative summons. A buzz, a creaking—then: "Hello—Weston—I—can't talk—conference!"

The voice was scarcely audible or recognizable, but Carewe's.

"Listen—chief," Lynn replied piercingly. "Like hell you're in conference! Jolly the men who're blackmailing you. But careful. Don't try to arrest them. They'll kill. . . . I've got their plot jinxed. . . . I've shut off the mills. . . . The cement has stopped running. . . . Pipe system, tampered with by that bastard Brown whom I'd ought to let drown—will not collapse. . . . Nor will this mill be blown up! Boulder Dam saved, Chief!"

Lynn did not expect an answer, but it came whisperingly over the wire: *"Biff—Weston! . . . Don't tell it."*

"Okay, Chief. . . . Come down and see me."

Chapter 11

Almost in collapse, now that the terrible strain was over, Lynn waited for whatever might transpire. When Sproul began to move Lynn bound his hands and feet securely. That done, he set to waiting again, for the telephone, for someone to come, anything.

The big cement mill seemed empty, strange in its incredible silence. Workmen at their posts inside and outside were waiting for things to move again. This step was unprecedented. It created surprise. But none of the workers deserted their posts.

"Some situation!" muttered Lynn. "Nobody knows! Nobody but me and Carewe! Not even Flynn! . . . Say, this suspense is awful. . . . But it's all right. The dam is saved. If the racketeers get the weekly payroll—well, Uncle Sam can stand that."

The moments seemed to drag by. Lynn felt a lessening of potential peril in each one. If only Carewe could handle the racketeers! They would escape surely. But no matter! What Lynn prayed for was that the chief would not be shot or blackjacked.

Lynn gazed darkly at the ghastly Sproul, conscious now, a bloody mess.

"You said you weren't in on the money end. What was it to you, then?" demanded Lynn, prodding Sproul with an ungentle boot.

"I work for the emancipation of the working man. Labor must rule in this country."

"Baloney. You're one of those crazy Communists. Are you Russian, German or what?"

"I'm a naturalized American."

"You're a liar. . . . What was that Bink Moore?"

Sproul did not reply, from which reticence Lynn guessed that Moore was just a tough nut in the pay of Sproul or someone like him.

"You can be made to talk," Lynn warned darkly, beginning to pace the floor again. The tension of silence and inaction began to tell upon him. "Why the hell doesn't someone phone—or come?" he muttered. "The mill's shut down. They must all know by now."

It seemed to Lynn that hours had elapsed since he had pushed in those red buttons. But when he glanced at the clock he found that the time was less than five minutes. His excitement, of course, had led to that mistake. It occurred to him that he might be making another, for instance, in regard to Moore. That worthy had scurried down the steps, hugging his package like a man who did not want to fall with it. Obviously, Lynn thought, he must have made his escape up the river along the railroad tracks. But had he? Gone less than five minutes!

Lynn ran across to the west side of the mill building and leaned out of a window. The group of workmen on the platform at the end of the sand and cement runway stood in tense postures, talking vehemently among themselves. At sight of Lynn they began to gesticulate.

"Anything wrong, Weston?" one of them called shrilly.

"I'll say. Did you see a man run up the tracks? He had on a black slouch hat pulled down. Carried a package," shouted Lynn.

"Yes. He started to come this way. Then ran toward the dam. Presently began to walk. You can see him now."

Lynn, suddenly aflame again, sprang to the foot of the stairway leading to the upper floor.

"*Smith!*" he yelled. "Come down quick!"

An answering shout from above succeeded to thumping footsteps. In a moment Smith appeared on the second floor, through the open spaces, and then came leaping down from steps. Gray with cement dust, his expression could not be determined. But as he halted breathlessly to confront Lynn his tenseness attested to his feeling.

"Smith, there's hell to pay, but I can't take time out to explain now. Watch the mills. Expect phone calls. Answer that I shut off the power and it must not be turned on. Don't let that guy in there get away. I'm after another one."

"By thunder!" ejaculated Smith, smiting the powder from his hands. "Hop to it, Weston!"

Lynn wheeled away, flashed by the cement mixer to run out and down the steps. With a flying leap he mounted the flatcar and crossed it to jump down on the other side. Then he started toward the dam, his gaze roving everywhere, and his mind whirling with conjectures. If Moore was really between him and the dam, there would be no escape for the scoundrel except through or up over the dam. No doubt the pipe tunnel, which was to have been filled with cement, would be impossible. But there were stairways and scaffolds and lifts going up the looming gray wall.

His searching eyes fastened first upon the far points. The lofty rim of the dam was bare of human figures. No climbers on the zigzag stairway! The inverted lift was coming down the perpendicular wall. On the wide plank walk leading to the tunnel, and the platform that hid its mouth, scattered laborers were standing in the same waiting posture Lynn had identified in others. Something was wrong. The work never stopped on Boulder Dam. Lynn crossed the bridge over the river. Close to the right canyon wall a flatcar with its tanks of cement and its puffing engine

168

caught Lynn's attention momentarily. He saw more men standing motionless. But he was seeking a form he would recognize instantly.

Lynn broke into a trot. He must not lose any more time. Once beyond the cofferdam he could command the whole space between that and the real dam. It was a huge space, full of water in spots, mounds of rock and lumber, piles of debris, a man-made jungle where even an elephant could have hidden. Lynn slowed again along the road, his sight oscillating like a compass needle.

One of the thousand-foot cables had been stopped with its cement bucket swinging in mid-air. This was a sight Lynn had never seen before. He had done that. And it appeared to him that the many faces turned his way belonged to men who accused him of it. He could hear the low rumble of the river as it narrowed into the diversion tunnel. Lynn gazed back to make sure there was no man whom he had missed. Across the pools of muddy water between the false and true dams he scrutinized the uneven benches under the canyon wall. All the laborers were between the middle of the dam, where the pipe tunnel opened, and the right-hand wall. There must have been half a hundred of them. Among them or hiding somewhere was Bink Moore.

"Hey, Weston!" boomed a voice that made Lynn jump. "What'n hell are you up to now?"

That voice came from Flynn. But Lynn's flashing eyes failed to locate him. They would have done so in another moment had it not been for a figure skulking behind a lumber pile. The dark garb, the slouch hat, corresponded with what Moore had worn. Lynn yelled back to Flynn:

"Look out for a guy with a package!"

No doubt Lynn's piercing voice struck Flynn mute, as well as his workmen who had come in sight to swell the squad. Lynn stood above them, perhaps a hundred steps distant. And he could reach their position only by following the road which curved in toward the tracks under the wall. This Lynn caught out of the corner of his eye while peering sharply for Moore.

"Biff, I saw that feller," Flynn shouted excitedly. "What'd he have?"

"Dynamite, boss! Watch your step!" answered Lynn, striding on again, to leave the road and face a declivity of mud and rock. His feet sank in it, and he nearly lost his balance because he did not look where he was going. When he righted himself again he saw the object of his search come out from between two piles of lumber to a spot where most probably only Lynn could see him. Lynn was about to yell his discovery when he was tongue-tied at seeing Moore hurriedly unwrap his package and fumble over something. This done he came boldly stalking out from under a scaffold, headed for the first of the zigzag stairways leading up over the dam.

Lynn divined his purpose at the same instant he thought he grasped Moore's quick attention to his time-clock bomb. Moore meant to go up the stairway, and he was going to get rid of that bomb, either to block possible pursuers or to destroy the intricate pipe system that could be seen winding into the tunnel. It might be that he had a powerful enough bomb to destroy it and the tunnel and possibly that section of the dam. Lynn had long been versed in reading a man's intentions from his actions. This man had nerve here if he had not shown any at the mill. He had keen judgment, too, for neither Flynn's squad nor the laborers at the mouth of the tunnel could keep him from reaching the foot of the zigzag stairway. It was Lynn's quick mental reservation, however, that this Red had not calculated upon a thunderbolt of a football rusher.

"Stop—Moore!" Lynn rang out stentoriously. "If you throw that bomb I'll wring your neck!"

For answer Moore strode only the faster, dropping the pair of overalls that had served as a wrapper for his package. Lynn caught a glint of something bright. Then with tremendous bounds he made off up the slope of talus. Leaping over rocks and piles, splashing through muddy pools, Lynn ran with all his marvelous speed to head off the Red from his objective. In one glance Lynn

170

had known that he could do this. Moore, too, had broken into a run. But it availed him little. When he saw that he would be cut off he checked his flight. But Lynn sped on and intercepted him halfway between him and the foot of the stairway.

"Lemme by!" screeched Moore, "or I'll blow us both to hell!"

"Bah, you—dirty Red!" panted Lynn. "You wouldn't—have —the nerve!"

Moore crouched with the shiny apparatus held before him, ready to set it off, while he sidled toward the stairway. At that moment Flynn and his gang came in sight up over the bank.

"Stay back, boss! Stay back!" Lynn yelled sharply. "The lousy Red might throw that bomb!"

Flynn spread wide his brawny arms to hold his men back. His ruddy face went pale.

"Hellsfire, Biff! Get back yourself!" he roared. "Somebody come with a gun!"

Lynn realized that if ever he had been put on the spot it was then. Warily he watched Moore who was cat-stepping sidewise toward the only avenue of escape. Lynn calculated the distance that separated them as fifty feet. The object Moore held so carefully was as big as a football, and it looked heavy. He could not heave it far, and if he threw Lynn could get away from there while it was in the air.

"Moore, you better think fast," warned Lynn. "You can't get away with it. . . . Drop that thing, or I'll bounce a rock off your head!" and Lynn stopped to snatch up two good-sized stones. He let drive with one. Moore just managed to dodge the bulletlike missile. Flynn let out a bellow which loosed hoarse cries from both watching gangs.

Lynn snatched up another stone. With one in each hand he edged toward Moore. He was wondering, calculating. If he could hit Moore with either stone and upset him, or even destroy his equilibrium momentarily, he could cover the distance between them in a few lightning swift bounds. Did the Red have nerve

171

enough to set off the bomb? Not in his own hands! Lynn knew that unerringly.

"No closer—Weston!" hissed Moore. Under his wide hatbrim in the shadow his face gleamed gray, and his eyes were two gimlets of fire.

"You lousy Red! You haven't got the guts!"

"Another step—and—I'll . . ."

"Come on! Pass it! That's right down my alley. . . . You're not Red. You're yellow!"

The man gazed about like a cornered rat. Lynn, quick to take advantage, let fly one rock and then the other. The first whizzed close to Moore's head. If it had connected it would have killed him. The second struck him on the leg, a glancing blow that toppled him over. The instant it hit him Lynn was leaping like a tiger. Moore with a hoarse bawl of rage and terror righted himself on his knees, and jerking something on his bomb he swept back his arm to throw it. At that instant Lynn was upon him, to launch a tremendous kick at the bomb. It went hurtling high and far, while Moore went down from Lynn's onslaught.

The bomb struck the rocks a dozen yards away. Then a wave of wind, like a wall, knocked Lynn flat. Simultaneously a tremendous blast shook the canyon foundations. A huge puff of yellow smoke and dust went mushrooming aloft. Stones rattled like hail on the wall of the dam. And over Lynn a barrage of gravel and shale hissed and whistled. Instinctively he rolled over on his face, just as a rain of rocks began to fall. Heavy ones thudded all around him. Those that hit him hurt but did no damage. Then the booming echoes of the explosion banged from wall to wall.

Lynn leaped up to grope about in the dust cloud to find Moore. But he could not locate him. Flynn's trenchant yell, edged with tragedy, pealed out: "By God—he's done for Weston! There he goes—*up the stairs!*"

Harsh and lamentable cries followed sharply upon Flynn's yell. Lynn groped around, feeling for the stairway. Presently he found it and started up. The dust cloud began to clear. He ascended out of it. And there, halfway up the second zigzag, Lynn spied Moore. That sight lent wings to his fear. Up he flew, covering twice the steps that Moore covered. From below pealed up a hoarse bellow from Flynn.

"*Atta boy, Biff! Kill him!*"

His yell raised a storm of men's voices in sustained passion, husky, deep-throated, a long roar that rivaled the explosion in echo.

Lynn flew on, gaining yard by yard. His stride ate up four steps at a time. But Moore floundered over the rim, almost falling. He wheeled then with a little automatic gun barking. Lynn, halfway up the last zigzag, dared not stop even if he had wanted to. His dodging, bobbing form offered no good target. Lynn heard the bullets zip on the stairs, tug away his hat, burn through his garments. But not one of that volley stopped him. Moore turned tail before Lynn surmounted the rim.

He saw the Red halfway across the uneven width of the dam. Boarded squares obstructed his passage toward the downriver side. He lost time while Lynn's judgment in avoiding obstacles enabled him to gain. Then that checkerboard of cement, with its uneven squares and fences, saw a short and dramatic race. Moore reached the ladder first, to start down, hatless and disheveled. Lynn went over, perhaps a score of steps behind.

He gazed deliberately down, locating the platforms, the plank walks, and the half-dozen ladders protruding here and there above the edges of the cement squares. Far below he saw laborers and trucks and engines, the muddy torrent rushing out of the exit of the diversion tunnel, under the bridge, and the road, which strangely enough, appeared empty. Moore might reach it, but even so he would never get away. Still, Lynn, relentless and grim, had wit to take no chances. His old football yell pierced the canyon space and like magic stopped the work and the din. Lynn saw many upturned visages, like ruddy gleams, hundreds of feet below, and to these he waved and pointed down at the man whose flight for life could not have been mistaken.

173

"Step on it, you yellow Red!" Lynn called derisively to Moore. The tremendous exertion, following Moore's fiendish attempt to blow him into atoms, had unleashed the savage in Lynn. He gained on the man. He was halfway down that ladder when Moore leaped off to a loose boardwalk where he fell, to scramble up and plunge upon another cement square. Along this he ran to the next ladder. Lynn reached it when Moore had descended halfway.

The ladder was long, and it was not fastened to the square. Lynn pushed it out a couple of feet, peering down. Moore, feeling the movement, looked up with livid face, expressive of ghastly terror. For a moment Lynn felt prey to the fascination of blood lust. One powerful shove would send that ladder over a hundred-foot declivity straight down to the rocks and debris below. But whatever Moore was, tool of unscrupulous men, radical, Red, or what, Lynn could not murder him. So he drew the ladder back and turned to go down.

Here he had lost a little ground, and such was Moore's frantic haste that Lynn did not gain on that ladder, or the long trestle across a chasm between cement squares, or on the way to the next ladder. This was a short one. Halfway down Lynn leaped off. And when Moore arrived at the fourth ladder Lynn was gaining fast. If he had not seen that himself he would have learned it in the clamor of the laborers. A leather-lunged truck driver, standing beside his truck on the rock bench of the bed of the river, bawled out to his fellows, "*Hell-rattlin' Weston! Now fer the clinch!*"

If before this the spectators of that chase had not translated its true meaning, then Lynn's marvelous action, if not his fame, and the desperate flight of the pursued, would have made clear a relentless justice and a craven terror.

At the top of the next and last ladder Lynn surveyed the field as of old. If Moore ran off to the left he would be hard to catch, especially when he got down to the river and the boats. But fear of the laborers would preclude his thinking of that. If he ran into the black caves of the uncompleted tunnels with their branches he might escape through to points above the dam. But

Lynn made certain that the man would be fool enough to take to the road across the bridge.

"*Head him off!*" yelled Lynn, through cupped hands around his mouth.

At that command laborers began to move on both sides of the road, but owing to distance on the left and obstructions on the right they could hardly cut Moore off. Lynn turned his back to descend that ladder. Bent on speed he attended solely to the wide-spaced crosspieces. And when he leaped down to wheel as on a pivot there was Moore racing onto the trestle bridge. No car, no workman in sight there!

Lynn broke into a run thinking that if he had only had his old speed this race would be short-lived. When he fell into his stride to see the distance between him and Moore lessening as if some unseen power dragged at his quarry he sustained a somber glee. He would catch this Red before he had gotten halfway up the hill.

The bridge was something over a hundred yards long. Lynn's thoughts were not consistent. Duck soup! I'll do this in ten flat! And will I lick that beady-eyed little bastard? Trucks coming down the hill! Of all days where in the hell are the four thousand workers on this dam? Made for Biff—this whole deal!

Moore, slowing perceptibly, ran off the bridge to disappear to the left. The road split there, one branch going up the canyon wall, the other down the river. Another bridge below crossed to the Arizona side.

At the top of his speed Lynn flashed out upon the road. He was in time to see Moore, close at hand, pointing his automatic at the driver of an empty truck. Lynn made the gravel fly up that gradual slope. He reached the car with such momentum that he had to stop himself with spread hands. Moore had gone round to the right side. The driver had started the engine.

In one sweep Lynn flung open the truck door. "Hold! Stop—her!" he panted explosively.

"Hell, man! He's got a gun!" protested the driver, a young fellow pale about the gills.

"Not—loaded! . . . Stop, damn you!" Lynn had to leap on the

175

running board. One darting hand shut off the ignition. With the other he reached over the driver to get hold of Moore. But Moore eluded him and slipped out on that side. Lynn ran around the truck.

He encountered Moore at close hand. The Red had picked up a piece of scantling, the end of which contained a long spike. He brandished this improvised weapon—was bringing it down. Lynn, at the end of his rush, swerved a little and launched a tremendous kick. Moore went down like a ninepin, and the scantling rebounded from Lynn's back. In another second Lynn fastened a brawny hand on Moore's shirt, jerked him erect and swung on him. Moore sank unconscious.

It was then Lynn relaxed. The intake of whistling breath almost burst his breast. He was as hot as fire and dripping sweat. The viselike grip of passion seemed loath to let go its hold. Brain and body seemed clamped at the line between collapse and recovery. He leaned against the truck.

The driver, looking out, saw how the situation had ended. He slid out on the right side.

"Where've I seen you, buddy? . . . Excuse me for fallin' for his stuff. If he'd had a load in that gun—good night! At that he tried to brain you."

Lynn spied the little automatic gun lying on the gravel. He picked it up. At that juncture a yell almost drowned by the sound of the river pealed down from above.

"Somebody yellin', buddy," the driver said with added excitement. "Flynn—on top of the dam! I'd know that bozo a mile away. . . . Say, what'd I bump into?"

"Looks like—Reds—are working at Boulder," panted Lynn.

"Reds? Uh—huh, these labor agitators! I've been talked to, buddy. But nothin' doin'."

Lynn had spied Flynn on top of the dam, standing in black silhouette with a couple of his men. No doubt they had seen the last of Lynn's chase, especially the end of it at the truck. Whereupon Lynn walked out clear of the truck and waved his hand to his boss. Flynn waved back authoritatively and began a hurried descent on the ladders. Lynn felt glad to sit down. The mental as well as the physical strife had told upon him.

"Gosh! I thought—I was in good shape," he muttered.

"Say, bo!" exclaimed the driver, "what the hell ya want?"

"I might have caught him—in the dam."

"Yeah? Well, you ketched him soon enough, I'll gamble. I heerd it. He'll never come to—the bloody little shrimp! Where'd I ever see you, buddy?"

"I don't know, I'm sure."

"You're such a big bloke. An' fast! Reminds me of them wrestlin' friends at the Olympic. I used to work in a garage near there in L.A. Been here only a . . ."

He rambled on while Lynn's mind began to clear. He had pulled another running stunt. Fine for Carewe and Flynn and Boulder Dam! But what about Anne? He must keep it from her, at least about the exploding bomb. I'll get it yet, Lynn thought somberly. Boulder Dam thrust so many things across his path. These damned Reds! Had they gotten a foothold here in this greatest and best-paid labor project ever conceived? What was the U.S. coming to? And then presently his brooding was disrupted by sight of the stalwart Flynn, striding off the bridge, his hair up like the mane of a lion. There were two workmen with him, one of whom was his foreman, Slade.

Flynn strode up, his heavy boots crunching gravel. His ox eyes flared as he bent them upon the unconscious Moore.

"I seen the last—of it—from the dam," he said, out of breath. "Is he dead?"

"Aw! I hope not. I only socked him one."

"I'll—make him talk. . . . Do you know anythin' about him?"

"Yes, strange to say. His name is Bink Moore. I have a cowboy friend who gave me a line on him and Sproul. But for that . . ."

"Sproul? Who's he?" Flynn demanded gruffly.

"He's the guy who came to the mill with Moore. They were hell-bent, believe me. But I was too wise, boss."

177

"Wise! Is that all? . . . Did you get Sproul?"

"I'll say. He's over at the mill, tied up. And Smith is on the job."

"Humph! Let's throw Mister Moore in the truck. . . . Looks like he fell off the rim to hit on the rocks. . . . Slade, you an' Jim go back to the dam. I'll phone from the office. . . . Weston, come up with me. We'll ride with our Red pard here while you tell me what it's all about. . . . Driver, step on it!"

Lynn's story was interrupted once, up on top and halfway to town, when Flynn halted the truck at the great storehouse for pipes. Presently Flynn came out, less somber of aspect.

"Okay at the mill," he said. "Smith reports no change since you left. Not a phone call!"

"That worried me," Lynn replied.

"I gave Smith orders to call in all the workers there an' not let another man near the mill till I come."

"Good! Lord, but anything might happen. There might be a hundred of them. He can't trust anyone."

"Don't you believe it! These Reds are damn scarce at Boulder. . . . Go on with your story."

When Lynn finished they had arrived in town.

"Biff, you haven't done nothin'," Flynn observed thoughtfully. "Nothin' at all! . . . We'll take this bird to the hospital an' put a guard over him. Then the office!"

It was really only a few minutes before Lynn entered the big office building at the thudding heels of Flynn, but measured by his dread it seemed a long time. The orderly progress of business in the many offices appeared to be going on as usual. When Lynn passed open doors along the corridor leading to Carewe's office his hope surmounted his dread. Surely there had not been any shooting or violence. What could have happened? He was on pins and needles of acute curiosity and apprehension. It would be too much to ask of fate that his intervention had saved Carewe and the payroll. But in another moment, when Flynn burst into Carewe's office, to confront the chief and his associate leaders of the Companies, Lynn realized in a flash of sight and reason that this was so.

"Big Boss, how's tricks?" Flynn boomed poignantly.

The chief's face did not have a healthy hue. His large eyes held a dark havoc, and his long shapely hands trembled. But his smile was reassuring.

"Hello, Flynn. And if there isn't Biff with you! . . . Tricks, did you say? Well, it was a grand slam."

"It was, huh? Well, I can tell you about a few slams, believe me. But first. Mill an' dam okay, thinks to this —— —— grease lightnin' young gentleman with me. I'll report at your request. Have you any orders . . ."

"But Mr. Carewe," Lynn burst out, unable to contain himself. "Did they get your payroll?"

"They did not. It was in the safe," Carewe rejoined with great satisfaction.

"Whew! That's a relief. You look okay to me. But did they—how many—who?"

Lynn broke off his passionate eagerness in confusion.

"Don't be distressed, son," the chief said with a warm smile. "But before we go into conference with Flynn and hear your story let me relieve your mind. Just after you phoned the wires were cut at the telephone exchange downstairs. The man who did it overheard you. He had been stationed there to cut the wires. But he did it too late. The two gangsters who had me cornered were forcing me to get the payroll when their accomplice rushed in to tell them the mill was shut down. 'Grab what dough you can!' he advised. They were a cursing trio. They held me up with guns —forced Mr. Roberts to open the safe and made off with the payroll. But downstairs the telephone girl, Miss Ford, bless her! had put two and two together. She had run out to give the alarm. And as luck would have it she ran into a couple of Boulder Dam police and a truck full of laborers. The police hid waiting for the gangsters, and the laborers blocked the road with trucks. But it never came to a chase, nor a fight. The police held up the gangsters, and that's all."

"Bella Ford!" Lynn ejaculated ecstatically. "Will I give that girl a rush?"

Flynn threw out his chest and with a huge spread hand seemed to push Carewe and his associates back.

"Chief, thet's no story. No story at all!"

"Well! I'll bet you're right. . . . Go ahead. Tell yours."

"I will, after Biff here tells what happened at the mill—an' how he was ready for just what came off."

Lynn's narrative was briefly told, if anything, mitigating his part, but the effect of mere facts alone was tremendous.

"My God! We must keep this secret—this inside stuff. Treachery of workers! It means more than mere racketeering."

"Chief, I'll bet we—Biff, I should say—has scrambled the leaders of that Red gang. It was a tough spot for us. We'll nail Brown an' wring confessions out of him an' these two Reds. An' after this we'll keep stricter tab. Close shave, Chief, but Boulder Dam will go up. . . . An' now listen to my story. Get an earful of this."

Whereupon Flynn related in Homeric manner the facts and the sensations of Lynn's terrific conflict at the mill and his chase after Bink Moore.

Not improbably, Carewe had been overwrought, and being an inventive genius, subject to the flights and emotions of all dreamers, he betrayed a great nervous reaction at the blunt portrayal of peril to his treasured Boulder Dam and to Biff Weston. At first he was mute, but he waved a forceful hand at the blushing Lynn, who was about to protest against Flynn's elaboration of the facts. Carewe arose to pace the floor, his broad noble brow carded by blue veins, his restless hands clasping and unclasping. Finally he faced Lynn.

"Biff, I had hoped to have you here in the office with me," he began laboriously. "But in the stress of this great job there isn't anything in the office worthy of you. Even *my* job wouldn't be big enough. . . . You stick to the building—the physical thing out there with Flynn and his toilers. It would be a blunder to take you off that now. . . . I and the heads of the Six Companies are going to lean on you, boy. . . . It seems banal, and I know not what, to speak of reward here. All the same I'll boost your salary to the limit my associates will sanction. . . . And when Boulder Dam is done you'll be my chief engineer in the building of another."

"Aw—well!" faltered Lynn, and overcome by gratitude and emotion he rushed out.

Chapter 12

"Step on it, buddy," Lynn shouted to the swarthy driver. "I must see my girl!"

"Thought you looked sorta wild. Gawd help you, pard. I was thet way once," declared the driver, and he did step on it, to Lynn's consternation and alarm. The truck roared so loud there was no use in trying to make himself heard. All Lynn could do was to hold on. In less than a few minutes the driver slowed down and halted at the street corner to let Lynn off.

"Whew! Called my bluff, didn't you?" ejaculated Lynn.

"Thet wasn't much. I drove an ambulance in France. . . . Good luck, pard. Hug your dame once for me."

"I will—and thanks a lot."

In a few minutes more Lynn reached his house, out of breath, happy and tremendously excited. He bolted in shouting, "Anne —Anne!"

She did not answer, nor come. He waited for a moment, panting. Then he called again. No answer!

"*Anne!*" he called, sharply louder.

His elation, his thought of a sweet embrace which now he

would have, died a sudden death. The appearance of the living room alarmed him further. Her apron lay on the floor. Anne did not throw things around. Her tan suit, her hat, her shoes, had not been moved. Lynn's blank incredulity succeeded to a terrible fear. He crushed it down, and rushing out he bounded to Mrs. Brown's back door. It was open. Broom in hand she answered his quick rap.

"Anne! Is she—here?" he rang out.

"For the land's sake! You frightened me. . . . No, Anne isn't here."

"Where is she?"

"I don't know, Mr. Weston," the woman replied gravely. "She left in a big car with four men not an hour ago."

"Oh my—God!" gasped Lynn, staggering under the blow he had anticipated.

"Didn't you know? I thought at the time it was queer. I heard the car. Thought it might be my husband. He hasn't been home for two days. I'm worried. They drove in between the houses. Then I heard quick steps. Someone went in your house. Anne screamed sort of short. I went to my door here. Looked out. There was a driver and two young men in the front seat. Eyes like gimlets! The engine was purring. I was surprised and stumped. Friends of yours or Anne's called, I thought. But when she came out, white as a sheet, with a slick dark-looking man dragging at her arm I couldn't help calling out to her. But she never even looked at me. Her eyes looked like blank holes. 'Scram!' said the dark man, as he shoved Anne into the moving car. The door clicked shut. They were gone. . . . I couldn't get the look of Anne off my mind. Now I know something dreadful has happened."

"White slavers," panted Lynn, collapsing against the house. "They had Anne before."

"Mercy! That sweet, lovely girl? How awful! . . . The dirty skunks! Mr. Weston, they haven't been gone an hour. Hurry. You might catch them."

"What kind of car was it?"

"A big one—plain black. I don't know what make."

Lynn staggered back into his house and dazed by the catastrophe he sagged upon the bed. It took a moment to clear his befogged brain. Then his thoughts leaped like scintillating arrows of fire. Bellew had gotten Anne into his clutches again. She had been right. Her intuition had been unerring. Lynn saw that he should never have been lulled into a false sense of safety. He should have believed Anne's grave assertion about the relentlessness of these racketeers. They had no fear of law or life, or any human ties. They were wolves with rabies. Bellew had discovered Anne's hiding place. He had laid his plans well. His power to force Anne to go willingly with him was the easiest of all conjectures to answer. Bellew had threatened to kill Lynn—that if she did not go freely he would take Lynn for a ride and kidnap her. The only way Anne could save Lynn's life was to surrender herself! She was hardly more than a child, and her gratitude to him was so great and her fear she might ruin him so poignant that she would have agreed to anything to save him. Moreover, she would do away with her life at the earliest opportunity.

When all the hideous, sickening facts dawned fully upon Lynn he sank to such misery as he had never dreamed himself capable of feeling.

Lynn cried out in agony. He felt that he would go mad. But before he did he worked out of spiritual torture into a determination for revenge and to save Anne before it was too late. That released the physical force of Lynn. It bound his grief in abeyance. He could not abandon himself to loss while he had life and strength and unquenchable white-hot wrath. And that spurred him to action.

Lynn nearly drove the wheels off his car until he reached the reservation limits. The guard was one Lynn did not know. Four months had passed since he last passed that spot.

"Did you see a big plain black car go by about an hour ago? Several men and a bareheaded girl with chestnut hair?"

184

"Piped that car, all right," returned the guard with interest. "It had three men beside the driver. I didn't see no girl. But they went through fast. Slowed up just before they reached me—then put on the juice. I was sore as a pup and yelled."

"Did you catch their number?"

"Catch nothin'. They threw her in high, and the wind nearly ditched me."

Lynn was moving when he heard the guard's last words. He beat a mile a minute on to Rankin's Palace, where he slowed up to drive in and have a look at the parked cars. The one he wanted to see was not there. Lynn drove on. There appeared to be twice as many camps and shacks in the pass as when he had driven by there last. This was no man's land. He caught glimpses of habitations back in the seclusion of the hills. And nearer the highway he sighted little motley groups of men who were assuredly not laborers. From there on to the turnoff for Ben Sneed's ranch Lynn hit a pace that threatened to dismember the car and scatter the pieces along the road. He drove into Sneed's place.

There were a dozen or more cars in sight, none of which answered the description he had in mind. Green grass and red and golden flowers surrounded the Spanish house, with its white arches and brown-tiled roof. Lynn got out and strode in, and he certainly did not hide that he was looking for someone. This drinking rendezvous had all the richness and color of a swell Los Angeles speakeasy. A score of men and women were draped around the tables. Sneed, with hawk eyes on Lynn, came from somewhere to meet him.

"Young fellow, aren't you butting in sort of precipitously?" he queried.

"Hello, Sneed. Yes. I'm looking for someone."

"She's not here. Beat it."

"Is that a guess, Sneed? Or do you happen to know?" Lynn ventured curtly.

His query and look were not lost on the shrewd bootlegger. Lynn was on edge, and it took all his training to control himself.

185

This handsome, suave Sneed had offered ten thousand dollars for Anne. He had no conception of how close he was to being banged flat as a sack against the adobe wall.

"I don't forget faces. Where'd I meet you?" replied Sneed.

"At the Monte. I had the great pleasure of gambling with you several times. My name's Weston."

"I remember. Haven't seen you around for a long time."

"Been working at Boulder."

"What do you want here? I don't run a gambling joint."

"I'm looking for a man."

"With a woman?"

"My sweetheart."

"You have that look, Weston. If they're here take them outside before you mess up the place."

"She wouldn't be here drinking," Lynn returned with piercing eyes on the bootlegger. "She'd be upstairs—locked in."

"Not so loud!" Sneed hissed with a slight start. And leaning toward Lynn he went on. "I don't run a roadhouse either."

"Yeah! Sneed, a man who tried to buy an innocent girl for ten grand would run any kind of a dive."

"That's how it'd look," the bootlegger returned coolly, and he drew Lynn aside out of hearing of his guests. "*Bellew?*"

"He's the man I'm after."

"That gray-eyed girl! He's got her back?"

"Yes. She's my sweetheart."

The hand on Lynn's arm closed like a vise. Then Sneed with snapping eyes gave vent to a string of cold hard curses that left no doubt of some kind of sincerity.

"Weston, you wouldn't believe that I tried to buy the girl from Bellew to marry her myself?"

"No, I wouldn't," retorted Lynn.

"That'd be too much to expect of a man. All the same it's true. She hit me deep. And Bellew swore he wouldn't take a hundred grand for her. . . . And she's your girl?"

"Yes. Since last spring. We've been living at Boulder, where I'm employed."

"Then it was you who rescued her from Bellew. And she told you about that offer of mine?"

"Yes."

"Bellew told me he had her sent out from L.A. That his agent there claimed she was a homeless, friendless girl, out of work—willing to come to Vegas as a waitress. Is that true?"

"No. Anne belongs to one of the best families in California. She belongs to the Junior League of L.A. She was a welfare worker, and she was downtown studying social conditions when they kidnaped her."

This plausible story of Lynn's deeply impressed the bootlegger.

"Bellew has pulled a boner—the second time."

"I'll say he has. The girl is going to marry me. And I'm John G. Weston's son. If I don't get her back at once and unharmed —why, even Nevada will be too hot for you racketeers."

"Here, get this straight, Weston. I'm no racketeer. I sell liquor. I'm an on-the-level bootlegger. You can get the dope on me in Vegas."

Lynn knew this was true, as far as reputation in Las Vegas was concerned, and he felt inclined to give Sneed the benefit of the doubt with regard to his association with the racketeer.

"Bellew is hijacking my trucks," continued Sneed. "If you knew my game you'd understand what that means. But if you can trust me I'll help you get your girl back. On your part you must keep this out of the papers."

"Sneed, I've heard only good spoken of you. I will trust you," Lynn returned earnestly. "Still, it sticks in my craw that you wanted to buy my girl."

"It needn't. I'd have forced her to marry me, which is the best any underworld man can do for a woman."

"All right. Then get this. Whatever I do must be done right now. Tomorrow will be too late. Anne will choke herself to death with a strip of bed linen."

"No! If she wasn't your girl she might do that. One girl in a thousand will do it. But she'll know you'll hunt her."

"Bellew has threatened to kill me. That's how he got her to go willingly."

"He will kill you, too, if you step in his way. Don't overlook that. He's a real Chicago gangster. And his bodyguard, Gip Ring, is a gunman. Nobody knows how many men Ring has bumped off."

"If I can get close enough to Bellew and Ring they'll never bump any more men off," Lynn declared in dark passion.

"Bellew has a busy night ahead of him without holding a kidnaped girl. He'll have to be in Las Vegas. His gang will be watching the roads for my trucks. And my gang will be watching them. The hell of it is I don't know which way these trucks are coming in."

"I'd figure Bellew would hardly let Anne out of his sight, trucks or no trucks. Can you find out where he'll be?"

"Yes, but how quick I can't say. He has half a dozen hangouts in Vegas. He's never seen in the daytime."

"That woman who stole Anne's clothes—who keeps these girls Bellew gets—she'll be the one to find."

"I don't know her. There are a dozen women like her in Vegas."

"My God! I'll go crazy," Lynn burst out in a frenzy as the ghastly hopelessness of the thing rushed over him again. The talk with this cold-blooded bootlegger brought on the horror. Lynn sank upon a chair and buried his face in his hands. Cold sweat dripped from his brow through his fingers. Sneed was talking, and Lynn could not distinguish what he said. But the man seemed to be a friend in need. Lynn had to grasp at straws. He had to follow a blind belief that God or fate would lead him to Anne. The thought of death for himself did not stay before Lynn's consciousness long enough to be realized. He stood up again and wiped his face with big stiff hands that shook.

"Don't go all to pieces, Weston," Sneed was saying. "It's a

188

tough break. The gamble is a thousand to one against our finding her—in time."

"Bellew hasn't—that chance—to live out the night," Lynn replied hoarsely, and on that deadly thought he pulled himself out of the depths. "Will you meet me at the Monte in half an hour?"

"I'll be there. Weston, go slow!"

"Sneed, if you ever cared for mother—or sister—or wife—think —for God's sake—*think* of some way to help me now. . . ."

Lynn broke off and rushed out of the place to his car. His desperate appeal to the bootlegger rang in his ears. Voiced aloud it made real his tragic extremity. He had been unworthy of the noble opportunity that had befallen him. Whatever had been his alarm in the beginning time had lulled into a security that had been false. All his pride in his toil and the promise of future success had been fatuous egotism. What did he care for success, or life itself, if he lost Anne? He loved her. He knew now. Too late! Lynn's remorse and grief were so insupportable that he scarcely knew what he was doing. As he turned into the main highway he narrowly escaped a crash with a car that had the right of way. The driver, vigilant and capable, swung out just in the nick of time. He yelled a lusty curse at Lynn.

"What a squeak!" muttered Lynn, his chest sinking. "Am I losing my nerve? . . . That big car would have strewn me along the road."

Such proximity to death goaded Lynn's flagging spirit. This was no dream, no nightmare, no story. It was as real as the white road, the cars and trucks humming by, the green and red desert on each side. Things just happened. Automobile accidents were common. Lynn remembered an eloping couple, just married at Las Vegas, who had been hit by a gasoline truck and killed. What had the young groom been thinking about? Probably he had his arm around the bride. Surely she had been happy, dreamful. But they were dead less than a quarter of an hour after their marriage. Nature and chance worked out destinies despite poor mortals. It was all in the mind. If you did not think right and quick you were lost. Lynn had no time for grief, for doubt, for panic. While there was life there was hope. Yet in that six-mile drive into Las Vegas he almost strangled with sobs. The fact of the catastrophe created the hell in his heart. Anne would lose no time killing herself, as much to free Lynn from the peril his protection of her entailed as to escape the heinous degradation of white slavery. She would fool Bellew. She would throw herself out of a speeding car or choke or smother herself to death. And that bald realization seemed to scream at Lynn the loveliness of Anne's character and person. He prayed to God that she could do away with herself before . . .

But that thought encountered a wall in his consciousness. Imagination failed to augment his anguish here. His fighting heart surmounted all. He could not give up. There was something beyond fatality working on him. Like a man falling from a height he grasped at it, as at a rope.

As Lynn showed down upon entering Las Vegas a truckload of roistering laborers passed him. That reminded Lynn that the day was Saturday. Las Vegas would be full of workers from the dam. Judging from the crowded main street, with its lines of moving and stationary cars, Lynn concluded it was already full. But he was still a mile from the center of town. He did not recognize the street as one he remembered. Las Vegas appeared to be extending its residences, stores and especially gas stations and garages out into the desert.

Lynn drove to the police station. He had formed no line of procedure. He knew he had to follow his blind, intuitive urge. He believed that his intensity of passion must enable him to read the minds of crooks, almost to see through walls. But he would try to get help from the sheriff.

So crowded was the approach to the office that Lynn had to elbow his way in. Slipping through a mass of men was one of his fortes. He gathered that this was a busy day for the enforcers of the law. And some of the men he pushed past were surely outside the law. Lynn got in the office by main strength. Sheriff Logan sat at his desk, with one man whispering in his ear and another close. The Texan had a worn visage and harassed expression. He recognized Lynn.

"Sheriff, I *must* see you alone—at once," panted Lynn. "Matter of life or death!"

"Howdy, Weston. You look it. You would butt in heah today. We're swamped. Jail blockachock. Hevron got shot last night. And a girl was murdered in the Diamond. Supposed to be a society girl from L.A. The reporters dug that up. Then there's rumor of a big hijacker's row tonight. And two thousand wild men from Boulder rolling in on us. What can you add to all this?"

"Sheriff, give me your private ear?" Lynn queried earnestly.

"Tend to the phone, Mike. And stall off anybody. Come heah, Weston." The sheriff led Lynn into a small side room and shut the door. "Spill it pronto. I don't like your look."

"Sheriff, my girl was kidnaped by white slavers—at Boulder City—not more than two hours ago."

"Your girl?" echoed the Texan.

"Yes. My Anne. Nineteen years old. Very beautiful. Wavy chestnut hair with streaks of gold. Big gray eyes."

"Pal, you gave me a scare. The girl murdered in the Diamond had black hair. . . . What else?"

"Last spring Anne fell into the hands of Bellew. But she escaped without any harm done to her—except the fright. I saved her. We have been living at Boulder. Bellew is the man."

"Bellew! So this is another of his rackets? —— —— —— ——!" The Texan swore vociferously and slammed his cigar on the floor.

"I'll say it is, Sheriff. . . . Anne was brought here in a big plain black car, with four men. Mrs. Brown, our neighbor, saw them —saw Anne come out and get in the car. . . . The man who came out of the house with her had a pale hard face and black sharp eyes."

"That describes Bellew. Go on," flashed Logan.

191

"Anne evidently accompanied him willingly. To me that's easy to understand. Bellew has threatened to put me on the spot. . . . Poor kid! . . . She has sacrificed herself to save me."

"And they say these heah are the good old United States! . . . Why Goddamn my pictures—a man cain't even keep his own! . . . Weston, this is terrible. No wonder you look like a death's-head."

"You'll help me—won't you?" Lynn asked huskily, swallowing hard.

"You bet your life I will. Oh, boy, if I only had a company of Texas Rangers heah. I'd clean out this burg if I had to throw up my job to do it. . . . But this is not Texas, worse luck. I have five deputies, two of whom just went to the hospital all beat up. Bellew rides around and gambles with a bodyguard. Never seen him without his four slick-dressed Chicago gangsters. One of them Gip Ring, a killer."

"Gip Ring! What does he look like?" Lynn queried eagerly.

"He's only a boy. Cain't be over twenty. Handsome as a girl. Light complected. Eyes like cold slate. He dresses natty."

"Sheriff, we must search the town for her at once."

"That's easy. I can make out a search warrant. But it'd be better to locate her first. I've got to have proof. The goods on Bellew."

"You have what I told you."

"Shore. But you don't even know it's really Bellew who got her. These gangsters are bad medicine. They'll shoot at any provocation. Bellew has all kinds of rackets. But he has never even been accused yet, let alone arrested. He's back of two of the gambling hells heah. I'd gamble myself that one of his gang put Hevron on the spot. We're bucking an unprecedented situation heah. The town is wide open, growing like a weed, lousy with money and an underworld population—transient while this Boulder Dam work is on. We've been hoping that a clash between Bellew and Sneed might rid us of some undesirables. Perhaps it'll come off tonight."

"I must act at once, Logan," Lynn rejoined bluntly. "If the law won't help me I'll go it alone."

"You'll get drilled from a coat pocket," retorted Logan, red and restive under the collar. "My hands are tied heah. The city managers will not stand for any big publicity mess. This Diamond murder has upset them. We're whitewashing the thing. . . . But all the same if you get proof Bellew has your girl I'll go after him. I'll threaten him with jail. I'll make him return her or keep him locked up. These gangsters hate confinement."

"But Anne protests that Bellew is mad about her," Lynn returned hotly. "Sneed saw Anne. Offered ten grand for her. Wanted to marry her, so he says. But Bellew wouldn't take a hundred grand. . . . I stopped to see Sneed. Think he's on the level. He offered to help me get Anne back, provided we avoided publicity. Looks like these racketeers and bootleggers are not the only ones who fear the newspapers. . . . Well, get this, Logan. I'll stir up the —— —— stink any Western town ever had. I'll *kill* this man Bellew!"

"Take my gun," replied Logan, his eyes gleaming with fire, and he drew and thrust a big blue gun into Lynn's hip pocket. "By God, you stir my Texas blood. . . . But listen. Make Sneed find out where Bellew has the girl. Then come for me. Use your haid. Take every one of these smooth young fellows for a gangster. Watch that hand in the coat pocket stunt. Don't expose yourself outside where you can be riddled from a car. The way you feel I'll gamble on you against the whole outfit."

"I felt you wouldn't fail me," Lynn returned gratefully. "Sneed was to meet me at the Monte in half an hour."

"If you're seen with him you'll be a marked man by the Bellew gang."

"They won't know me."

"Don't fool yourself. A big racketeer knows his stuff. If Bellew found your Anne in Boulder City it's a safe bet he knows all about you. But smart as Bellew is he won't suspect swift contact with you. He'll expect the usual police inquiries. Gangsters laugh at the law. It just doesn't operate."

"I'll beat it now. See Sneed and then—" Lynn left by a back

door Logan opened for him. He went round the block and up Main Street to the Monte Palace. It was humming like a beehive. Lynn checked his strong impulse and interrogated it. His reaction to anything or anyone must depend upon what either roused in him. If he had a chance to look into the eyes of a gangster who knew of Anne's seizure by Bellew he knew the secret could not be kept from him. One of his greatest gifts as a football star was to grasp a situation instantly and act upon it. Football was more than play: it was drama and not seldom a tragedy.

Lynn slipped in between the swinging doors of the Palace. Just inside the entrance his sharp eyes glimpsed Sneed almost hidden by four men. Beyond them the place reeked with smoke and rum, with whirring rattle of roulette wheels and hum of low voices. Faces and noises came in a wave. Sneed swept out a white hand to drag Lynn inside the circle.

"Just had good news," he announced, cool and radiant. "My trucks are coming through from the Arizona side. They didn't split at Victorville, but went to Needles, crossed and on to Bowman. They'll come back by way of the ferry above Boulder Dam. And get in tonight on the one road that won't be ambushed. What a break! Bellew has already sold my booze. Sold it before he got it hijacked! He'll never get it. And he'll be ory-eyed."

"I'm glad for you, Sneed. But how does that lucky break help me?" Lynn returned impatiently.

"Wait a minute. Don't jump down my throat. If I'm not bughouse this deal means curtains for Bellew. He has been too brazen. He has overreached himself. He'll have to split his gang to watch the roads. When the trucks are in my storehouse outside of Vegas, one of his gang, whom I have bought, will get word to him where the big shipment of liquor is stored. They'll run rings around a fire engine getting out there. And my men will be there hidden."

"Fine! I'd like to be with them. But my imperative job is to locate Anne at once. How can you help me do that?"

"We'll locate her before dark. Bellew will lay low. He never mixes in fights. All he does is give orders. But he's on the spot

194

right now. He can't keep his hideout secret with my men scattered about watching. Bellew will have to have reports—send out orders. When we locate him we'll watch till his hijackers go out on this holdup. . . . Good! Here comes Sacky."

A sallow-faced individual, not young, characterized by eyes like little bright beads, approached from Lynn could not tell where. He just arrived. And Lynn had a feeling that this man radiated news.

"Ben, I found Decker," said the so-called Sacky. "He was eatin' at the Chink's. He saw Bellew in a car this mornin'. Three fellows with him. Decker recognized Gip Ring. The other two he didn't know. But one of them, an oldish chap, part greaser, he'd seen with the woman who runs the employment agency. They drove west out of town on the Boulder Dam highway. This was at eight-thirty."

"Weston, things are getting hot," said Sneed, his eyes snapping. "That's as much proof as you'll get till you catch him with the goods."

"It wouldn't be enough for the police officers?" queried Lynn.

"Hell, no. They wouldn't arrest Bellew on a bet. . . . This woman who runs the employment agency may be in on this. We want to watch her."

"Anne told of being met at the bus station by a dark-faced man who took her to the woman's place."

"We're on. That's the man who can locate your girl. . . . Scatter, all of you, and report to me. Weston, I've a front room upstairs. I'll watch the street from there. You might go the rounds—"

"Would that fellow Decker guide me around town?"

"Yes. But what for?"

"All I want is to catch sight of Bellew or anyone who was in that car with him."

Sneed shook his head gravely, but he did not voice what was in his mind.

"Sacky, take Weston to Decker and hurry back."

Lynn found himself out in the crowded street, hurried along

by a hand at his elbow. They walked toward the east end of town.

"Weston, it's a cinch Decker will show you one of these men before nightfall," Sacky was saying. "What are you goin' to do when he does?"

"I'll make him tell where they took Anne."

"How'll you make him? A gangster never squeals."

"I'll break every bone in his body," Lynn returned grimly.

"They all carry guns. And they shoot."

"I'll beat him to it."

"My hunch is this. Don't tackle Gip Ring, or Bellew either. He's never alone. Hunt for the oldish man—the greaser. . . . You are in a tough spot, young fellow. I'm for you. We're all for you. And that goes outside of Sneed's eagerness to get Bellew on his own account."

Sacky led off the main street round a corner, where, halfway down the block, they came to a Chinese restaurant. Several men lounged in front of the place. Sacky approached one of them, a slim youth whose good looks were scarcely to be expected in a bootlegger's gang.

"Deck, this is Weston," said Sacky. The young fellow offered his hand to Lynn. "Ben wants you to guide him around town till you find one of the men who was in Bellew's car. Weston will do the rest. My advice is pass up Bellew and Gip. Hunt for the other two."

Sacky's hurried departure indicated his gladness at having completed his mission. Another hint to Lynn of the risk in this underworld adventure! Lynn took advantage of the moment to tell Decker about Anne's abduction in the first place, then the present misfortune, and what an innocent girl she was, and finally how pretty, which tribute Decker interrupted.

"I've seen her. . . . Let's have a drink."

"You've seen her!" Lynn ejaculated in quick eagerness. "Where? When? Sneed didn't tell me that."

"He didn't know. I kept that to myself. I'd heard about his offer to Bellew for her. And I meant to turn seeing her to my own

196

account. But this is a horse of a different color. . . . She was in Bellew's car—in the back seat. She looked out, and I had a good shot at her. Say, that dame will never be safe in this world."

"When—did—you see her?" choked Lynn.

"About eleven. He was driving in from Boulder."

"Describe her," said Lynn, clenching his fists until his nails bent on his calloused palms.

"Oval face—white—red lips like a bow—big eyes, wide apart, dark gray or blue—chestnut hair with curls flying. A strong, sweet, passionate face, Weston, and I don't wonder at your being pale about the gills. And she's your twist—your girl?"

"Yes."

"Pretty young, isn't she? Sixteen about?"

"She's nineteen. . . . Decker, I can't offer you much, even a grand. . . ."

"Stow that talk. You can't buy me for a job like this. . . . But you can buy me a drink."

"I've been on the water wagon myself. But a drink might perk me up."

"You'll feel better when you get your hands on Bellew. I see you're packing a gun in your jeans. Put it inside your jacket. . . . There . . . You must have come right from work. That's a husky pair of hobnail boots you're carryin' around."

"Didn't have time to change. Can we buy a drink these prohibition days?"

"Sneed has three trucks loaded full of liquor on the way here. What do you suppose he does with it?"

"Sells to speakeasies, I'd say."

"Partly. And he'll have fifty grand in his sock for these three trucks alone. Money in bootleggin' here? Well, I guess. There's millions in it."

"But who buys—I mean—drinks so much?"

"Lord only knows. Not a half goes down the gullets of the dam workers, that's a fact. There's a large floatin' population. Lot of swell people motor here. Do they sop it up?"

A stiff drink of whisky not many years old injected something raw and hot into Lynn's internals.

"That'll do for a starter. I reckon we'll need a finisher. But we're sober on this job. . . . It's ten to one I can find one or more of these men. What's comin' off when I do?"

"I'll make up my mind when I see him," responded Lynn.

"Your idea is to find out where they hid the girl?"

"Of course."

"And then go after her?"

"Yes."

"Say, boy, you've got your nerve. I kinda like you. But hell! Any guy would go through fire and gore to save that girl."

"Gosh, the town's crowded," Lynn replied as they left the speak-easy. "Never saw so many!"

"Saturday aft. Then these murders have got people out. . . . We'll begin here at the Empire. I'll go in first. You follow, but don't let it look like you were with me. You're just a sucker huntin' for a game. Keep me close. I'll tip you off when I find your man."

"All set. Let's go," Lynn replied darkly. His consciousness admitted of no failure in this hunt.

There were two hundred or more Boulder Dam workers in the Empire—a lean-faced, brown-skinned, bright-eyed crowd of men mostly young and all still sober and on the chase of relaxation and pleasure. At least half the gamblers did not belong to this fraternity of toil, and there were numerous wolves in the dark. The turn of a card, the roll of a ball, the swing of a wheel, dominated the individuals in this long bright blue-hazed hall. But in different ways!

Decker took his time. He looked an idler, a careless watcher, easy and familiar, and he was not approached by anyone or asked to sit in on games. On the other hand, Lynn, who had never visited town in the rough garb of a laborer, was importuned by many. He had to shake off one insistent gambler. Another man openly offered to procure liquor. Then, during this slow search,

Lynn heard various snatches of talk about the murders which had the town agog.

At last Decker led the way out. "Have patience and hang on to your nerve," he said after a keen glance at Lynn. "That joint is a favorite hangout for some of Bellew's gang. Not today!"

The Arizona Club, the Nevada Parade, the Atlas and Calumet, and the Boulder Dam, all on the west side of Main Street, failed to yield any of the men Decker sought.

"Three o'clock," said Lynn's guide. "Pretty early yet."

Off the thoroughfare one block they entered a quiet zone consisting mostly of private houses. Parked cars were numerous. A few pedestrians, all laborers in their good clothes, passed them by. Lynn heard music from somewhere, loud voices singularly vacant and mirthless, and a girl's mocking laughter. Decker led on until he came to a large plain house at the corner of the street. It looked like the dwelling place of a town merchant. They were admitted by a Negro and shown to a well-furnished sitting room.

"Tell Mame that Deck wants to see her," said Lynn's guide.

"Yas, suh. I was gwine to," returned the darky.

Lynn heard a clink of glasses and gay laughter through partitions and down the long somber hall. The step and entrance of a girl quite pretty except for too much paint, and lightly though modestly clad, shocked the blood to his heart.

"Howdy, Mame," Decker said familiarly. "Sorry to have you waked up."

"Well, if it's not our champeen booze peddler! Who's Handsome here with you?" the girl replied with gaiety, her too-sharp eyes upon Lynn.

"Friend of mine, Mame," replied Decker, low-voiced. "Name is Weston. He's in trouble. And I'm askin' you—maybe you can give us a tip."

"Trouble? What the hell you take me for—a mind doctor or a sky pilot?"

"No kiddin'. He has just lost his girl. Young—peach of a kid —innocent as you once was." Decker lowered his voice to a

199

whisper. "She was kidnaped this morning, out at Boulder—by Bellew. Brought to town. I saw her in his car, less than two hours ago."

"*Bellew!* On that racket," hissed the girl, her eyes glittering.

"You're tellin' me! Mame, have you seen Bellew lately?"

"No. He doesn't visit any more."

"Mame, I thought you might give us a tip. We've got to find her before night. Can you help us, Mame? We'll never squeal. And we'll do somethin'—"

"I'll be grateful to you all my life," interposed Lynn.

"Say, Handsome, you don't need to sell me on the idea," the girl returned with emotion. "I'd risk my life to save your girl—for *her*. And by God, I've got your hunch."

"*Mame!* Spring it on us—quick!"

"There was a girl I got friendly with who was brought to Vegas by a dago or greaser named Vitte or Vitto. Something like that. Anyway he's in with the dame who runs an employment agency here. Deck, find that bozo Vitte!"

"I'll say we will. He was in Bellew's car this mornin', when I saw the girl. . . . Mame, you've linked it up for us. Girl, you're a peach to come clean with that."

"Thanks, Mame—and good luck to you," Lynn said feelingly.

As they hurried out the girl followed them to the door. "Handsome, you're big enough to beat up that greaser. And as for Bellew—I hope to God you make mincemeat out of him."

"Now let's shake the rest of the joints for Vitte," Decker declared when they got out. If we can't find him, then we'll go for the dame who runs the employment fake."

"Decker, are you sure you can identify this Vitte?"

"Sure as death. I'm a scout for Sneed. And do I have to know my onions. I could put Vitte on the spot for you even if I haven't seen him. I have, this mornin'. And I'd seen that bird before. Come on, pard. It's gettin' so hot my feet burn. And let's have that finishin' drink."

They had it and Lynn personally thought he had swallowed a

200

dose of aqua fortis. From the speakeasy they crossed the street to the Monte. "I'll run upstairs, report to Sneed and then look this place over," said Decker. This gambling hall catered mostly to a higher class, or else a more sporting class, and at five in the afternoon was not crowded. Lynn was looking on when Decker returned surprisingly soon. He was pale and breathless. "Gip Ring playin' roulette here," he whispered in Lynn's ear. "Sneed says that means Bellew is under cover somewhere, and your girl, too."

"What I feared," gasped Lynn. "Show me this Gip Ring."

"Sneed says lay off Gip. He'll kill you."

"But let me see him—just see him," begged Lynn.

"Got yourself in hand?"

"Yes. I swear I'll not break out."

"Oke. Let's not waste time."

In another moment Lynn was curiously gazing at a notorious Chicago gunman. This Gip Ring was young, dapper, and had the look of a fresh egoist of a movie star except for the peculiar force-fulness of expression. The lines of Ring's face were cut as in gray stone, and his cold piercing eyes moved with the oscillations of a compass needle. He appeared absorbed in his game, yet he saw everyone and every move. The right corner pocket of his sack coat sagged distinguishably to Lynn's sharp sight.

"Not so much to look at, eh?" Decker queried as he led Lynn out into the street. "But he's a hophead, and a killer for fair."

"What's a hophead?" asked Lynn, expelling the smoky air of the gambling hall.

"Dope. Heroin or opium. That accounts for the cold nerve of these gangsters. Some of them show yellow through when they're not het-up."

Decker ran the gamut of all the clubs on the opposite side of Main Street without giving Lynn a cue. When they came out of the Elite the white and neon lights of the street proclaimed the end of day. Lynn felt his nerves ready to fray out.

"Pard, I'll say you're a sticker," Decker rasped out. "It's tough, but we're hot. There are more joints below. But let's breeze over to the employment agency."

They were soon out of the center of the light and action of Las Vegas. Decker pointed to a building, queer of shape, as high as three stores, yet the upper third was blank of windows. Half of the main floor shone light. The entrance appeared to be on the side street. Decker stepped in the open door, followed by Lynn. The interior looked like any employment office, especially the two benches placed near a door marked private. To the right of this door a stairway went up into the dark.

"What ees your bizness?" called a sharp voice, unmistakably with an accent.

Lynn and Decker turned to encounter a man who apparently had been sitting near a table. He was under thirty, swarthy of face, small of feature and had eyes like black daggers.

"My friend wants to hire a waitress," announced Decker. Then turning to Lynn with a singularly gleaming smile he added. "Here's your man!"

All Lynn's subjected inward force seemed to burst in his veins, through which hot darts and gusts rushed. As he stepped forward he saw the man's swift hand slip into his right coat pocket, an action unobtrusive to any but vigilant eyes.

"Who ees it?" the man demanded shrilly.

"Weston. I want to ask—"

He could not keep the ring out of his voice, which cut short at the other's sharp exclamation.

"Stick eem up!" he hissed.

"Sure. They're up," Lynn replied as he elevated his hands high and stepped closer casually. "Are you a holdup gent? We've been directed here to . . ."

"Don't shoot, Vitte. The dicks are comin'," Decker called sternly.

Chapter 13

Lynn saw Vitte's sloe-black eyes redden with the swift intent of murder. The corner of Vitte's sack coat shook with the invisible hand and gun hidden in the pocket. As it raised and stiffened Lynn kicked up with all the tremendous strength and speed years of training had given him.

His heavy boot landed on Vitte's hand and side with a sodden bam! The alien might as well have been struck by a catapult. That kick lifted him off his feet and hurtled him through air, crashing down table and chair and landed him against the wall. And when he landed Lynn pounced upon him like a huge terrier on a rat. One swift wrench rendered Vitte's gun arm useless, if it had survived that onslaught. Then Lynn jerked him halfway up and panted. "Talk or I'll—kill you! Where is she?"

Decker checked a swing of that mallet fist. "Weston, don't bust him. Make him tell us."

Lynn shifted his left hand to Vitte's lean neck where its clutch shut off hoarse utterings. The man was still conscious enough to sense the imminence of death. When Lynn released that viselike grip on his throat he gasped: "Gerl eez—upstairs—Bellew!"

"I'll take his gun and hold up anyone," said Decker, swift and dark.

"Run for help. Sheriff Logan!" Then Lynn hit the half-sitting Vitte a clip that knocked him senseless. Decker knelt to get the man's gun, while Lynn leaped for the stairway.

There was a light at the top of that first flight. Lynn turned toward the second flight. The steps were carpeted and gave forth no sound. It grew dark up there. He felt his way—his groping hand on the bannister. He reached a level. There, breathing deep, Lynn halted to get his bearings. The pitch-black darkness gradually lessened as his eyes grew more accustomed to it, and presently vague outline of corridor and wall became visible.

Then he heard a sound—the whimpering of a girl and the menacing voice of a man. Lynn's whole frame leaped as if galvanized when he recognized Anne's husky contralto. He looked around to see how much room he had to plunge his whole weight and power against the door from which the sounds came. He had to burst it open in one lunge. It appeared to be an ordinary door. He could break it down. Then it occurred to him to try the knob. He did so noiselessly. The door was unlocked. Lynn opened it and stepped into a brightly lighted room.

Across this room stood a man with his back to Lynn. He appeared young of build, as showed in his lithe shoulders stripped to his undershirt. His head, dark, sleek, shiny, resembled that of a cobra about to strike.

Beyond him against the wall Lynn saw Anne. Her hair hung disheveled. Her face was ashen, her eyes great gulfs of havoc.

All this Lynn saw in a single flash. Then Anne became aware of his presence.

"*Lynn!*" she cried wildly.

The racketeer whirled on pivoting feet. Lynn looked into a cruel visage that appeared transforming under his gaze. Its heat and triumphant mastery, its sadistic line of hard lips, its lurid eyes of black fire—these marvelously changed as the man realized that he was trapped. He had no weapon on him save a whip. His frame appeared that of a stripling compared to the build of the intruder. His vaunted bodyguards were absent. Far greater racketeers than he had made fatal mistakes. He had made his. All this and the fact that his gun was in his coat on a chair beyond the bed showed in his changing expressions as easily read as print.

"Who're—you?" he demanded hoarsely, lowering the whip.

"Weston," Lynn replied in a voice that came to his ears like a whisper.

"Take your dame—and get out. She hasn't been touched. . . . Lay off me, or I'll put you on the spot."

Anne slid along the wall and slumped down, her head and shoulders falling behind the bed, which had been pulled away from the wall.

Suddenly Bellew leaped like a cat, cleared the bed, gained his coat. He yelled piercingly as he whipped it off the chair and felt with a too-hasty, too-shaky hand for the gun that was certainly in his pocket. He got to it just as Lynn, clearing the space between, landed upon him. They went down in that tackle and brought up short against the wall, with Bellew's gun hand in a grasp that made it useless.

On his knees Lynn shoved the livid Bellew against the wall and swung back that brawny arm with its sledge hammer fist. Bellew made a frenzied struggle to release his hand. But he could not even work the trigger of the automatic. He must have sensed his doom, for his pallid face grew ghastly with its distorted convulsions, its dripping sweat. Yet such had been the school that had developed him, such had been the far divergence of his class from manhood, that he betrayed in eye and voice his thought to escape destiny.

"Hold on—Weston! Take my gun. Take your girl. She's oke. . . . Lay off me."

Lynn swung blindly, his fist colliding with Bellew's face. It was a kind of blow that caused extreme pain. Bellew went to pieces from its effect.

205

"Don't hit—me! ——— ——— ——— bully! . . . Let go, ———
——— you! There's fifty grand in this coat. Take it. . . . Let me
go. Beat it with your girl before my gang gets here. . . . They'll
kill you."

Bellew found desperate strength to writhe his gun hand loose
enough to shoot. Lynn felt a blow—the hot sting of a bullet. It
loosed his dammed-up fury. It also awakened him to his and
Anne's peril—that he was wasting precious moments on this
wretch. He swung again, finding the man's chin.

Bellew went lax in his grip. Then Lynn heard shouts below
and thudding feet on the stairs. He had only time to jump erect,
dragging Bellew up in front of him, when Gip Ring ran into the
room, his gun ready. At his call three others followed, with
bated breath and eyes glinting.

"Boys, he's done for Bellew, but we've got him," the gunman
announced crisply, as his piercing gaze grasped the situation.

"He's not—dead. Only beat—up," panted Lynn, playing for
time. He held the limp Bellew to cover him and edged a couple
of steps near the electric snap. His quick thought was to switch
the room into darkness, leap to close and lock the door, and take
his chance with these gangsters. As he edged over, Gip Ring and
his three allies moved cautiously the other way. Twice Ring
leveled his gun, but did not fire, no doubt owing to the extreme
danger of hitting Bellew.

"*Look out, Gip!*" one of the three yelled just as Lynn, dragging
Bellew, lunged for the electric light snap. Ring fired. Lynn heard
the thud of the bullet hit Bellew. Next instant he had seized the
snap and wrenched it off, plunging the room into total darkness.
Then he dropped Bellew. In another bound he reached for, felt,
the door. With swift hands he closed it and put the key in his
pocket. All this quick action to the tune of the *rat-tat-tat* of the
gangster's gun. Lynn crouched close to the floor.

"Gip! Don't shoot!" one of his partners shouted excitedly. "You'll
hit us!"

"Think, you hops. Open the door!"

"He locked it. I heard him."

"Hear him pantin'? He's layin' for us by that door."

Lynn made haste to subdue his accelerated breathing. His predicament had marvelously changed to his advantage though it was still precarious. These gangsters would be sure to do themselves injury. He crawled silently along the wall. It was well that he did, for Ring shot again, and his bullet struck close to where Lynn had been crouching.

"Bellew, where are you?" asked the gunman.

No answer!

"You hit him before the light went out. . . . Like as not killed him!"

"Hell!" rasped the gunman. "Snap, stop your peevin' and get wise. We're put on the spot. Locked in the dark with a gorilla! It's every guy for himself."

"Gip, I haven't a rod!"

"Okay, Ring. God help you if you bump into me," hissed the gangster called Snap. He certainly had a weapon.

Lynn felt that one of them was moving near, probably toward the center of the room. He flattened himself on his left side against the wall, with his hands free so that he could seize the first leg that touched him. Lynn realized he would need to be so swift, so violent, that he must render the placing of a gun against him impossible.

He heard suppressed breaths, stealthy steps out from his position, then a soft colliding of two bodies. A gunshot flashed and cracked in the blackness. Lynn saw three standing figures die out in the flare.

"Hophead! You hit *me!*" cursed Ring, and red flashes alternated with the rattle of his automatic. It ceased. One of the gangsters, groaning, crawled away from the center of the room.

"Gip, you're the hophead," sang out Snap, deadly and fierce. "You plugged the Kid."

All the answer Ring made to this was a quick mechanical clink of fresh shells being fed into his gun. The room smelled of burnt powder. Shouts down below and out in the street penetrated the tense silence. Lynn thought reinforcements for himself or Bellew had arrived. If both came at once there would be a clash downstairs. The suspense of inaction grew insupportable. He had to get hold of one of these gangsters. He had to force the issue.

Noiselessly moving to his knees he prepared to crawl upon the gangsters. His idea was to move swiftly, but without a sound, and make powerful sweeps with his right arm, then with his left, until he caught one of them by the leg. Something of Lynn's former fury succeeded this deliberate strategic move. All his great muscular force set tensely, as he slid six inches on one knee, and made a half circle with his right arm.

"Look out, Gip! Behind you!" yelled Snap, and he shot into the blackness.

"Give him the works!" yelled Ring.

By the flash Lynn located both men. The one facing him must have been Ring, for he leaped away from Snap.

That action precipitated the finish. Lynn crawled and swept, crawled and swept. . . . Then his powerful right hand, at the end of a sweep, cracked on a leg. The impact, swift and strong, knocked the leg out from under its owner like a tenpin. The man went down, his yell of terror broken by his sodden fall. Lynn had hold of Gip Ring's leg. His left hand swept to the aid of his right, while the gangster was spinning on the floor. Lynn saw red flashes, but the shots sounded like tiny spat-spat-spat. Faint yells pierced his bursting ears.

He swung Ring along the floor until the gangster crashed into the bed. That impact made of Ring's rigid, resisting body a thing like a limp string with a weight on the end. But the gangster Snap was shooting at random. Lynn rose erect and swung Ring by the leg. The gangster's slight frame had no weight for Lynn at that moment. He whirled and swung and moved swiftly toward the zone of red flashes.

Suddenly a tremendous shocking smash staggered Lynn. He had swung Ring into Snap or the third fellow. A gun clanked hard on the wall and fell ringingly. Whoever Lynn had hit went hurtling over the bed to bang the wall solidly. Lynn heard a body slither to the floor, then silence. The man must be unconscious, Lynn thought.

Lynn dropped Ring's limp body to the floor. For a moment he felt dizzy. He could not inhale enough breath. Then the congestion left his brain.

He got up to feel for the door, not having any idea which was the direction. First he reached a wall, and his seeking hand ran into the broken electric light snap. That he remembered was near the door. Then he stumbled over something. A body! His feet tangled in a coat. Bellew's coat! Lynn snatched it up, stepped over the body, and found the doorknob. His mind cleared. It took only a moment to get the key out of his pocket, unlock and open the door. A yellow light from the landing below showed the corridor and stairway. There seemed to be an uproar on the main floor or out in the street.

With left hand on the wall, and feeling low with his right, Lynn began a circle of the room. He collided with the bed. That end was closed to the wall. He crossed the bed and felt for Anne on the floor. His groping hands failed to locate her. And he had almost succumbed to mounting panic when he felt a still form. He called her, and she answered faintly, *"Lynn! Lynn!"*

"Darling, I—I thought you'd—fainted. Are you hurt?" he gasped.

"No. Are—you?" she whispered.

"If I am I don't know it." Still holding to Bellew's coat he lifted her up. Then he made for the dim yellow space in the darkness.

He gained the corridor, the stairway; he ran down. At the second landing he heard a woman's shrill voice, high-pitched and angry. A clamor rose from outside. He was not out of this mess yet. Anne's body clasped close to him made his aware of the gun inside his coat. He had utterly forgotten the weapon Logan had given him. But would that have helped him materially? Nevertheless, he held Anne with his left arm and drew the gun. Down the second flight! He turned.

Then he was at the head of the main wide stairway. Decker

blocked it, trying to keep a furious woman from ascending. She appeared to be a hag bereft of her senses. She fought Decker, got by him, and started up. Over her head Lynn saw Logan trying to keep the crowd out. Two men lay on the floor.

The woman, frenzied beyond credulity, tried to intercept Lynn, tore screechingly at Anne. Lynn did not waste even a shout into her demonical face. He knew she must be the woman from the agency. He gave her a push, and she fell against the wall and sank to the ground.

Lynn ran down, jumped over her, to face the exultant bootlegger and the cool Texan.

"By Gawd, pard, I swore you'd pull it. But you're all bloody."

"Heah, Weston. Follow us. . . . We've got to rustle. Bellew's gang's on the way."

Lynn kept close to his guides as they tore a gun-fronted passage through the crowd. But it appeared to be only a curious and not a menacing crowd. Outside beyond the sidewalk in the open street, Lynn began to stagger with his burden.

"Boy, you're hurt. Let me take her. Heah's my car."

Lynn laid Anne in the back seat of the car, and as he covered her he found Bellew's coat under the blanket. He took that up.

"Logan, will you—take her—to some safe place—to your home —hide her—look after her—till I . . ."

"Shore will, boy. Hop in. Let's rustle," the sheriff replied as he slipped in behind the wheel.

"I'm shot. . . . Don't know how—bad."

"Rush him to the hospital, Decker. Grab any car heah. . . . Weston, one more word. How about Gip Ring and Bellew?"

"I took—them for—a ride," Lynn returned with a faint smile, as he accepted Decker's support. "See . . . kept Bellew's coat— gun—for souvenirs, and here's your gun. . . . I didn't need it."

"I'll say you're shore from Texas. . . . I'm off. Don't worry about Anne!"

Logan drove away as the curious crowd began to congregate. And Decker led Lynn across the street.

"I can walk—if it's not far," said Lynn.

"I'll bet two bits you could run, if you had to. But nothin' doin'. We'll ride," replied Decker, and he appropriated the first available car.

Lynn sank down in the seat, conscious of a joy and gratitude that counteracted a growing sick weakness and throbbing burns in shoulder and leg.

"I've been shot—all right," he said, more to himself than to Decker.

"See you have," replied that worthy. "Bloody shoulder. But what the hell? What's a bullet to a guy like you?

"Logan told me you'd been a football player. I'll bet you run amuck through Bellew's gang. Am I bustin' for news? Pard, stay put long enough to tell me that."

But Lynn grew so sick and dizzy that it was all he could do to hold on to his consciousness and the heavy coat across his knees. The weight of it, the significance of which he had forgotten, kept him from fading into oblivion.

Chapter 14

By the time Decker arrived at the hospital Lynn had recovered somewhat from his dizzy spell and walked unaided into the presence of the physician and his aid.

"Gentlemen, I've been shot," he announced coolly. "In this leg, somewhere below my hip—and here on my left shoulder."

"You're bloody enough to be shot all over," replied the elder doctor. "Come into this room. Let's have a look. . . . Who are you?"

"Weston, from Boulder Dam. I'm not so tough as I look."

"Doc, this guy doesn't belong to the class he's been fightin'," Decker cut in dryly.

They removed most of Lynn's clothing and made a careful examination. "Nothing very serious," was the smiling report. "Both bullets went through clean. Small caliber steel bullets, I'm sure."

"I've played through footballs games with worse hurts than these," replied Lynn. "Fix me up, doctor, and let me have a bed here tonight."

"Pard, it's turned out oke," Decker said beamingly. "Am I tickled pink? . . . I'll blow now and run back to the ringside. I can't wait to see how you gave them the works."

"Come back soon. Tell me. Send Logan," called Lynn to his departing ally.

"Oke."

In half an hour Lynn's wounds had been dressed, and he was resting on a clean cot in the hospital ward with an attractive and most solicitous nurse in attendance. There were other patients present, but none nearer than several cots from Lynn.

Left alone, practically, he lay there as wide-awake and keen as he had ever been in his life. The coat he had clung to—Bellew's coat—and which the doctors had been curious about, hung close over the iron bedpost. Lynn felt conscious of throbbing pain, but it was nothing to what he had often been used to endure. A wrenched tendon, a twisted knee, a muscle torn loose—these injuries so common to football players hurt a great deal more than bullet wounds, at least those Lynn had sustained. He knew he had a headache, yet he had to think about it to feel it.

As he relaxed and settled down to wait for Decker a sense of blessed relief and infinite gratitude closed his eyes and uplifted his spirit to the heights. Anne was rescued, unharmed, safe by now with some good woman. That for the time being was all he could think of. A miraculous, if not divine, instinct had directed him to her. Lynn tried to recall what had happened in the room. But he could not get events in sequence. They were all jumbled up.

The nurse came back to hover over Lynn, to feel his face with soft hand and to take his pulse.

"You must try to sleep," she said.

"Sleep! With what I have to think of? . . . Nurse, I never want to sleep again."

"Are you in pain?" she asked, puzzled.

"Gee! I forgot I'd been shot. . . . I'm just happy. . . . Nurse, you better stay away from me. I could hug and kiss anything feminine that happened along. And you're a peach."

She smiled down upon him and smoothed back his damp hair. The doctor passed and stopped to inquire.

"A little out of his head. But no fever," she said.

213

"Doc, the little lady is wrong," interposed Lynn. "I'm wide-awake and sane. Say, I've got Einstein beat for brains. . . . Wait till you hear how lucky I've been."

"Weston, we've already got an inkling of that," the doctor replied kindly. "You must have had some fight. Report just phoned in for us to make ready for two men."

"Two? But there were three men, counting Bellew," returned Lynn, racking his memory.

"Patrol wagon took one to the morgue," Lynn's informant concluded and passed on.

"*Morgue!*" Lynn ejaculated with a gasp, and suddenly his mind seemed to be illumined. Ring must have killed Bellew with that first shot! The realization was interrupted by the advent of Decker, big-eyed and radiant.

"I've got all the dope, pard," he announced. "Oh, boy! Are you a hero? No wonder this pretty dame is makin' eyes at you. . . . Nurse, this is Biff Weston, football star and Boulder Dam worker —and is he some guy besides that? You're slow if you haven't fallen for him."

"Maybe I'm not so slow as I look," she returned with a laugh. "But I'm on duty. I mustn't let you excite him."

"Nurse, it'd excite me to send him away," Lynn interrupted pleadingly. "Please don't."

"She couldn't. It ain't in woman's nature, with your handsome mug like that. . . . Nurse, you set on that side of him, and I'll set here. . . . Weston, you're on the tip of every tongue out there—the ——— ———est, chain-lightningest cyclone that blew the roof off a town!"

"Anne! . . . Logan! Where'd he take her? Is he coming? Hurry, or I'll biff you one," exploded Lynn.

"Just came from the station, my friend," Decker replied laconically. "Logan took Anne home, I reckon. Gimme time, pard. I ain't no radio broadcaster. . . . Barnes, a deputy of police headquarters, gave me this message from Logan: 'Tell Weston if he wants I'll take Anne home to his mother.' "

"Good Lord!" Stunned for a moment, Lynn could only lie there until his thoughts moved again. "To Mother! Of all ways for things to work out!"

"Pard, I'd think your home and mother would be the best place for your harassed little girl now," Decker replied seriously.

"No! That wouldn't do. You see Dad was sore at me more than a year ago. . . . But Mother? *She* will take Anne in. Come to think of it, there's no one in the world I'd like Anne to be with so well as Mother, if—if . . ."

"Okay, then. Logan will keep her at his home till you say. You live in L.A.?"

"No. Pasadena. Half an hour this side."

"Sure. Don't worry, pard. You can trust that Texas Jack. He's hipped on you. And that'll be that. . . . And now, considerin' there are a *few* little things in this world besides your little girl, suppose you let me tell you some."

"Nothing else really matters, pard," said Lynn, somehow warming to the presence and meaning of this rough friend in need.

"Nurse, get that. He called me pard. *Me!* A low-down booze scout! . . . Weston, take a snootful of this dope. . . . Just saw Sneed. He's crazy. I steered him off you for tonight. He'll want to stuff a handful of yellow grands in your mitt. Look at that! . . . He gave it to me. First grand I ever had. . . . Well, his trucks got in. Did they get in? Ha! Ha! I should smile. Johnny Devoe was drivin' the third one, some ways back. Bellew's hijack gang held the two trucks up. But they couldn't stop Johnny. Not even a rattlin' machine gun. Johnny stepped on her—ducked and piled right into Bellew's car. Sneed said he made a hell of a mess, but didn't bust a bottle. But when the police got on the scene they found only the mashed car. The hijackers made a getaway, crippled and dead—if there were any, in another car."

"I'm glad. Sneed is a good sport, even if . . ." Lynn stalled over that unforgivable offer of ten thousand dollars for Anne.

"That's a preliminary, pard, but it ain't nothin'," went on the irresponsible Decker. "I seen them put what's left of Bellew's

215

bodyguards and that dame in the wagon. Bellew's dead. The others are hospital-bound, pard."

"Dead! My God! But I only bashed the others."

"Gip Ring and Kid Barton were both shot, too! . . . Weston, did you use your gun?"

"Logan's gun? No. I forgot I had it until too late."

"Well, they shot themselves. The dicks have that figured. . . . Bellew was shot, too."

At this juncture the nurse, despite her intense sympathy, insisted that Lynn be left alone.

"Righto," declared Decker, rising with alacrity. "I've got the most off my chest. And all's well. Pard, I'll come tomorrow. . . . Nurse, I could go for you in a big way. Can I date you up?"

"Go along with you," she returned. "How do you know that I haven't a husband?"

"You ought to have one if you haven't. Think it over, girlie. . . . Good night, pard, and let me say meetin' you injected somethin' hot into my life."

Lynn asked the nurse for ice water and that she turn out the near light. Presently in the semidarkness he lay, compelling his racing thoughts to slow down. Throbbing pain in the dead hour of night was an old associate of Lynn's. That could not keep him awake. But this astounding thing he had done—and what the result would be—these kept him awake for a long while.

Lynn awoke bright and early. For a moment the unfamiliar surroundings roused bewilderment until he smelled iodoform. He was on a hospital cot; and over him rushed a vivid sequence of the events that had brought him there. His shoulders seemed free of pain, but when he moved his leg it hurt. Nevertheless he hoped his injuries were trifling.

The day nurse, whom he had not seen, proved to be a woman of ample bulk and cheery face.

"Good morning, dearie," Lynn said gaily. "Pardon my effervescence. I suppose that night nurse told you I was nutty."

"She recommended that I sit on you, if necessary. That you were an obstreperous patient."

"Obstreperous! I pass, nurse. I'm okay, though. Patient or not I want to wash and shave. Where's the bathroom? . . . And oh, yes, I want ham and eggs, toast and coffee."

An hour or more later the younger physician visited Lynn and redressed his wounds, saying that the shoulder wound had closed perfectly and that the one in the leg showed no inflammation. He was doing well indeed.

"Weston, you're a superb specimen. The kind of physical marvel whom we surgeons like to operate on."

"Yeah? Well, you've had your little party with this anatomical marvel. . . . When can I go home? Out to Boulder?"

"Not soon, I'm sure. And then only provided you go to the hospital there for a couple of days. Just a precaution. Your wounds are not superficial. Both the bullets went through. Any internal infection will make itself manifest quickly."

From that hour Lynn had little time to ponder over his adventure, as one visitor after another called to see him. He did not have much to say to detectives and reporters and turned the tables on them by asking questions himself. A Los Angeles newspaper man was expected any moment. A Catholic priest and a Presbyterian minister visited him simultaneously. Lynn was courteous to these kindly-intentioned men, but disclaimed any great need of their services at present. Then Ben Sneed came—a markedly different Sneed, as he appeared to Lynn.

"Weston, I got my consignment of liquor safe, and I owe it mostly to you," he claimed, earnestly. "Bellew was heeled for me last night. Only he ran into you and didn't click. . . . I'm slipping this envelope under your pillow."

"Yeah. What's in it?" Lynn rejoined brusquely.

"Some lemon drops and peppermint gum," replied the bootlegger with a laugh.

After a moment's reflection Lynn overcame his resentment at the idea of Sneed's rewarding him. Why be a stuck-up chump? He was on his own now. He had certainly worked in Sneed's interest, although unwittingly. And if he meant to keep whatever there was in Bellew's coat there did not seem to be any reason to refuse Sneed's gift.

"All right, Ben. Much obliged. Some lemon drops will go fine. . . . What's the news this morning?"

"All quiet on the Vegas front. It sure beats hell how this burg can quiet down. They know how to run this town. It's like L.A. after an earthquake or a busted dam. Nothing much happened— very few casualties! You know the dope, Weston. It's the only way to run any town that drags down big from tourists and travelers. Same with Vegas. These old birds would die of the jitters if the truth got in the papers."

"I get you. But what's the inside dope? What do the police know? What's the underworld saying?"

"Aplenty. That pretty dancer who was murdered the other night. A Greek half drunk hit her with a pick. She was well connected in L.A. But they hushed it up. Hevron was put on the spot by Bellew. As for Bellew, the dope this morning is that he croaked. His funeral will not be a grand Chicago gangster ceremony with flowers. Not much."

"I suppose my name is associated with the row last night," Lynn asserted regretfully.

"Is it? I'll tell the world. What could you expect? It's great stuff, Weston."

"But where did they get the story?" demanded Lynn.

"Decker mostly. And did that scout of mine sell you to the public? Here he comes now. . . . I'll beat it, Weston. Deck looks like a politician who's just pulled a big one. Once more, take my everlasting thanks. I'm in your debt for all time. So long. I'll be seeing you."

"Mornin', Biff. I see you've blossomed out in the papers. Punk stuff in these locals. Wait till my story comes. . . . How are you? Swell, if your looks can be believed."

"I'm fine, Decker."

"Tough nut to crack, I'll say. What did Ben slip you?"

218

"I didn't look. He put an envelope under my pillow here. Lemon drops, the damn fool said."

"Ha! Ha! Lemon drops? They're yellow in color at that. Mine was.... Weston, I'm tellin' you Sneed is a good man clear through. He's as clean as Bellew was dirty."

"I'm beginning to get that, Decker. I always liked Ben until I heard he'd offered ten grand for my girl."

"You ought to have been sore. Ten grand for that little dame? The piker!"

"Have you any news about Logan?"

"No. Sorry. But Logan will be here soon. You can gamble on that. Just be patient."

Lynn had rather a bad hour succeeding Decker's news. Still in the end he reasoned it all out and accepted it on the score that he had been placed in an exceptionally terrible position and that fighting for his own life would have justified any violence, let alone something he held more sacred—and that was Anne. If only it did not get into the papers! Even that dire calamity softened to the counsel of common sense. His erstwhile proud family would have to acknowledge the outcast son and take their medicine. Lynn brooded over the thing until he wore out its shame. What had he to be ashamed of? As his feat began to draw a little away and he could get a perspective he felt proud of it. What would Flynn say in his booming voice—and the engineers of the Six Companies—and the coach, the old stickler for a man who never let go—and that big ham Speed Folsom who had been elevated into Lynn's backfield position and glory—and lastly, what would Gordon P. Weston say—his Dad, who would have been a good sport but for his prissy relatives—his father who had ridiculed his athletic prowess and the fame that it had given him? "Go out and biff yourself into a job!" he had said, stingingly. "Kick, you big stiff! Kick aside your competitors for a grubstake. Go out on your own!"

Lynn felt those words ringing in his ears. And they were still ringing there when Logan, the sheriff, appeared with the young doctor, making their way to Lynn's cot.

"How aboot you, son?" the big Texan asked feelingly, and his hand gripped Lynn's.

"I'm okay, Logan. Just begun to fret. But now you're here . . ."

"We're settin' pretty, eh, Weston?" replied the sheriff, sitting down and waving the nurse away. "I took Anne to my house and turned her over to my housekeeper. A good woman. Anne went to sleep pronto. I advise you to send her to L.A. She'd be safe there for the present, until this Bellew gang is run out. I phoned L.A. for information—for your father's number in South Pasadena. Called. Your mother answered. She was alone. So I had to break it, which I did without telling her you'd been shot—what'll be in the papers, shore. She told me to bring Anne with all haste. I'll bet your home is some swell place for a Boulder Dam worker!"

"Logan, I can't thank you enough," Lynn replied with emotion. "That's a good idea—sending Anne to Mother. But how'll I send her?"

"I'll be glad to take her. Have business in L.A. anyhow."

"You are a friend to those in need," Lynn declared gratefully. "If I've done something for you and Sneed, believe me, it's little to what you've done for me. . . . But before you take Anne let me see her. . . . I'll—I'll marry her if she'll have me."

"Good! That'll be fine. Have you? Say, son, I could tell you somethin'. . . . As for your gunshot holes—shore you don't know you have them. These doctors do, believe me. They're afraid of infection. Weston, what a hell of a Texas Ranger you'd make. You could pack as much lead as Cole Younger or Buck Duane. Put her heah, son! You've reversed my faith in the younger generation."

"Wow! Logan, let go my mitt," wailed Lynn, squirming to get his bruised hand away. "Beat it, will you, pard—and fetch Anne."

"Be heah pronto."

The Texan strode out, leaving Lynn with swelling heart and ringing ears. Would Anne marry him? He thought she might. And in time he could win her love. That fight with Bellew's outfit was an expression of the tremendously passionate love he had suddenly found he bore Anne Vandergrift. What a blind fool he had been not to realize it! But she had been just like a still, transparent pool of water. A man could fall in love with a girl like that and never know it until some great passionate crisis of life awakened him. How would Anne feel toward him now—after this second rescue from Bellew? She had liked him, respected him, been eloquently grateful from the very first. Still that was not love. His heart was beating too high to sink under suppositions. But surely she would consent to marry him. Once his wife—then he would take care of her and the future. How magically bright that looked! She would have a home, a husband.

In the light of this marvelous prospect the moments sped by, leaving no room for thought of his family and their reaction to his fight and the romance of his life.

Presently the quiet of the hospital broke to murmuring voices and soft footsteps. Lynn turned his head toward the sounds. Anne had entered with the nurse. And Logan, his brown face beaming, towered behind them. When had Anne looked like that? Her white face—how dark her eyes! When they sighted him on the cot they devoured him with an incredible hunger. Always Anne's eyes had intrigued Lynn; now they stopped his heart. She ran ahead of the nurse and reaching his side she caught at him with nerveless hands.

"Oh! Lynn!" she cried faintly.

"Hello—Anne! . . ." replied Lynn. "How white you are! Your eyes . . ."

"I'm all—right—Lynn," she faltered and sat down upon the bed beside him.

"Weston, I just told her you'd been shot. Not so easy, son!" Logan interposed feelingly. "I'll just hang around, in case you want me. We should be starting for L.A. pretty pronto."

"Okay, Texas," Lynn replied with assumed cheerfulness. Sight of Anne had magnified her preciousness.

"Lynn, I didn't know—I didn't know—you'd been shot," cried Anne, clinging to him. "Oh, you are so pale. . . . I don't believe

221

Mr. Logan or the doctor either. . . . Are you suffering?"

"Girl, I don't know I'm shot," Lynn said vibrantly. "But I have been, and these guys know best. I can take it, you know, Anne. . . . I—you see—well, there are reasons why I must not risk chances."

"Chances! Oh, indeed you must not. But *who* can make you take care of yourself?"

"You can."

"Lynn! I—I never could before," she returned, a little mystified.

"Well, you can. And I'll prove it. But listen. Logan thinks you should be taken to my mother. I guess that will be best, until I'm well and there's no more danger from these white slavers. Logan will run them out of Nevada. . . . I'll miss you, Anne. But I'll run over to L.A. as soon as they'll let me."

"Lynn, I—I don't want to go."

"Sure you don't. But you must. My mother and sister will be swell to you. . . . And—and if you'll . . . well, I won't worry while I'm here getting well."

"I will go," she said, and it was evident that the decision was not an easy one to make.

The nurse intervened gently to press Lynn back and smooth his pillow.

"At least you must lie still," she said kindly.

"Thanks, Anne. . . . You're just one swell kid," Lynn replied thickly. "But that's not all. . . . What I—I mean is . . . Anne, will you marry me?"

"*Lynn!*" A wave of scarlet burned her white neck and face, and her eyes dilated.

"Right here and now," Lynn went on ringingly. "Logan will fetch license and minister. . . . Then I'll let you go to my mother— be free from dread. . . . Please, Anne. That will settle your problems."

"It would—but—but I'm not thinking of myself," she murmured softly, while the blush slowly receded, leaving her whiter than before. Her eyes dropped. "Your family should be considered. . . . I'm nobody. I . . . ."

"Anne, *will* you?" he interrupted passionately. "Think of yourself first—and then me. . . . Will you marry me?"

"Yes," she whispered almost inaudibly, as if overcome by something tremendous in her.

In just twenty minutes from that happy moment, in the presence of Logan, the radiant nurse, and the smiling hospital inmates on the surrounding cots, Lynn had made Anne Vandergrift his wife.

Despite their importunities, he had sat up for that ceremony. When it was over he lay back spent and weak, more from the strain of his emotions than from physical disability.

"Now you've done it—Anne," he whispered to the stunned girl, rapturous under the blue-gray spell of her eyes. "Run along with Logan now. Give my love to Mother—after you introduce yourself as Mrs. Lynn Weston. . . . The governor will fall for you in a heap. Look out for my old college chums. They'll make a play for you. . . . I'll send you money and come as soon as I'm able."

"Oh—Lynn!" Anne cried bewildered.

And at that moment Flynn and Carewe came in, ushered by the day physician. They did not need to be told what had just happened. Carewe's look of deep concern changed to a warm smile. And Flynn's dark frown vanished. The interchange of greetings and congratulations that followed left Anne a flushed and lovely bride.

"Logan, take her away—pronto—before I climb off this cot," Lynn cried gayly. "*Adios,* Mrs. Lynn Weston. I'll be seeing you."

It was sweetly manifest to Lynn that Anne could not move out of her tracks of her own volition. Logan and the minister led her away. Anne looked back once. Her lovely flushed face, and something darkly eloquent in her eyes, gave Lynn a hope too big for his breast. She was gone out the door, and his Boulder Dam friends bent over him.

"Biff, you ain't done a damn thing," declared Flynn.

"My boy, you have knocked the pins out from under me," added Carewe. "But the great thing is—are you badly injured?"

"Chief, I swear I'm not," Lynn replied earnestly, deeply touched by Carewe's concern. "I'm used to hurts. I'd never get blood

223

poisoning. I've bled a lot. But what's that? In a week I'll be running the mill."

"No, you won't," returned Carewe. "Flynn has dug up a *real* job for you."

"Biff, I'll tell the world," interposed the boss. "But you're not to hear about it now."

"Chief, I forgot all about my job. Imagine that. I forgot Boulder. . . . Is she okay? Is the cement mill running? And that damned water pipe system I couldn't figure out?"

"All's well, Biff. New pipes in. Water on again. Tunnel full of cement."

"Thank heaven!" Lynn ejaculated in utmost relief. "I can't wait to hear it all. . . . But Brown? Did you get him?"

"We haven't yet," answered the chief. "Evidently he has left Nevada. And Mrs. Brown left for parts unknown."

"Well! I'm sorry for her. But I've cussed myself many times for not letting Ben Brown and his bag of tools go to the bottom of the Colorado."

"Biff," added Flynn. "It looks like both Brown an' Moore were not pronounced Reds. Just ignorant men inflamed by such agitators as Sproul. By the way, you damn near killed that gazabo."

"Yeah?" The remembrance of that lean-jawed Communist brought a grimness momentarily into Lynn's happy mood.

"Biff, the news of your fight reached me this morning," said Carewe. "You had been shot, so the man informed me. Decker was his name. A friend of yours! But he didn't say you had not been killed. I phoned Flynn, and he hurried into town. He read the morning paper's account. And we heard various reports. I needn't say how happy we are to get the truth. You're a rather remarkable fellow. All's well that ends well."

"Chief, about my new job?" Lynn queried eagerly. "I hope it's not in the office."

"Ask Flynn—but not until you come back," Carewe rejoined warmly. "You are laid off for a while—with pay. Do you need any money?"

"No, thanks, Mr. Carewe."

"Well, Biff, may I suggest that as soon as you are well you go to L.A. and give that little bride the happiest honeymoon any girl ever had. And here I mustn't forget. I heard your father had a big stock of building materials on hand just when the depression hit us. Well, I sent a man over to his yard, and we'll buy out his whole stock. Suppose you engineer that sale. Subject to our buying schedule, of course. . . . After that come back to your new job. I have in mind a home for you and Anne at Boulder, where you'll be comfortable and she'll be safe. Under guard till Boulder Dam is built!"

"Oh! *Chief!*" burst out Lynn. "Grand! My heaven—this is too much. I . . ."

"Biff," Flynn interrupted with a twinkle in his eye, "if I'm to be your boss till this job is done, I'm givin' you a hunch you'll be tied down. No more vacations! I can't spare you. So take a month! Send for money if you need it. An' mop up a lot of champagne!"

"Say! What're you guys up to?" gasped Lynn. But they departed without satisfying his curiosity.

For a long while Lynn lay there wrapped in the dream of his marvelous good fortune. It was useless to try to understand it, useless to give the credit to his labors and his unending fight against himself.

After a while when he appeared alone he drew from under his pillow the envelope Sneed had slipped there. It was not sealed. Lynn opened it—shook out three brand new green bills, each marked with the number one thousand.

"Golly! What do you know about that! Grands! First I ever saw! Three grand! That booze-selling, pie-faced bootlegger! Yeah, this *is* a tough break for little Biff!"

He carefully deposited the bills in his deepest pocket. And then he was inspired to take up Bellew's coat—weighed it—speculated upon it. There was a heavy object in the inside pocket. Also he had put the little whip Decker had given him into another pocket. Something clinked against the bed. Lynn removed from the right side pocket a pearl-handled gun.

"Bellew, you didn't get to it in time," he muttered darkly and lay the shiny deadly-blue little weapon on the table. Then he put it back again. At length Lynn felt this thick lump in the inside pocket. It was a wallet, stuffed full of something that gave to the pressure of his hand. Then he remembered and suddenly became wet with cold sweat. "Fifty grand he offered me—the lousy . . ! 'Take it—and your girl.'" How the words shrilled in Lynn's vibrant ears! "By God—I wonder now!" Making sure no eye was on him Lynn opened the long wallet just so he could peep at the interior. His startled gaze caught sight of a thick, densely pressed packet of thin green-edged slips of paper. "Holy—Mackerel!" gasped Lynn, overcome. "They're bills, so help me heaven! Grands! I'll bet my shirt! . . . What is money to these racketeers and bootleggers?"

He closed the wallet and squeezed it in his strong brown hands, subject to another kind of sensation—a perplexing distress that exploded into the midst of his exultation.

"On the spot again. Lynn Weston!" he soliloquized. "Do I run back to Vegas and turn this over to the city officials or the police? . . . Like hob I do! . . . This money is mine. I earned it. Where Bellew got it I don't care. From other racketeers, and it's not tainted money for me."

He raved on until his intelligence and reason displaced his natural exultation. Time would decide what was right for him to do with this money. But he had not the slightest doubt that fortune had come to him. As a boy the pot of gold at the foot of the rainbow had haunted him. *Treasure Island* was his favorite story of adventure. He had fallen out of his ill-guided college days into romance. Boulder Dam had been his guiding star. He had played the game. And as the gods of chance would have it and as Helen Pritchard had so tauntingly expressed it, he had snatched love out of the empyrean.

"And will I hang on to the ball? I'm telling you, coach!" he whispered.

Epilogue

In course of time the day came when Lynn, with Anne and their little boy, stood on Observation Point, among hundreds of other spectators, to view the finished Boulder Dam.

The splendid macadamized road, with its white carved stone parapet, ended in a wide curved level for the accommodation of sightseers. Years before Lynn had stepped out of Helen Pritchard's car at that point, into a changed life. He remembered that fateful step, and the succeeding ones flashed in vivid procession through his mind. He lifted the boy up on the parapet, and holding him there he braced himself for the shock he knew he must sustain.

Boulder Canyon appeared to have been closed by a dazzling white barrier of stultifying magnificence. The bronze walls, smooth, clean, shining, ended against the great dam that reached the blue sky, against which were silhouetted the snowy turrets and towers of the lofty boulevard that crossed the dam from rim to rim. What a sheer blank enormous precipice of man-made granite curving from wall to wall!

At the foot of the dam a white five-story building fitted in like a blunted triangle, its two long wings extending downriver under

227

the walls, its sculptured beauty reflected in the wide pools of water between. High on the right wall of the canyon, hundreds of feet up, two white-faced electric plants stood one above the other, and from the portals of each shot three great streams of water, long round jets that curved in parabolic beauty to turn from green to white, and spread into magnificent waterfalls, and fall with low thunder into the river. The upper trio of spouts, each as large and beautiful as Yosemite Falls after it took its leap, shot out with vastly greater volume and force clear over the lower electric plant, with its trio of lesser spouts; and under the dazzling sun they shone and scintillated and glowed, creating the most exquisite man-made rainbows that had ever graced the earth.

Lynn's heart was full to bursting. Boulder Dam was beautiful in the extreme. It had sublimity, grace, translucent changing color, and perpetual melody and movement. But all this, and Lynn's elation, could not restrain his mind from envisioning the grand scene five hundred thousand years hence.

The canyon yawned there black and dark under a pale and failing sun. The wide V-shaped gap was open as it had been in the beginnings of time, after the great inland water had cut its tortured way to the sea. On the canyon walls colossal scars showed the action of a recent glacial period. Far up the canyon gleamed the pale green teeth of the retreating ice, sinister and deadly, yielding only to another age.

Below foamed and thundered the rapacious river, augmented to its old volume, no longer red but dirty white, remorseless and eternal.

Life had failed on the earth. Inscrutable nature had gone on with its work, patient, terrible and endless. A mournful wind swept across the gaunt desert, down the naked halls and shingles, across the barren flats.

But the earth, with its long past age of creation, its dreamers and builders who had passed on, was only a tiny globe in the universe. Other planets were evolving. And that divine Thing felt by Lynn in his vision had no beginning and no end. The spirit moved ever toward perfection and immortality.

Zane Grey

"Ohio's Writer of the Purple Sage"

BY ERWIN A. BAUER

There are still a few old-timers around
Ohio that remember a certain bright young ball player who
almost made the major leagues around the turn of the century.
They knew him as "Pitchin' Pearl" Grey because he had a fast
ball that "fairly smoked." It seemed certain that stardom was in
his future. But somehow, somewhere, he was sidetracked.

You might say that Pearl Grey was fortunate to be sidetracked.
Most baseball players are forgotten as soon as they can bat and
run no more, but Pearl's achievements will be remembered as
long as America and adventure are synonymous. As Zane Grey,
writer of the purple sage, he became world famous. More people
read his books and stories than those of nearly any other American
author.

Before he died in 1939 Grey composed more than five million
words for publication, including seventy-one books which were
translated into nearly every modern language. These printed
works were made into countless movies and eventually into a

229

television series. America has been depicted to readers throughout the world by this man who first saw the light of day in 1872 in Zanesville.

Psychologists nowadays make much of a man's heritage and background. They like to point out the obvious effect of early years on a man's entire life. Well, Zane Grey's early years were spent in the rolling blue-green hills along Ohio's Muskingum River. Evidently this was a good training ground for a life that raced through sixty-seven years and touched some of the strangest places on the face of the earth.

Grey's ancestors were of genuine pioneer stock. His father's family came as Irish immigrants to Pennsylvania, settled there, but eventually pushed on to the greener pastures of Ohio. An adventuresome, pioneer spirit was even stronger on his maternal side. His mother, the former Alice Josephine Zane, was a direct descendant of Colonel Ebenezer Zane.

Ebenezer was the defender of Fort Henry through many a siege, and later he conceived the idea of building a wilderness road—Zane's Trace—to open the Ohio River valley for settlement when hostile Indians still lived there. After the road was a reality, he received a land grant from Congress which included the present site of Zanesville.

Zane's boyhood in Zanesville was lively and largely unrestrained. His home was at 363 Convers Avenue in a part of town called The Terrace. Young Grey didn't spend much time indoors. With a gang of boys known as the "Terrors of the Terrace," he dug secret caves, organized clubs with mystic rites—became something of a nuisance in the community. He also authored his first story during this period on a strip of wallpaper, but his father destroyed the "manuscript" as a punishment.

Young Grey's father, "Doc," had taken up dentistry late in life, but his heart wasn't in it. He was really a rough-cut backwoodsman, hunter, farmer and preacher—all of which appealed to Zane except the last. At a tender age Doc taught him to hunt and fish.

Young Grey spent his boyhood climbing in hardwood hills thereabouts, swimming in the steamboat locks, or fishing in the murky Muskingum and Licking rivers, which join at Zanesville. On other occasions he'd raft down the Muskingum to Duncan Falls where giant catfish were available.

Since he was christened (unaccountably) Pearl, he at first had to defend his unusual name to be accepted by his contemporaries. A "terror" as a boy, he became one of Zanesville's outstanding athletes and a lifelong outdoorsman.

Although fishing was his first love, Pearl was far better at baseball. During his high school days the Grey family moved to Columbus, and it was there he developed into a star. One summer afternoon in the sleepy village of Baltimore, just south of Buckeye Lake, Grey almost lost his scalp, but got the biggest break of his young life.

Baltimore and a nearby town took their baseball seriously— and their teams were intense rivals even though the other town always won. One day Grey appeared in the Baltimore lineup as a "ringer" and both pitched and batted the team to victory. But the opponents found out he was a "furriner" and started collecting tar and feathers. Somehow Grey escaped to Columbus, where a University of Pennsylvania scout who had seen the game was waiting for him with an athletic scholarship.

After graduation from Penn, where he earned a degree in dentistry, Pearl had offers to sign with several big-league teams. But relatives convinced him that, in the long run, pulling teeth was more profitable than pitching. As a result he opened up an office in New York City.

Business was slow and dreary from the beginning. But it must have been a balmy, springlike afternoon when existence in the big city suddenly became unbearable. Many years later Grey recalled thinking that the hills would be light green, and dogwoods would be blooming back in Ohio. Without further ado, he snuffed out the gaslight in his drab office and walked out. He never filled another tooth. Instead he kept going until he reached the Lackawaxen River in Pennsylvania, which reminded him of home. There he stayed to fish and relax.

While living on the Lackawaxen, Grey began to put some of his experiences and his thoughts on paper. He did so laboriously, in longhand, a practice he was to continue all his life. *Field and Stream* magazine bought one of his first writings.

But fame and fortune didn't come immediately to Grey. His first full-length novel, *Betty Zane,* a frontier story about his great-great-aunt, sold well later, but initially he had to have it published at his own expense. Mostly he received rejection slips in wholesale quantity, an unhappy experience that many writers frequently share. Some are discouraged, and some only become more tenacious. Grey was one of the latter.

His wife Lina, whom he married in 1905, encouraged him in his work even though it meant personal sacrifice. He credited her determination with keeping him going during the discouraging early years.

Then Grey met a lecturer called Buffalo Jones who talked him into traveling West. A week later he stepped off the train at a desert whistle stop in Arizona's Tonto Rim country. It was like landing in a new world.

For several months Ohioan Grey mingled with cowpokes, Indians, sheriffs, and prospectors. Farther north, in Montana, Teddy Roosevelt was doing the same thing for the first time. It was still the unadulterated Wild West that both of them saw. Grey roped wild horses, hunted lions, helped find a herd of lost buffaloes in the Tonto Basin. Once, as the victim of a practical joke, he rode an unbroken stallion and was almost trampled in a stampede.

It was a rough, dirty and saddlesore existence, but it was inspiration for *Heritage of the Desert,* his first successful novel. *Riders of the Purple Sage* soon followed and sold two million copies, an unprecedented sale at the time. Zane Grey's reputation was made.

Beginning in those first novels, Grey set a pattern for his

232

heroes that never varied and, in a sense, described the author himself. Always these men were hard-bitten and resolute, extremely moral, square-jawed and blue-eyed. Invariably they toiled on the side of law and justice.

The villains were stereotyped, too. They were contemptible, with no respect for law, order or women. Almost without exception, the women were steadfast, virtuous and shining inspirations to their men. Heroine after heroine in dozens of novels that cascaded from the presses suffered, persisted and was finally rewarded with lasting happiness.

Many men set out to acquire a fortune and in the process forget why they wanted it in the first place. Grey was different. One of his editors and closest friends pointed out that Zane just wanted to travel and go fishing wherever he pleased. Anyway, that's surely what he did.

The man who at first caught bullheads and bass on the Muskingum bought a 190-foot three-masted schooner and visited the far corners of the globe. He fished around the bleak and lonely Perlas Islands and rocky Galápagos, off the coast of Ecuador. He trolled off New Caledonia, Australia, New Zealand, and Tahiti, catching giant marlin and sharks which remained as world records until modern advancements in tackle made it possible to catch bigger fish. At one time Zane Grey held nearly every deep-sea fishing record.

He was especially interested in young people and often wrote that an outdoor background early in life would mold them into happy, useful citizens. His *Zane Grey's Book of Camp and Trails* was one of the first volumes on camping written especially for boys.

Zane Grey was a conservationist when few people knew what the word meant. He attacked water pollution in an era when it was officially ignored. He was alarmed as he saw more and more of primitive America disappear.

Zanesville—and Ohio—had one last chance to see Zane Grey in 1921. World War I was finished, and the famous man who had left his birthplace as a boy returned at the invitation of Zanesville's Rotary Club. A world-wide wanderer was coming home. Nearly everyone in town turned out for Zane Grey Homecoming Week.

Grey spoke at a vast banquet in the Masonic Temple, attended a Rotary luncheon, walked again the streets he had roamed as a boy. But Zane was most touched, he revealed, when he appeared before 3,000 cheering children, free from school for the day, in the then-new Weller Theater. Grey spoke briefly; then a film adaptation of his novel *The Desert of Wheat* was shown. Movies based on Grey's novels have been Saturday matinee fare ever since.

When Zane Grey died of a heart attack in 1939, both he and his books had become symbols of a type of rugged, outdoor adventure that is part of the tradition of the American frontier. But somehow, whether he was writing of frontier days in the Ohio Valley or the rolling plains of the West, he always seemed to see them through the eyes of a tow-headed boy clambering along the banks of the Muskingum River. And through his eyes millions of others have seen them since.